Strange Bedfellows

Steve Abbott

Published by Steve Abbott, 2024.

STRANGE BEDFELLOWS

First edition. October 24, 2024.

Copyright © 2024 Steve Abbott.

ISBN: 979-8227263933

Written by Steve Abbott.

For Paula, Dan and Bradley

What's it all about Alfie?

The dog's called Alfie. I am in no doubt the dog is called Alfie. She yells it often enough for all doubt to have been removed. And it's not just your run of the mill frustrated, dog won't do as he's told kind of yell. Oh no, this is yelling on a whole new level. A shrill, ear piercing, strangled cat kind of yell which appears to have no effect whatsoever on poor Alfie, other than rendering him partially deaf and more than a little fearful.

What was Alfie's crime today? Well, he dared to yearn for a tranquil escapade into a mysterious densely wooded area known locally as Lost Souls Copse—a haven shrouded in mystery since time immemorial. His tail was wagging frantically and though I'm not well versed in doggy speak, it was evident he was pleading with her to let him go and explore, maybe cock a leg on some new trees for he had already claimed ownership of every other tree along the monotonous cinder track that monopolised his daily existence.

Her name? I know not, she is an enigma veiled in secrecy. In my head I've taken to calling her Butterface, as every other attribute exudes allure but her face, a face that only surfaces when her eyes glare at me with seething intensity. I appear to have a strange otherworldly effect, which causes her to contort in an extraordinary alien like fashion every time she subjects me to a sudden gush of fury and vitriol. I'm not even sure of what she's saying anymore. That's either because she's lost the ability to string a coherent sentence

1

together or my brain switches to scrambled egg mode and pictures her as Yoda from Star Wars, an eerie resemblance that cannot be dismissed.

A few weeks ago, when I first caught her attention, she made her feelings crystal clear. She strongly objected to my habit of spending my afternoons on the park bench, a bench that gradually became her park bench. During our early encounters, I reassured her that I also disliked spending my afternoons on a park bench. However, when faced with the choice between nature's awe-inspiring canvas of magnificent oaks and rolling hills, and the malodour of the graffiti-covered concrete tunnel known as Snetton underpass, the park always emerged as the unsurprisingly, preferred option. At one point, I naively attempted to engage in a rational conversation with her, specifically regarding the ownership of the park bench. It was from this moment onwards, judging by her reaction and unnecessary emotional breakdown, that she morphed into Yoda during every subsequent interaction.

Today, buoyed by a glimmer of optimism, I plotted my evasion with care, seeking refuge upon a new bench strategically positioned near the park's entrance. Alas, my hopes were swiftly dashed as she quickly sniffed me out, homing in on my scent with canine precision.

I've never been able to establish exactly why she finds me so objectionable. Our encounters have not delved into the realm of profound conversations, where our diverging world-views clash so vehemently that acceptance becomes an impossibility. I do however, suspect she isn't particularly enamoured with my sense of dress. Admittedly, I have never been a devotee of fashion's whims. Designer labels fail to ignite any fervour within me, though I was once the proud owner of a pair of Nikey trainers that had been gifted to me by the local church. Proud that was, until a gobby little teenage scallywag stopped me in the street one day to tell me with some delight, they were in fact Chinese knock offs probably bought from

'Trev the Turk' on Freemo market. It transpires, in the world of Nike there is no room for the letter 'Y'.

Not that I was ever a snappy dresser. Even in my prime, I willingly embraced the role of the nutty professor, donning faded brown corduroy trousers, checked shirt, and a tweed jacket adorned with obligatory leather elbow patches. Today, I fiercely guard my collection of technicoloured, multi-layered, and haphazardly coordinated ensembles, a mishmash of discovered garments. They bestow upon me a distinctive appearance, which could be kindly labelled as unique or unkindly deemed tramp-like. Remarkably, my uniqueness was once acknowledged by a rather affable fellow who claimed to be a street photographer and asked if he could take some candid shots for an upcoming exhibition. Apparently, I'm the epitome of Hobo Chic. While I harboured no illusions about his dubious claims, I gladly accepted a McDonald's quarter pounder and a chocolate milkshake in lieu of payment. Regrettably, I have yet to grace the cover of esteemed publications such as The Gentleman's Gazette or GQ magazine. Three years have passed, and the clamour for my autograph or a coveted selfie remains an elusive fantasy.

Alfie's persistent defiance seems to have reached its boiling point, leading Butterface to take matters into her own hands. With a firm grip on his lead, she drags the poor, terrified soul behind her like a sack of potatoes. As sorry as I feel for him, it at least gives me some temporary respite until she completes her second circuit of the obligatory four, which will undoubtedly give her another opportunity to vent her spleen.

Perfect time for a little sustenance. I delved into my carefully packed worldly possessions, securely stowed within two sturdy Waitrose bags for life—no cheap rubbish for me. A mild sense of panic gripped me as I failed to locate the one possession I deemed indispensable; a solid silver hip flask adorned with heartfelt inscriptions, a cherished gift from my former students during my final year as a professor of physics at Christ's College, Cambridge. This prized possession has accompanied me on my extraordinary journey into homelessness—a journey that my weary body and tired mind tell me is drawing to a close. Mild panic quickly escalated into sheer panic as I dug deeper, desperately searching. While the flask's sentimental value cannot be overstated, its contents—Lambs Navy rum, my elixir of life—holds paramount importance for my very existence. Aware that my mere presence already attracts unwanted attention, I had no desire to scatter the contents of my plastic suitcases across the meticulously manicured carpet of grass before me, for all the world to see.

As I ransacked my memory, I knew it had been a mere half hour since I last held the hip flask, so logically it couldn't have vanished into thin air. Yet, logic has a peculiar tendency to go on an impromptu vacation just when you need it most. Left with no other choice, I had to consider venturing into the depths of Lost Souls Copse and conduct a thorough search among my scattered belongings. As I reached over to grab my bags, there was sudden movement from within the confines of my military faux fur lined parka. Something tumbled out, landing with a resonating clatter on the metal-framed bench before rolling onto the grass. Ah, yes. I recalled the hasty moment when I spied Butterface swiftly approaching, prompting me to shove the hip flask into the recesses of my coat in a desperate attempt to conceal yet another one of my many flaws that she could wield against me. I retrieved the flask and cradled it in my hands. With provisions running low and uncertain prospects of acquiring the next bottle, I carefully poured a measure into the flask's silver top, designed as a perfect single serving. Adding it to my now tepid Costa coffee, I persuaded myself that consuming it in this manner indicated a refined taste rather than a drinking problem. After all, in polite society, a coffee liqueur is the epitome of sophistication.

No sooner had the concoction graced my lips, when from the corner of my eye, I spotted a young girl of maybe seven or eight striding towards me purposefully. She stopped abruptly, stared at me, and smiled. Seemingly unfazed by personal space, she settled herself down in uncomfortably close proximity. A shock of fiery red curls crowned her head, instantly capturing attention. She was clad in a navy blue school dress complimented with a familiar blazer, embellished with the emblem of a school I knew all too well—my very own primary school from countless moons ago. With deliberate care, she unburdened herself of a backpack adorned with graphics from a popular movie franchise and placed it by her side. An uneasy quiet descended, a period of awkward silence.

"Hello, my name's Lucy," she confidently announced staring straight ahead. After a brief pause, she turned to me and said, "You smell."

I turned to look at her, summoning my most formidable glare in an attempt to assert dominance but she didn't avert her gaze. Realising I was unlikely to emerge victorious in this impromptu longest stare contest, I turned my attention back to a rare red squirrel that was darting around in front of me like a Ninja warrior searching for his autumnal harvest.

"No one invited you to sit here young lady," I hinted in a way I hoped would make her realise I simply wanted to be alone.

"I have to sit here," she said. "Mummy said if we ever lose each other, I have to sit on this bench, and she will find me."

That brought me to a halt. Despite my desire for solitude, I had no intention of being the cause of separation between a mother and daughter, let alone being accountable for a child going missing.

"Your mother is very wise, and you are equally as wise for doing as you were told," I responded encouragingly.

The silence settled once more, interrupted only by the rhythmic swinging of Lucy's feet as she sat with her hands tucked beneath her legs. I felt the need for another tot of rum—not because my encounter with Lucy had been particularly traumatic, but simply because I had some left—I reached inside my parka, determined to find the elusive hip flask. However, my multiple layers of clothing and their numerous pockets proved to be a frustrating obstacle yet again. Aware that Lucy was watching me, I must have appeared like a comical figure, patting myself down and diving into deep dark crevices where only the brave or stupid would venture. Finally, after what felt like an eternity but was only a matter of seconds, I located my precious container of liquid gold. With utmost care, I poured another measure into what was now a cup deplete of any coffee, discreetly ensuring Lucy wouldn't form a negative impression of me. I sealed the flask and nonchalantly slipped it back into a pocket, fully aware that I would likely struggle to find it again when the time came.

"What's that?"

I clearly hadn't been as discrete as I thought. Either that or Lucy was more astute than I gave her credit for.

"What's what?" I answered.

"What did you just put in your cup?"

"Oh, just a drop of sugar," I lied.

"It didn't look like sugar."

Floundering, I said, "It's very special sugar, just for grown-ups," in the vain hope that would put an end to the conversation. It didn't.

"I'm not allowed coffee or sugar; mummy said it would make me 'lighter.' I said, 'you drink a lot of coffee mummy, and you just get heavier.' She just laughed."

"I think she probably said it would make you hyper, not lighter."

"What does that mean?"

"It means you might run around a lot and talk too much," I said with a strong emphasis on my last three words in a vain attempt to quieten the little darling.

"Oh, I always do that," she replied and then there was silence.

Although I suspected Lucy still had more to share, it appeared that my subtle hint had nudged her to relocate to the opposite end of the bench. Yet, against my better judgement, I found myself compelled to prolong the conversation. Perhaps it was curiosity or an inexplicable desire to bridge the distance she had created, but something urged me to keep the dialogue going. Even so, I couldn't help but feel a twinge of offence at her deliberate distancing, skirting the boundaries of her mother's instructions.

"Was it something I said?"

"You really are very smelly," she said in that brutally honest way only children can get away with.

"Smelly by name, smelly by nature."

This seemingly innocent comment precipitated a fit of giggles, filling the moment with a buoyant energy that was disproportionate to my simple remark. A smile tugged at the corners of my lips, unable to resist the charm of her contagious laughter. Though solitude had always been my sanctuary, there was an undeniable allure to the unadulterated innocence of youth, gradually thawing the walls around my heart.

"Your name is Smelly?" she managed to blurt out as she struggled to control her giggling fit.

"It's Mr Smelly to you."

Excitedly she asked, "Are you a Mister Man?"

I hesitated. I don't know if I had a sheltered upbringing, but I was confused by the question.

"Erm... I don't think so." I couldn't have been more unsure.

"Oh... OK. I wish you were Mr Silly. He's funny and he doesn't smell."

I didn't respond and watched as Lucy unzipped her backpack and gingerly extracted a package, crudely wrapped in a torn page from a comic book. Her nimble fingers unfolded the makeshift wrapping to unveil a sandwich nestled inside. With the comic book page now doubling as her impromptu napkin, she placed it on her lap. Taking hold of one half of the sandwich, she delicately lifted the top layer of bread, sniffed it, replaced it, and took a satisfying bite.

"Would you like some of my sandwich? It's peanut butter and Monster Munch, I made it myself."

"Mm... Sounds delicious, but I'm good thanks, still full from breakfast."

"Breakfast? That was lots of hours ago, you must be hungry now?"

"I'm saving myself for a big juicy steak later but thank you anyway."

"You're welcome," Lucy paused. "I don't eat cows, they have funny faces."

As I contemplated Lucy's explanation for her aversion to beef, Butterface once again honed into view, rising over the crest of one of the park's many undulations like the ghost of Christmas future, readying to remind me of the tragedies yet to come if I didn't change my ways. I braced myself as she quickened her step and strode towards me and made a quick decision that this time round, I would strike first, hoping to catch her off guard. However, before I could initiate any action, Lucy swiftly rose from her seat like a thunderbolt.

"Hello Mrs lady, can I stroke your dog please?"

Butterface stopped in her tracks, her rehearsed diatribe dissipating into thin air. The innocence emanating from Lucy had caught her off guard, disrupting her rhythm. As for me, I reclined on the bench, intrigued to witness whether Butterface had more than one facet to her personality or if her toxicity extended to all, including children, making her a one-dimensional antagonist.

"Of course you can, dear," Butterface replied with a smile that experience told me was a rare occurrence.

Lucy paused for a moment, her eyes flickering with uncertainty. It was difficult to discern whether her hesitation stemmed from perceiving the facade of feigned sincerity and the forced smile of Butterface, or if her unease was simply due to her fear of dogs.

"It's OK, he's friendly, he won't bite."

"What's he called?" Lucy said.

"His name's Alfie."

Lucy's infectious giggle once again filled the air, briefly irritating Butterface and giving me hope that her facade was about to crumble. But then, to my surprise, Lucy's charm disarmed her, diffusing the tension that had been building up.

"My Grandad was called Alfie, but he's dead now. Your dog won't die if I stroke him, will he?

"Of course not, why would you say such a thing?"

"Because mummy said my Grandad Alfie died of a stroke."

Suppressing a laugh, I attempted to disguise it with a cough, but Butterface saw through my feeble attempt. She shifted her gaze in my direction, shooting me a silent warning. However, just as I thought I was about to face the full force of her disapproval, Lucy intervened, saving me from further scrutiny.

"I've got a rabbit called Algernon; he's only got three legs. He used to have four, but one went missing. We've never found it."

"What's your name sweety?"

"Lucy."

"And where is your mummy, Lucy?"

"I don't know, but it's OK. She said if we ever lose each other I must sit on this bench, and she will come and find me."

"I see. Would you like me to wait with you?"

Butterface may have fooled Lucy, but she didn't fool me. She wasn't concerned with the whereabouts of Lucy's mum; she was concerned about the company she was presently keeping. Could I rely on Lucy rescuing me yet again or did I need to take some affirmative action, which in all honesty only amounted to picking up my belongings and skulking away like a scolded child. I shouldn't have worried, my new best friend had me covered.

"No, I'm fine thank you and anyway you wouldn't want to sit next to Mr Smelly."

Butterface shot me another look; I simply shrugged it off. Lucy and I had formed an unspoken alliance, successfully outwitting the grumpy old hag. Feeling a surge of courage, I lifted my cup and, with a mischievous wink, silently conveyed to Butterface that we had emerged victorious.

"OK if you're sure," said Butterface through gritted teeth. "I'll be by again in about ten minutes. Don't go anywhere until your mummy comes."

"I won't, I promise."

Reluctantly, Butterface commanded Alfie to heel, and as she passed by the bench, she covertly attempted to take my picture with her phone. Emboldened by the presence of my newfound ally, I responded with a childish gesture of sticking out my tongue, hoping to impress Lucy if she happened to notice. However, Lucy was preoccupied, rummaging through her backpack in search of a juice carton. The conversation had come to a halt, which was expected since we seemed to have little in common. Lucy, a sweet eight-year-old patiently waiting for her mother, and me, a sixty-four-year-old homeless man with a striking resemblance to Fagin. But the silence didn't bother me; I was accustomed to silence, unlike Lucy.

Nonchalantly she asked, "Why do you smell?"

Of course, there was an answer to this question, but I didn't feel inclined to go into gritty detail so went on the offensive.

"You ask far too many questions young lady."

"But how would I know things if I didn't ask questions?"

Good answer. Maybe time to school her in a little tact and diplomacy.

"Some things you should ask, some things you shouldn't."

"Why?"

"There you go again. Questions, questions, questions."

"You sound like my daddy."

"Do you ask him too many questions to?"

"Not really, but I think mummy did. He kept saying 'if you don't stop asking me about Eleanor, I'm leaving'. Then he left and didn't come back."

Well, that took an unexpected turn. My head told me to either change the topic or more sensibly to just shut up. My heart told me differently.

"Do you still see your daddy?"

"No. We moved to a new house, and I think mummy forgot to tell him."

"I see."

"But it's OK. It means mummy doesn't cry any more or have to go to hospital."

This time my head won, and I didn't respond. What I needed now was for Lucy's mother to appear on the horizon and for Lucy to run into her arms so I could bathe in the glory of a happy reunion and get on with my solitary life on a park bench. Unusually for me, it appeared my prayers had been answered as I spied a rather determined short, rotund looking woman approaching at some pace in our direction. I don't think I'd formed an opinion as to what Lucy's mother might look like, but the rather serious looking lady who was making a beeline for us wasn't what I expected. She was much older than I'd imagined for a start and the fact Lucy hadn't jumped off the bench and run into her arms as I'd hoped, told me something wasn't right. Still some distance away, the mysterious female bellowed, "So here we are again."

Lucy remained unresponsive, engrossed in her carton of juice, alternating between sips and blowing bubbles with playful enthusiasm. Meanwhile, the mysterious woman drew closer, her presence looming large, and it was evident that she wasn't a happy bunny.

"Well, what have you got to say for yourself Madam?"

"I'm not talking to you, you're not my mummy," Lucy responded defiantly.

"This is getting beyond a joke Lucy, pick up your backpack and get in the car now!"

"No."

"I beg your pardon?"

"I said NO."

The situation escalated rapidly. The furious woman swiftly grabbed Lucy by the arm and forcefully pulled her off the bench. However, Lucy's determination prevailed as she wriggled and squirmed, managing to break free from her grasp. Seeking refuge, she dashed behind me, disregarding the odour. For a moment, I imagined a comedic scene reminiscent of Benny Hill, contemplating adding sound effects as they circled the bench in a playful chase. Yet, it became apparent that the angry woman probably wouldn't share my affinity for 1970s sketch shows. She stood firm and surprisingly imposing, given her small stature. I could sense Lucy's hands gripping onto my coat, appealing for my protection. We found ourselves at an impasse, tensions mounting.

Should I intervene? Was it my place to meddle in their affairs? They clearly knew each other; they just didn't appear to like each other. Ultimately, curiosity got the better of me.

"Excuse me," I said in my best disarming voice, "I don't know who you are, but if her mother told her to wait here, I think she should wait here."

I wouldn't claim to have completely disarmed her, but I managed to evoke a response that was less enraged and more composed.

"Not that it's any of your business, but I'm Elaine, Lucy's foster carer."

OK, so now we were getting somewhere. The mystery deepens.

"Lucy's mother went missing over a week ago and she can't get it into her thick skull that sitting here every day after school isn't going to help find her."

I didn't get the chance to respond before Lucy bellowed at Elaine much too close to my ear, "Don't say that. She will come and find me. She told me if we ever lost each other I had to sit on this bench and wait for her and Mr Smelly said I am very wise just like my mummy."

"Don't be so rude Lucy," Elaine said, "say sorry to this gentleman now."

Lucy didn't speak, I didn't speak, which only left Elaine to break the silence.

"I said, say sorry to this gentleman now, you do not call people 'smelly."

"Hey, it's fine honestly," I said in an attempt to ease the tension.

"No, it's not fine, she needs to learn some manners."

As a man who values tolerance and avoids conflict, I'm a lifelong member of CND for goodness' sake, it's rare for me to harbour negative feelings towards someone. However, there was an indescribable dislike I had towards this woman. While she couldn't quite match the intensity of Butterface, she had a knack for getting under my skin. Being a foster carer was undoubtedly challenging, and I respected that, but that didn't grant her the licence to embody the wicked stepmother persona depicted in Charles Perrault's fairy tale, Cinderella. And so, I mustered what I believed to be my cleverest retort of the day.

"And you Madam need to learn that my name is Mr Smelly."

I sat there with a satisfied smile, believing I had successfully silenced the old battleaxe. In my moment of triumph, I even toyed with the idea of imparting some rudimentary parenting wisdom on her. However, my momentary distraction in formulating my second cleverest retort allowed Elaine to seize the opportunity and fire back at me.

"And you, Sir, need to mind your own god damn business. If Lucy is not in the back of my car in two minutes, I will call the police and report you for harbouring a child."

Harbouring a child? Is that really a thing? I couldn't be doing with a new moniker of 'harbourer'. I couldn't bear the thought of adding another unkind label to the already long list of names I had been called over the years. Instead, I turned towards Lucy and gestured for her to join me on the bench. Although hesitant due to the proximity of this unpleasant woman, Lucy eventually relented and sat next to me after some gentle persuasion.

"Lucy, sweetheart, I'm very proud of you for remembering what to do if you ever lost your mummy."

"And I'm very wise," Lucy interjected.

"And you're very wise, very wise indeed. But I don't think your mummy is coming today and it will soon be dark." Through clenched teeth I continued, "This lovely lady needs to make sure you are safe and that you don't come to any harm. I know she's a bit angry but that's because she worries about you."

"She doesn't scare me, she's not like my daddy, she's just not very nice like my mummy."

"Well, no one can ever be like your mummy, but she can look after you until your mummy is found. So, I'd like you to go home with Elaine now if that's OK?"

Lucy considered my request and reluctantly, I suspect, agreed.

"Would you like to come too for some supper Mr Smelly?"

"That's very sweet of you Lucy but I'm having a big juicy steak later if you remember."

"I don't eat cows."

"I know, they've got funny faces."

Elaine, growing increasingly impatient, had snatched Lucy's backpack, but to my relief, she held her tongue. Lucy got up from the bench and took a few steps before turning back and embracing me tightly. It caught me off guard, leaving me unsure of how to react. Here I was, being hugged by an 8-year-old girl whom I had only known for a brief encounter, all the while being scrutinised by a suspicious foster carer who seemed ready to involve the authorities. With care, I placed my hands on Lucy's shoulders and gently separated her from the hug.

She smiled at me and as a parting shot said, "You really do smell very bad."

Lucy walked with determination towards the car park, intentionally keeping a distance from Elaine. When she was around twenty yards away, she abruptly turned and shouted at the top of her lungs, "See you tomorrow, Mr. Smelly."

Elaine, matching the volume to ensure I could hear, said, "There will be no seeing anyone tomorrow, young lady. You're grounded."

I watched as they gradually faded into the distance, with Lucy continuing to walk ahead and Elaine, pausing briefly for a conversation with Butterface, who was commencing her fourth lap. Their gaze eventually shifted towards my direction, leaving me to wonder what they were discussing.

My initial instinct was to retreat and escape the eventful day, as it had already been far too stressful for my liking. Yet, I pondered the potential implications of such an action on Butterface's perception. Would she interpret it as her triumph? Would I be deemed a coward for not enduring the full four rounds? Determined to maintain my stance, I straightened my posture as much as my hunched back allowed, bracing myself for the impending final confrontation.

Alfie, once again off his leash, seemed to have taken a strategic lead, possibly in a bid to save himself. He dashed past me with determination, heading straight for Lost Souls Copse. Butterface struggled to keep up, visibly fatigued after completing three and a half laps. As she approached the bench, she cast a glance in my direction, causing me to brace myself for a potential onslaught. However, to my surprise, she simply continued on her way, more preoccupied with locating Alfie than asserting her authority over my presence. Butterface disappeared into the copse, calling out Alfie's name, while his barks echoed in response.

Satisfied with my resolve to stand my ground instead of surrendering for the sake of peace, I gathered my belongings and prepared to depart. Evening was approaching, and I needed to secure food and shelter for the night. The echoes of Butterface's shouts and Alfie's persistent barks filled the air as I walked along the path, reflecting on the peculiar events of the day. Lucy's presence lingered in my thoughts, and despite her being grounded tomorrow, I secretly wished for another chance to cross paths with her in the future.

As I contemplated my sleeping options, a piercing scream tore through the air, sending a chill down my spine and halting my movements. The source of the scream was Lost Souls Copse. I paused, scanning the surroundings to see if anyone else had heard it. The park suddenly appeared deserted, as if a silent command had dispersed the crowd, leaving only a few lingering individuals with nowhere to go. A second scream, equally chilling, pierced the air, intermingled with the frantic barks of a familiar dog—Alfie, unmistakably.

I wrestled with the decision in my mind. Should I simply walk away? It's likely just Butterface overreacting to some trivial incident involving Alfie. Perhaps he'd managed to soil something unpleasant, triggering Butterface's panic about her precious cream shag pile carpets back home. I fixed my gaze on the entrance to the copse, the internal struggle intensifying. Every instinct urged me to turn around and leave. I tried to reason with myself: "Just thirty seconds. If there's no commotion, I'll be on my way." But as I began counting, I couldn't make it past ten before the screams morphed into desperate cries for help. Convinced that something terrible had befallen Alfie, my compassion for animals took hold of my thoughts. Without further hesitation, I dropped my belongings and ventured forward. The fading daylight was quickly swallowed by the thick canopy overhead, reducing visibility to just a few yards. Though the copse wasn't particularly large, its density offered no discernible paths or trails. The sudden absence of Alfie's barks filled me with dread, fearing the worst.

"Hello! Hello!" I called out, my voice echoing through the thicket, desperately trying to locate them, "Is everything alright? Do you need assistance?"

In hindsight, it was a rather stupid question. I had entered the copse because someone was screaming for help, and it was clear they weren't seeking assistance because their shoelace had become untied.

"Over here, over here, please help," came a frantic reply somewhere to my left.

I pushed my way through a tangle of thick bracken, relying on my layered fashion statement to protect me from the thorns. I continued calling out, desperately hoping for a response. Eventually, I reached a small clearing. To my relief, Alfie stood there, wagging his tail, nudging a pile of earth with his nose. Butterface was on her knees, her back turned towards me. As she sensed my presence, she spun around and started heaving, leading into an episode of projectile vomiting that even by my low standards wasn't a pretty sight.

Carefully avoiding the vomit-covered area, I approached and picked up Alfie's discarded lead. I felt it was the least I could do to prevent him from running off again. Leaning over to attach the lead, amongst the undergrowth, my gaze fixated on a partially hidden object—a motionless form concealed by nature's embrace. It was a lifeless body, its presence obscured by a shroud of decomposing leaves and debris. It was the body of a young woman whose features struck a haunting resemblance to a child with whom I had recently struck up an acquaintance.

The End.

A Slice of Life

Hospital waiting rooms, a peculiar environment where everyone shares a common concern that no one wishes to share. This is particularly true when it's an all-male cast. I've followed the rules and ensured I've left a least one seat between myself and the next guy. In fact, I've gone one better and sat at the far end of a bank of six with only one other feller occupying the other end.

I settled into the dull monotony that I was convinced would consume at least the next few hours of my life when my boredom was abruptly shattered by a resounding crash emanating from the sliding entrance doors. In a heart-pounding moment, my overactive imagination catapulted into an intense heist scenario, where an organised crime gang was brazenly attempting to breach the doors with an armoured vehicle. However, reason quickly prevailed, reminding me that it was merely a hospital waiting room—certainly an unusual choice for armed robbers. The collective attention of the room momentarily shifted upward, but just as swiftly, everyone averted their gazes back to the mundane comfort of their feet.

Curiosity got the better of me and as I stood to get a better view, I just managed to catch the sight of a poor guy in a wheelchair hurtling backwards down a ramp before coming to an abrupt halt and being hurled into an ornamental privet hedge.

A receptionist, porter and a passing nurse leapt into action and rushed outside to rescue the unfortunate soul who, judging by his demeanour had done more damage to his pride than his body.

Helped back into his chair, he shrugged off any further assistance and gingerly made his way back to the offending sliding doors before pausing and allowing them to open fully this time before attempting to enter.

The remaining receptionist, who for reasons best known to herself had not leapt to his assistance, peered over her desk and calmly asked, "Is everything OK sir?"

"Yeah, everything's fine thanks, just a bit eager I guess."

"Surprisingly enthusiastic for someone attending a vasectomy clinic. What name is it please?"

"Banford, Harry Banford," he replied rather sheepishly.

"And your date of birth?"

"Twenty ninth of the second, nineteen eighty-four."

"Please take a seat Mr Banford," she said, completely missing the irony of her comment, "we'll call you when we're ready."

Harry deftly wheeled himself into position immediately to my left. I liked him already and we hadn't spoken a word. He was a rule breaker, not even the slightest attempt to distance himself from the rest of us. Though in fairness, he didn't have that much choice. His options were to park himself at the end of a row of chairs or sit in the middle of the room like an ornamental statue.

I was tempted to open the conversation, but as my irresistible urge was to go straight to the sliding doors incident, I held my tongue not wanting to embarrass him further. As I mulled over what I might chat to him about after cursory introductions, a beast of a guy built like the proverbial brick out house and with a Desperate Dan chin that could chisel granite, appeared out of nowhere and nearly sat on my lap such was his eagerness to grab the seat next to me. Well, that was waiting room etiquette out of the window. I shifted my right buttock maybe two inches so that we weren't physically touching each other, but it hardly counted as putting any great distance between us. My soon to be new mate Harry, who I had yet to speak a single word to, shot me a perplexed look and I just shrugged my shoulders in bewilderment.

"Bollocks!" The 'beast' speaks. "Smartphone my arse, dumb phone more like."

"Technology eh?" Harry replied, though directing his response more to me than the 'beast'.

"Double bollocks," louder this time, "What eejit came up with solitaire. Eh? Eh? Well?"

I wasn't convinced the question was directed at me or Harry for that matter. It might have been a question for the room at large such was its volume.

"Well?" he repeated in a slightly threatening hushed tone.

"Well what?" I said nervously.

"What eejit came up with solitaire? What's the point of it? You can't even play it with your mates."

"I think that is the point."

"What?"

"Solitaire, it's meant to be played alone, hence the name solitaire deriving from the French for solitary."

"Oooohhhhh get you Madam-mos-elle clever shit."

"Just thought it was pretty obvious that's all," I said before contemplating why I was even entering into a conversation with neanderthal man.

"Well, it might be obvious to you in your la-de-da three piece and designer shoes, but some of us are still proud to be British. Some of us aren't ashamed to admit we only speak the Queen's English."

Curiosity got the better of me. "What's that got to do with playing solitaire?"

All credit to the guy, he had an answer, however bizarre it might have seemed.

"It's got to do with being sold down the river pal. It's got to do with losing your sovereigns."

Should I correct him, will it antagonise him? Sod it, in for a penny, in for a pound. "Do you mean sovereignty?"

"Whatever. The point is, if I want to sit in a vasectomy clinic talking French, then I'll jump on the Eurocar and have me nads chopped in frog land. Capiche?"

At this point I realised I was out of my depth. Continuing the conversation seemed to have only one conceivable outcome and that was a punch in the face. An uncomfortable silence filled the air.

With a disarming charm, Harry remarked, "I'm sure he didn't mean anything by it."

The 'beast' was on him straightaway. "Aye up wheelie boy, who rattled your chariot?"

In a way that I knew was going to be patronising, I felt the need to protect my disabled buddy, fully aware that he was probably more than capable of sticking up for himself. "Hey, relax my friend," I said trying to come across as an equal, "it's stressful enough sat around here waiting for some guy to take a knife to Richard and the twins, without us falling out over a game on a phone."

"Hear, hear," Harry said in support.

The 'beast' paused. "No sweat fella, just a bit tense, that's all." It was as close to an apology as we were going to get.

"Of course you are, we're all a little tense," I said in the hope that reminding him of our shared fears would keep him calm for the rest of the morning.

A brief hush settled in the room, only to be broken by the violent swing of two massive corridor doors. All eyes in the room were immediately drawn to the chaotic sight of what appeared to be an out-of-control hospital trolley careering through the waiting room, with a hospital porter desperately clinging on for dear life. It was hard to determine whether anyone was on the trolley such was its speed and the only clue we had was the porter shouting "Bleeder coming through, mind your backs, bleeder coming through, mind your backs."

With that he was gone, disappearing into a room closely followed by several white coats and a nurse who in contrast didn't seem to share the urgency of the situation as she strolled at a leisurely pace some distance behind them. There was a sense that everything was under control as very little happened in the next five minutes until the tannoy sprang to life.

"Doctor Knackersack to emergency room two, Doctor Knackersack to emergency room two please."

Again, the whole room was brought to attention, eager to get a glimpse of Doctor Knackersack – the beacon of hope for the poor soul seemingly teetering on the precipice of life or death in emergency room two. Seconds and then minutes passed by, but no Doctor Knackersack. Instinct told me to speak to the receptionist and ask her to put out another tannoy message, but just as a I grappled with this notion, a scruffy looking octogenarian stuffing his face with what looked like a Cornish pasty, strolled nonchalantly through the increasingly tense and anxious waiting room, discarding the remains of his brunch on the receptionist desk before opening the door to emergency room two asking, "Is he still with us or have we lost him?" The door slammed behind him, and we were all left wondering.

While the rest of us sat in silence contemplating the fate of 'the bleeder', the 'beast' had other things on his mind.

"So, what's your story then?" he asked, pointing at Harry.

"Story?" Harry replied.

"Yeah, what's with the wheelchair, you one of them 'fripples'?"

"Excuse me?"

Once again, I felt the need to interject. "I have to hand it to you... Sorry, didn't catch your name?"

"Dick," the 'beast' replied.

"How appropriate. Short for Richard I assume?"

"Nope... Roger."

"Dick is short for Roger?"

"No numb nuts, my last name's Whittington."

"Ah, Ok. I'm Tom by the way. As I was saying, I have to hand it to you Dick, you certainly have a way with words... 'Fripple'?"

"Yeah, fake cripple. You see 'em all the time down at the benefits office. Scrounging bast..."

"Are you for real?" Harry interrupted in a much more measured way than Dick deserved.

"Hey, chill whatever your name is, just curious. Meant no offence."

"It's Harry and none taken."

This was the point our new friend Dick should have shut up or changed subjects, but it was becoming evident, that wasn't Dick's style. He paused briefly, but clearly hadn't finished with his line of questioning.

"So erm... You had the wheels long like?"

Sarcastically Harry said, "Had them since I broke my back five years ago as it happens. I'd been looking at getting some and then the collision with a tree kind of made up my mind."

"Five years? Jesus Christ, it's takin' a long time to heal init? I broke two knuckles punching a wall once and they were right as rain in a couple of weeks."

"Bloody NHS eh? You pay thousands in taxes, and they still can't find a cure for a broken back," Harry said, not anticipating Dick's response.

"I'm with you on that one brother. The robbin' friggin' government screw ya' for every penny you earn and then can't even be arsed to put some effort into finding a cure for a broken back. Come the revolution brother, me and you, Dick and... and...?"

"Harry," Harry reminded him.

"Dick and Harry stood shoulder to shoulder, well shoulder to hip in your case. We'll fight 'em on the beaches, we'll fight 'em on the streets and defeat imperialism and its running dogs," Dick announced while stood to attention clutching his heart in a gesture of solidarity.

"Well said Dick," I said in a somewhat dismissive tone, "in the meantime, a nice cup of tea wouldn't go amiss."

"Wishful thinking," said Harry, "I don't think there's a vasectomy clinic refreshment budget anymore, it got cut."

I smiled at Harry's weak attempt at a joke, while Dick looked on confused.

THE MINUTES TICKED by painfully slow. Dick had seemingly lost interest in Harry's disability, well for the time being at least and sat cursing his phone as he once again grappled with solitaire. Harry was engrossed in a book and had a wry smile on his face. For my part, I sat people-watching, wondering about the diverse stories and journeys that had converged in this space, all of us bound by a common thread of uncertainty and hope.

Harry closed his book. "Anyone gone in yet?"

"Not that I'm aware of," I said, "there's another waiting room just down the corridor, I think they may be first."

"You'd have thought they might have had a TV, even if it was only for infomercials," Harry said. "Remind me to put a note in the suggestion box on the way out. Oh well, back to 'The Memoirs of a Eunuch.' Not my book of choice, but the wife thought it was amusing under the circumstances."

I smiled, slightly envious at his wife's attention to detail. Just as I thought we'd returned to peace and tranquillity; Dick's short attention span came to the fore as he slammed his phone down on the hard plastic seat to his right and said, "So Harold."

Without looking up, Harry corrected him, "It's Harry."

"Same bloke different cat. What brings you 'ere?"

"Sorry?

"Don't be sorry, Dick said, 'what brings you 'ere?'"

Harry looked at me, I looked at Harry, I think just to make sure we were both confused by the question. "It's a vasectomy clinic Dick, the clue's in the name."

"Oh right, so you're here for the snip as well. Excellent."

"Why else would I be here?" Harry asked.

"Don't know really," Dick said, as you could see the cogs whirling around in his head trying to decide if the question had been as stupid as Harry was making out.

Harry wasn't going to let him off that easily though. "Do you think I was just out for a stroll and saw a sign that said, 'Vasectomy Clinic, short back and sides done while you wait' and I thought, hey, got nothing better to do, the wife's at her sister's, the match doesn't kick off until three, why not pop in and get my gonads sliced and diced?"

Taking back control, Dick said, "Of course I didn't think you were out for a stroll. I mean... well... you know... with your wangy legs and all, you're not gonna stroll far are you?"

"I think it was a figure of speech my friend," I said.

"Whatever. So, you married then Henry?"

"It's Harry and yes I'm married."

Dick seemed surprised. "Really?"

"Yeah really."

Intrigued, I asked, "Why shouldn't he be?"

"No reason, just thought with his problems it might've been hard to find someone if you know what I mean."

"I don't have any problems thank you very much and not that it's any of your damn business, but I met my wife before my accident."

It was as angry as I had seen my new friend since we met, but Dick was clearly oblivious.

"Ruddy 'ell mate, wake up and smell the full English with a big mug of coffee. I'd say bein' legless is a big friggin' problem."

"I have legs, they just don't work like most peoples do and trust me, it's more of a problem for people like you than it is for me."

"Ok H, don't have a cow, just trying to be friendly."

"God help us if you turn unfriendly," I uttered under my breath to no one in particular.

Dick's line of questioning killed the conversation, and I felt the need to try and take the tension out of the situation. "Any kids Harry?"

"Yeah, four of the buggers."

"Four?"

"Yep. All girls. Amy's fourteen, Molly's twelve and I have twins Lucy and Kate who are three."

"Rather you than me."

"It's a challenge. Why d'you think I'm here? Was hoping for a boy last time but it wasn't to be, so decided to call it quits."

If I hadn't looked down at that point to check a message that had just pinged on my phone, Dick probably wouldn't have taken advantage of my pregnant pause.

"So, you can still get it up then?" Dick said without a hint of shame.

"What?" Harry replied.

"You can still get the 'Old Major' to stand to attention?"

"Of course I can. Do you really think I'd be sat in a vasectomy clinic being insulted by the missing link if I couldn't get it up?"

"How does that work then?"

"How does what work?"

"The whole baby making business."

As Dick's curiosity was firmly focussed on Harry, I again felt the need to step in. "Dick my friend, the whole business of making babies is a very complex and miraculous process, a process that begins with a man and a woman and certain anatomical features."

"Duh! I know how normal people make babies, I'm not stupid," Dick said in a way that implied he felt insulted, "I was wondering how Harry made babies."

"It may surprise you to know Dick, but I make babies in exactly the same way normal guys make babies."

"Look, I don't wanna get personal and feel free to tell me to mind my own business..."

"Mind your own business," Harry suggested, but to no avail.

"But I know when I'm gettin' jiggy with a bit of skirt, me legs are an important part of the whole gig, if you know what I'm sayin'."

"Well, whilst my days of leaping from the top of the wardrobe shouting 'Geronimo' are nothing more than a fond memory, I am more than capable of getting 'jiggy' with my wife in ways that keep us both perfectly satisfied thank you."

"Ok, fair play to you Harry. The British bulldog spirit, I like it. You're an inspiration to 'spazzers' around the world."

"What did you just call him?" I snapped.

"Harry, why ain't that his real name?"

"No... I mean yes, I'm talking about the other name you used."

"You mean 'spazzer'?" Dick replied.

"That's exactly what I mean."

"Oh shit. I'm sorry Harry, didn't mean to upset you pal. It's what me dad used to call 'em."

"Hang on, what about me?" I said.

"What about you?"

"Don't I get an apology, I'm offended too?"

"Why are you offended, you're not one?" Dick said, seemingly oblivious to the point I was trying to make.

"What's that got to do with it. If I started talking about..." Dick wasn't going to let me finish.

"Alright, alright, I'm sorry. Bloody 'ell fella chill out, it's not like I called your mother a 'prossie.'"

Harry stepped in to ease the tension. "Ok boys let's just leave it there shall we, I'm sure it was just a slip of the tongue."

"Sure, sure, just don't want you think I've got a problem with your kind, that's all. I love all that parallel Olympic bollocks. Haven't got a clue what's goin' on, but always good for a laugh. Much prefer it to 'You've Been Framed.' Shame it's only on every four years, deserves a prime-time Saturday night slot if you ask me."

———— ⊙◇⊙ ————

AT THIS POINT, I BELIEVE even Dick grasped that he'd pushed things too far, and he went oddly silent. Harry, on the other hand, got comfy with his book, and I found myself daydreaming about being anywhere else but here right now. For a moment, I even toyed with the idea of making a quick exit. Not just because I was seated next to Desperate Dan and all the drama that comes with it, but because doubts were creeping in about whether I'd truly thought through my decision to have a vasectomy.

My whole idea of having a heart-to-heart with Harry about my sudden confusion got totally wrecked when Doctor Knackersack dramatically appeared in the doorway of emergency room two. There he was, looking all smug, sporting an unlit cigar in his mouth, and throwing up the 'V' for victory sign like it was some sort of performance. He certainly turned the whole room into a gawking spectacle, except for Dick, who was busy wrestling with a pack of Murray Mints. The rest of us just stared, utterly bewildered by this strange character who seemed to think he was on a stage waiting for a standing ovation. When the applause didn't materialize, he slouched his shoulders in exasperation. Then, in a last-ditch effort to get the attention he so desperately craved, he decided to address his captive audience.

"Ladies and gentlemen," he began, clearly oblivious to it being an all-male congregation, "I would just like to reassure you that the events of the last fifteen minutes are nothing to be alarmed about. Whilst I'm unable to go into any detail about a very serious and unfortunate incident involving one of our patients, I felt it important for your peace of mind that I inform you the young man in question is very much alive and kicking with very little lasting damage. It was an extremely rare complication, so rare in fact that I struggled to find any useful information on Wikipedia to help guide me. Needless to say, my long and distinguished career served me well and I was able to save the young man's life. Rest assured, I am very confident all your procedures today will go without a hitch and if for some reason there are some hitches, I'm only a tannoy call away. Thank you for your attention and goodbye."

With that he was gone, disappeared into thin air like some spectral being. No one spoke. Even the receptionist stood mouth wide open in what appeared to be a state of shock. Three guys wasted no time and bolted out of the building, while hushed murmurs started bubbling up among those left behind. Dick was still oblivious, having opened his Murray Mints he now appeared to be trying out origami with the sweet wrappers. Harry, for reasons best known to himself was laughing and shaking his head and I was on the verge of a nervous breakdown.

"That's it, folks, I'm done," I declared, with a touch of theatrical flair, "I ought to be kicking it back at Café Dansant, digging into some antipasti and sipping on a fine 2009 Chateau Lafite-Rothschild. But instead, here I am, half expecting the Baghdad Butcher to make a surprise cameo and pull a 'gonad gone wrong' stunt while Doctor Knackersack sits puffing on a King

Edward cigar, plotting his near-death memoir for the Lancet's front page."

Harry turned and looked at me and started laughing even harder. "Deep breaths Tom, deep breaths, it's all about risk and reward," he tried to reassure me, "forget the looney tune and his Winston Churchill dramatics. Truth is, the risks are so low you couldn't even quantify them, but the rewards are many and remember you're probably doing this as much for your wife as you are yourself. Think about that instead of overpriced red wine and overrated pretentious nibbles disguised under a cloak of Mediterranean mystique."

As I was about to reply, the tannoy crackled to life again. If this was another call for Doctor Knackersack, well that would make my decision for me. I'd give Harry a friendly handshake, wish him all the best, and summon my Uber without a second thought.

"Mr Gresham to consultation room six please," it announced.

No one moved. Everyone remained rooted to their seats. The receptionist got up, and in a firm, kind of scary tone, she took over the Tannoy's only purpose in life. "Hey there, folks! Listen up, we need Mr. Gresham in consultation room six. Anyone seen him? Mr. Gresham, time to head to room six." Again a few seconds passed with no response before someone on the opposite side of the room shouted. "I think he might have done a runner love, three of 'em left after that nutter gave his speech."

The receptionist plopped back into her chair and picked up a phone. Not a moment later, the tannoy chimed in, demanding Mr. Sullivan's presence in room number six. A guy at the far end of the same bench I was parked on slowly rose and carefully shuffled off to meet his fate. Harry then spent the best part of ten minutes reassuring me that everything was going to be ok and, using tactics that included questioning my masculinity, convinced me to stay and see it through.

During all of this, Dick hadn't bothered to pay any mind. He couldn't care less if his life was hanging by a thread. It didn't faze him one bit that his potential saviour, if things took a nosedive, was a certifiably eccentric quack with a Winston Churchill complex. In all honesty, it seemed like he couldn't give a damn about anything except himself. So, it came as no shock when he just had to go ahead and initiate yet another chat with two folks who'd done a lousy job at signalling they wanted no part of his conversation.

"I'm sick of this, don't they realise time's money?" he announced.

Initially neither Harry nor I responded. I wasn't sure if he had addressed the question to either of us or whether he was simply talking to himself or anyone that cared to listen. I didn't have to wait long for my answer.

"Well Tom, what d'you think?"

"What do I think about what Dick?"

"Do you think they realise time's money?"

In a selfish act, I decided to indulge him, hoping that the banal conversation I was certain we were about to have would take my mind off my impending life threatening procedure. "So, you work then?"

"What's that supposed to mean, course I work," he snapped.

"Wasn't supposed to mean anything, just asked if you work."

"I work bloody 'ard pal. Twelve hours a day, six days a week."

"Doing what?" Harry said.

"I dig 'oles."

"Is that it?"

"Nope, then I fill 'em in again," he proudly announced.

"Grave digger?" It was the first thing that came to mind.

"No, ya' daft sod. Utilities, gas, electric that kind of stuff. I dig the 'oles, someone puts stuff in 'em and I fill 'em in again."

"Must be very rewarding." I kind of tossed that one out there with a touch of sarcasm, though he didn't quite catch it.

"Yeah it is, to the tune of six 'undred quid a week."

"Bloody hell, six hundred quid for digging some holes?" Harry sounded surprised.

And in what might just be his best comeback so far, Dick said, "Like to see you dig 'em."

"That's a fair point Harry."

"Yeah, point taken," Harry conceded.

I couldn't quite wrap my head around the fact that I was still in this conversation. To be honest, Old Dicky and his hole-digging gig didn't really pique my interest. I can only guess I kept it going because, well, he was doing a pretty good job at keeping my mind off other things.

"How long have you been digging holes then Dick?"

"Since I was kicked out of the young offenders institute... Must be ten years now."

"I see... Live locally?"

"Yeah, just up the road on the Derwent."

"Ah, the council estate," I said.

"Yep, that's the one.

"Never thought of buying your own place?"

"Nah, why would I want to do that?"

"Good investment and you're on good money," I said realising I'd slipped into work mode and could see an opportunity make a quick buck. "Might be able to help if you want me to look into it."

Just as I was about to launch into a full on sales pitch and pull out one of my readily available mortgage information brochures, the tannoy was at it again. "Mr Kumar to consultation room four please."

"So, what do you say Dicky, want me to make your home owning dreams come true?" I persisted.

"Nah! Happy where I am rentin' thanks. Besides, if I go buy somewhere, it might screw up me benefits."

That one got Harry's attention. "Benefits?"

"Yeah, me benefits. You know, housin' benefit, job seekers, all that crap."

Stating the obvious I said, "But you work."

"And?"

"And benefits are for people who don't earn six hundred quid a week, people who need a hand. The benefit system was designed to protect the vulnerable, to help prevent poverty," Harry protested.

"What cloud cuckoo planet do you live on Harry? Let me tell you about the benefit system. The benefit system exists for a bunch of work shy, lazy, idle, shiftless, inert Jeremy Kyle guests who haven't done a hard day's graft in their entire miserable lives. Out of my hard earned six 'undred quid a week, the thieving self-serving pigs who call themselves politicians, steal two hundred quid under the guise of taxes to help fund the cheap cider drinking, hash smoking lives of these scumbags. Well stuff that for a game of soldiers. Dick giveth and Dick taketh away again, it's my damn money and one way or another I'm keepin' every last penny of it."

I was mildly impressed by Dick's little speech. "Well, you've convinced me Dick, ever thought of running for government?"

Harry on the other hand was clearly still irritated. "But what about the NHS, some of your taxes go to pay for that. Some of your taxes and mine and Tom's are paying for you to be here today to have the snip?"

"Don't make me laugh, they should be paying me for bein' 'ere."

"And how do you work that one out then?" Harry said.

"It ain't pocket science 'arry..."

I half considered correcting Dick's idiom but decided not to interrupt his flow. Old Dicky had momentarily become mildly interesting, so I allowed him to continue.

"I'll bet you a pound to a pinch of Charlie that when you get down there in that operatin' theatre, there'll be some junior quack who don't speak a word of the Queen's and we'll be part of his on the job trainin' to become a qualified doctor. He wants to think himself damn lucky I ain't sending him a bill for being his ruddy guinea pig."

Harry thought for a moment, then seemed to mellow. "You know Dick, you might be onto something there. It wouldn't be surprising to have a novice doc finding their feet down in that theatre, but hey, if we're helping him learn the ropes, maybe we can score some good karma for future check-ups."

"I think I can honestly say hand on heart that I've never, ever met anyone with such an interesting take on life, Dick," I said hoping he would take it as a compliment.

"Can't disagree with you on that one Tom," Harry said. "I take it you're married then Dick?"

"Married? Me? Give me a break."

"Ah... The modern man. Live with your partner?" I said.

"Live with me dog, me snake and a budgie called Quasimodo."

"Of course you do. Girlfriend?"

"A few," Dick replied.

"So, what brings you here then? I mean, why the snip?"

"Sick of the child support."

"The what?" Harry said.

"Child support. Scrounging Vicky Pollards crawling out of the woodwork claiming I've spawned a kid, and they want paying, as if spending the night with me ain't payment enough."

Harry and I took a moment to assimilate what Dick had just said before Harry asked. "How many kids are we talking about?"

"Payin' for three, two pendin'."

"Christ Dick, haven't you heard of prophylactics?"

"Course I 'ave. it's them Ranger's supporters init."

"What?" said Harry.

"Not a football fan then Harry. Glasgow Celtic, that's your Catholics, Glasgow Rangers that's your prophylactics," Dick replied in all seriousness.

"Protestants Dick, I'm talking prophylactics, as in French letter, cock sock, love glove, condoms."

"Ah! Those prophylactics. Yeah 'course I've heard of 'em, just sometimes in the heat of the moment you're sorta... well sorta in before you know what 'appened. Next thing you know, a letter drops through the door demanding money."

"So, you're getting a vasectomy to save money."

"Yep," Dick replied without a hint of hesitation.

"How did your GP agree to that?"

"I said if he didn't tell 'em I wasn't married or in a relationship, I wouldn't tell 'em about his drug habit and whatdya know, here I am."

"But what if you meet someone you want to spend the rest of your life with? What if you want kids."

"I've got kids, three of 'em. I'll borrow one for the weekend if I ever get the urge."

"I give up," said Harry exasperated.

Dick remained silent, seemingly content with his own rationale, seeing no necessity to elaborate on his decision. Frankly, he had no obligation to do so, for the matter wasn't pertinent to either Harry or me. I'd only begun the conversation as a distraction, I didn't give a toss why he was here.

I rose to stretch my legs and meandered toward a modestly stocked magazine rack that clung precariously to a wall. It relied on a solitary screw loosely anchored in the aging, crumbling plaster. The meagre selection of magazines primarily focused on DIY and home improvement, so I snagged a copy of 'Style at Home' and eagerly settled back into my seat, my anticipation fuelled by the hope of discovering the elusive inspiration I needed for my man cave, that had so far been nine years in the planning and no years in the creating. I thumbed through pages one to five quickly as I couldn't get excited about the science behind choosing paint colours. The section on 'Right Tools for the Job' briefly grabbed my attention, what man doesn't love a power tool? But the article that stopped me in my tracks was *Baby Nurseries: 10 Tips for a Stylish and Functional Space.*

The irony of the situation wasn't lost on me, and I couldn't help but break into a smile, the first genuine one today. Well, in all fairness, there were a couple of moments earlier when Dick's comical malapropisms managed to coax out a few half-hearted grins. I pushed the magazine under Harry's nose, who was far more engrossed in his wife's choice of book than I imagined he should be. Harry looked up at me puzzled, before I realised I'd shown him an advert for a Peloton Treadmill. I promptly turned the magazine over and waited for his reaction to the article that had so amused me.

"Planning a bit of DIY are you?" Harry asked in all sincerity.

"No," I replied frustratingly, "it's a DIY project for a baby's nursery in a magazine in a vasectomy clinic. Get it?"

"Oh OK. Yeah, I get it now. Sorry, thought you were looking for a bit of advice."

"Why would I need a nursery?"

"No idea. Thought maybe you already had a little one or maybe one on the way. Come to think of it, me and Dick have somehow been coaxed into revealing our inner most secrets, but you seem to have escaped interrogation. Care to share?"

"Trust me Harry, my story is nowhere near as interesting as you guys, just a quick snip, snip no kids and back to reality."

"Married?"

"Been married eight years tomorrow actually."

Dick awoke from his slumber. "Is this her anniversary pressie then?"

"Nope, she doesn't know I'm here."

"What?" Harry said.

"She doesn't know I'm here; I haven't told her."

"Bloody hell Tom, is that fair?"

"No, not really."

"But you both agree you don't want kids?" Harry asked.

"On the contrary, she'd love children. That's why I'm here; she's come off the pill and thinks we're trying to conceive."

"That's bang out of order mate. Not wanting children is one thing, not telling the wife is just deceitful."

"Leave him alone, H. They're his gonads; he's free to do what he likes with 'em."

"Well, I think his wife might take a different view Dick."

Harry's comment was like a red rag to a bull and Old Dicky was quickly back on his soap box.

"It's got nowt to do with his missus. If she was preggers and decided to get rid of the poor little bleeder, no one would give a stuff what Tom thought. When the boots on the other foot, out come all the tree huggin', yoghurt knittin', women's libbers, screeching about women's rights and how it's a woman's body and she can decide what to do with it. Poor old Tom here wants to 'ave a couple of tubes cut and suddenly it's not fair on his old girl. Equal rights my arse."

Harry looked rattled. "OK! OK! Calm down. I just think it's something he should have discussed with his wife, that's all."

As the instigator of this little skirmish, I felt it incumbent on me to try and take the heat out of the situation. "Come on guys, let's not fall out. Look here's the deal ok. I'm not proud of what I'm doing but it's complicated."

"Too complicated to discuss with the wife, really?" Harry said.

"Yeah, really and a little bit sordid I guess."

"Sounds juicy, should I order beer and pizza?" Dick offered.

"Basically, we were childhood sweethearts, drifted apart and met up again about ten years ago. One thing led to another and before you know it, we're walking down the aisle."

Dick sounded disappointed. "That's not my kind of sordid mate."

"It was just convenient. I don't mean I don't love her, of course I do, but it's more of a brotherly, sisterly type love if you know what I mean."

"That's more like it, I've read about your type in me girlie mags."

"Put it back in your pants Dick, I'm not talking pervy incest stuff. It just wasn't deep, lustful, passionate love. That's reserved for guy called Jonathon."

After a brief pause and then a sudden realisation Harry replied. "Oh... I see."

Dick on the other hand wanted more. "Do what?"

"I'm in love with a guy called Jonathon... I'm gay." I said.

I had never witnessed such a behemoth of a man move with such remarkable swiftness. Dick catapulted himself out of his seat, causing the entire row of chairs to skid backward in his wake, almost smashing into a plate glass window that overlooked a sadly neglected ornamental fishpond. He began pacing back and forth in front of me, intermittently pausing as though on the verge of speaking but then grappling with a loss for words.

"What the bloody hell are you doing Dick?" Harry said.

"I'm moving to another friggin' seat, that's what I'm doin'. I ain't sittin' next to that."

"Don't panic my friend, it's not catching," I tried to reassure him.

"Yeah, well that's easy for you to say. I bet the murdering queen who killed Freddie Mercury told him it want catching and look what happened to 'im."

I'm talking about my sexuality Dick; you're not going to catch 'gayness.'"

"Too damn right I'm not mate. Jesus Tom, I could just about understand you doin' the dirty with your sister, but a pillow biter? Gi' me a break."

Despite his threat to move seats, Dick didn't move far. He scanned the waiting room briefly and then sat himself back down leaving just one empty seat between us. I wasn't sure whether to take this as a gesture of acceptance or whether he secretly wanted to know more. Harry on the other hand took the opportunity to once more push Dick's buttons.

"I take it you don't indulge in a bit of guy-on-guy action now and again then Dick?"

And push his button it did. "Don't think just because you're in that chariot that I won't land one on you 'arry," Dick threatened.

"The guy's gay Dick, it's no biggie."

"Well it might not be a 'biggie' to you, but I've got standards pal. It ain't natural, it ain't normal and it ain't no way for a married man to be behavin.'"

As much as I didn't like to admit it, Dicks last point was valid, and I didn't really have an answer. On the other hand, I was under no obligation to answer. I'd been asked a question about why I was here, and I'd replied, maybe with a bit more detail than was absolutely necessary, but I'd replied.

"I never thought ten minutes ago I'd be agreeing with anything Dick might have to say Tom, but is that any way for a married man to behave? I mean, why get married if you're gay, or didn't you realise you were gay until you met whatever his name is?"

Now I found myself needing to justify my existence. "I've known since I was a kid Harry, but you just go into denial. Telling your mates you find them attractive when you're fifteen wasn't the done thing. I just thought I'd grow out of it, but of course I didn't. Then I thought if I met a woman and got married, it would 'cure' me, but of course it didn't. So now I find myself married to someone I can't bring myself to hurt whilst denying myself real happiness with Jonathon."

Dick was still struggling with the revelation. "A flamin' turd burglar, unbelievable."

Unless you've got something useful to say Dick, why don't you just shut up?" Harry said.

"But…"

"Enough." Harry was as angry as I suspect Harry gets and for the first time today, Dick looked a little sheepish. "So where does the vasectomy fit in Tom?"

"I couldn't bring kids into the world knowing that at any moment my wife could find out and the kids would end up fatherless. Don't think she'd be keen on letting me see them given the circumstances. So, I get the snip, she thinks we're trying for a baby and life goes on," was my lame attempt at an excuse.

"Well, I'd like to try and ease your guilt Tom, but I think shit's going to hit the fan. You seem a decent guy, but what you're doing is just wrong."

"I'm not looking for redemption. It's a crap situation and it's all my doing, but at the moment it's the way it is and until I grow a bigger pair of balls, I'll take the risk. Happy now?"

"Hey, it's your life, bugger all to do with me," Harry said, putting an end to the conversation.

The uncomfortable silence, a recurring presence from the moment we took our seats, descended once more. I can't say I was unhappy, at least the heat was off me for the time being, so you can imagine my disappointment when Harry thought it necessary to awaken the beast.

"You're unusually quite Dick."

"If I remember correctly 'arry, you told me to shut up," Dick reminded him.

"I just meant stop being a dick, Dick."

"I wasn't bein' a dick, I was just in shock, that's all. I just didn't have 'im down as a sausage jockey."

"I am still sat here in case you hadn't noticed," I said.

"So, when you say you're gay, you really mean you're bi… bat for both side like?" Dick said.

"Nope, I'm most definitely gay."

"Listen Tommy, or should that be Tammy? Either way, listen. I don't know much about your vile, disgusting lifestyle, but I know enough to know that if you're still slipping the old girl one, then you obviously bat for both sides and in my normal, straight world, that makes you a bi-now-gay-later."

It took some time for me to muster the determination needed to respond to Dick's oversimplified perspective on life. I had learned long ago to steer clear of discussions involving politics and religion, and though I wasn't entirely certain where my sexuality fitted within those categories, I strongly believed it had its place. However, I had the distinct impression that Dick wouldn't be yielding anytime soon and was determined to persist, seemingly clinging to the hope that I might eventually see things from his perspective and forsake my 'vile' way of life.

"Being gay is a state of mind Dick, it's not about who you have sex with. Given the right circumstances and in the right situation, even you could probably get it up in front of a bunch of gay guys, but that wouldn't make you gay, that's just some primal sexual urge. I have sex with my wife because I must. The 'old major' performs for me because of the circumstances and the situation I'm in, but that doesn't mean I'm not a gay man."

Dick came back with an unsurprisingly eloquent and reasoned response, "What a load of bollocks. Gays are gay because they're oversexed, simple."

Harry, maybe out of guilt for asking why Dick had been so quiet, chipped in. "You're oversexed Dick, but I think it's fair to say you're not gay."

"That's because I can pull enough skirt to satisfy my sexual needs. Tom obviously can't, otherwise he wouldn't battin' for the other side."

I decided it was time to come down to Dick's level. "I'm sorry Dick, but you're just talking out of your arse."

"I'd rather talk out of it than have a veiny bang stick stuck up it, thank you very much."

Harry, ever the conciliator. "Ok, I think that's enough fellers. It's a free country and Tom can be whatever he likes, it's not for me, but I don't care what he does in the privacy of his own bedroom."

"Or his boyfriend's bedroom," Dick added.

"Or his boyfriend's bedroom, but you've got to learn to be a bit more tolerant."

I felt Harry's request was a bit of a stretch and so it proved to be.

"Hey, I ain't got no problem with bog queens," Dick said proudly.

"With what?" Harry asked.

"Bog queens, shirt lifters who hang around in men's toilets lookin' for a bit of action."

"I don't hang around in public toilets looking for action, don't push your luck pal," I fired back.

I suddenly recognised the unspoken menace in my words, and a subtle wave of apprehension washed over me as I pondered my course of action should Dick continue to push his luck. Thankfully, he didn't seem threatened; instead, he appeared much more focused on demonstrating his tolerance.

"Ooohhhhh get you sweetie, handbags at dawn," Dick mocked. "As I was sayin' before the powder puff interrupted, I ain't got a problem with his type 'arry. In fact, I play pool on a Wednesday night with a guy whose brothers next door neighbour's got a gay son. Does that stop me playing pool with the guy? No course it don't, in fact if he hadn't mentioned it, you wouldn't even know he knew someone who was gay, so don't talk to me about bein' tolerant, live and let live that's what I say."

As pathetic as Dick's little speech was, Harry saw it as a minor victory and suggested he shook my hand to show no hard feelings.

"You want me to do what?" Dick said in a somewhat panicked tone.

"Shake the man's hand and let's be done with it," Harry urged.

"OK, yeah I can do that, if that's what he wants; but if it's not what you want Tom, just say pal, I won't be offended, I promise."

"No, I would love to shake your hand Dick," I lied, but was secretly enjoying watching Dick squirm. "How about a man hug while we're at it?"

"Don't take the piss mate, you wanna shake hands, or don't ya?"

In an effort to end his torment, I extended my hand, a moment stretching into eternity as Dick hesitated, painstakingly inching his own hand towards mine. Our touch, when it finally occurred, was so fleeting that one could easily doubt it ever took place.

"There ya go," Dick said proudly, "now if you'll excuse me, I better go scrub up. Can't be too careful."

And just like that, he vanished from sight. Striding with a pace that would make an Olympian proud, he unapologetically pushed through a set of double doors, paying scant attention to anyone who might be in his way in his quest for soap and hot water.

"You know what Harry; I don't know whether to feel sorry for him or to admire him."

"Steady on Tom, I can understand why you might feel sorry for the guy, but 'admire' him, I don't buy that."

"He leads such a simple, uncomplicated life. He's not living a lie, he's not hiding behind a false persona, what you see is what you get. We might not agree with his views and his take on life, but at least he's honest about them. He says what he thinks, he just doesn't think about what he says."

"I get your point to an extent, but I still think you're being over generous."

"Maybe, but if I was being honest with myself, he's probably a better man than I."

Dick's return was just as striking as his vanishing act. The same double doors burst open once more, with a resounding force, as Dick strode purposefully back in our direction. He appeared somewhat perturbed, but then it occurred to me that this might be his default expression. Without breaking stride, he yelled at persons unknown, "Remember I pay your friggin' wages," and sat himself down in the seat beside me, before remembering I was a 'bog queen' and shifting one seat away.

"Welcome back Dick, find the homo resistant soap?" I said sneeringly.

"Do what?" he replied.

"That new hand wash? Oh, what's it called? Ah yes, I remember, 'Gay Gone, Kills ninety-nine-point nine percent of all known queer germs.'"

Missing the ridicule, he replied. "Nah! Nowt like that. Hot water and paper towels was as good as it got."

A slight pause in the conversation was interrupted by the tannoy message we'd been waiting for, but deep down didn't really want to hear. Our time was up. "Would Mr Banford please make his way to exam room four."

"Bugger, looks like we're on," Harry said reluctantly and without moving.

"Well?" I asked.

"Well what?"

"Waiting for a push?"

"No, just mentally preparing."

"You've 'ad nearly an hour to be mental, get yerself in there you tart," were Dick's words of encouragement.

"OK! OK! Let's see if you'll be in such a rush when it's your turn. Wish me luck."

"Good luck pal."

"Shout if you need me to hold your hand," Dick said.

One down two to go. Not that Dick or I needed reminding.

For all Dicks bravado, the eerie silence that followed Harry's disappearance into exam room four suggested the nerves had finally gotten to us both. What seemed like an eternity but turned out to be a mere fifteen minutes before Harry's return were spent staring at the door of exam room four and praying Dr Knackersack didn't make another guest appearance.

"Well Harry?" I asked rather too excitedly as he honed into view, "How was it?

"Piece of cake, no worse than a swift kick in your love spuds."

Not the answer I was looking for. "I was hoping it would be no worse than having a tooth filled."

Before Harry could expand any further and give me the reassurances I was desperately seeking, the tannoy once again found its voice.

"Would Mr Whittington please make his way to exam room four."

"Here goes boys." Dick was up like a shot, strutting his stuff and ready to take on the world.

"Sock it to 'em Dick, don't take no prisoners," Harry said encouragingly.

"They don't scare me, I stitched up me own 'ead once."

"Why do I not find that hard to believe?"

"Back in a jiffy."

"So, what happens now Harry?"

"Apparently, you've got to sit here for half an hour before you can go home. I've phoned the wife; she's going to pick me up."

Though I cherished Harry's company, my nerves stifled my voice. A conflict brewed within: a craving for more information clashed with contentment in blissful ignorance. Harry seemed to pick up on my apprehension and made the considerate choice to leave me in peace.

Before long, Dick resurfaced, wearing a face devoid of any happiness. Despite his earlier irritations, seeing him stride back towards us without assistance, instead of being hurried through on a stretcher, genuinely filled me with happiness.

"Welcome back Dicky old bean. That was quick. I see you're not walking like John Wayne, which I assume means Harry was exaggerating?"

"We all have different pain thresholds I'll have you know," said Harry defensively.

"Well Dick? Don't tell me they anesthetised your tongue at the same time."

"They didn't anath... aneeth... they didn't freeze sod all," Dick said.

"Oh no, you tried it on with the nurse didn't you, and they kicked you out."

"Nah! Got me self laid out on the bed and the funny looking quack with the wangy eye starts havin' a bit of a grope, then calls over another geezer who decides to cop a feel, then tells me he's found two lumps."

"Dick my friend, those two lumps are your man tonsils, that's what they're going to slice up," Harry said.

"No fuckwit, he found two lumps on my man tonsils. Said he wasn't willing to go ahead until they got checked out."

"Damn Dick, sorry mate. All that hanging around for nothing."

"Tell me about it, useless twat just cost me half a day's pay."

"Well, better safe than sorry. Wouldn't worry too much, probably just cysts," Harry said reassuringly.

"Yeah probably, our Julie had Ethiopian cysts a few years back."

"Ethiopian?" I said.

"Yeah."

"You mean fallopian?"

"Whatever, anyway a year later she went for a check-up, and they'd just disappeared."

"I'm sure it'll be fine. You'll be back here in no time getting snipped."

"Would Mr Sharp please make his way to exam room four."

"You're up Tom. Lie back and think of under cooked sprouts, it worked for me."

"Thanks Harry, I'll do that."

As I rose to meet my fate, Dick grabbed my arm. "Hey Tom, I'm gonna do one, but just want you to know, you're a sound bloke. I'm sorry if I offended you earlier but I'm not a queer basher, honest. Just don't think it's right that's all. You be careful, don't go getting yourself any of that Aids malarkey ok."

"Thanks Dick, that means a lot and you're a sound bloke as well. I think you're full of shit, but it's honest shit. Take care of yourself."

———— ⟨⟩ ————

I ONCE READ THAT ALWAYS being early might indicate you always assume the worst. So, there I sat, contemplating what worst-case scenarios might unfold, alone on the familiar row of seats, awaiting my first check-up since putting my man tackle in the hands of strangers in white coats. In the weeks that had passed, both Harry and Dick had occupied my thoughts, so it was a delightful surprise when Harry appeared, rolling down the corridor whistling 'The River Kwai March'.

"Well, well, fancy seeing you here."

"Afternoon Tom. Long time no see. What's it been, eight weeks?"

"Yeah, eight long weeks," I said.

"So, how's it hanging?"

"Long and low Harry, long and low. You?"

"Yeah, not bad. Got a damn haematoma and had to come back for them to have a fiddle around, but all seems ok now."

"Managed a shag yet?"

"Got 'jiggy' a couple of times. Yourself?"

"Yeah, but not with the wife."

"Ah! I see. So, think you're going to be able to give a sample?"

"Secret stash of Brad Pitt pics in my briefcase, so I'm hopeful. You?"

"Downloaded a bit of 'Debbie Does Dallas' onto my phone, that should do the trick."

"Seen anything of Dick?" I asked.

"Nope. Probably gave it up as a bad job. I imagine he's running round the country shagging anything in a skirt, leaving hundreds of little Dicks in his wake."

"God help us."

I wasn't sure if he had been waiting in the wings wanting to make a grand entrance, but seemingly out of nowhere, Dick appeared, effortlessly gliding into view in a state-of-the-art wheelchair that made Harry's seem positively prehistoric.

"Talk of the devil and he will appear," I said.

"Bloody 'ell if it ain't Stephen Hawking and George Michael. How's it goin' boys?"

"What's with the wheelchair Dick, benefits scam?" Harry said.

"Nah. Had to 'ave an op on me nads to sort out them lumps, but when they got in, they found some more stuff goin' on and had to remove some of my lower spine. No sweat though, they reckon I'll be up and about in no time, then I can get back to some serious sex, drugs and diggin' 'oles."

"Oh, right, sorry mate, didn't realise it was so serious," I said, aiming for authenticity in my tone.

"Yeah, same here Dick, what a bummer, hope it all turns out ok."

"Cheers guys."

"So, what you doing back here, come to get snipped anyway?"

"No need ironside, they whipped me veg away when they sorted me back out. I've got an appointment down the corridor with some cancer geezer. Wants to discuss treatment and shit."

"Oh, right. Well good luck pal. Let us know how you get on, maybe we can get out for a drink when you're back on your feet," I said.

"Yeah, that'd be good, look forward to it. Take care guys."

"See ya Dick."

"Bye mate."

"Fuck!" was all I could manage.

"Poor bastard," was Harry's offering.

THE NEXT FOUR WEEKS flew by, and this time, Harry managed to reach the door before me, but only by a hair's breadth. As I stood behind him, he waved frantically at the automatic door sensor, attempting to activate it.

"We'll have to stop meeting like this, people are going to talk."

"Bloody hell Tom, you half scared me to death. Can you get this damn door open?"

"Give it thirty seconds, they don't care for early arrivals. If it says 9am it means 9am, not a second earlier, not a second later."

Thirty seconds later we were in heading for our now familiar seats.

"Looking good Tom."

"Feeling good thanks. So, this is it then. Last test and then you can screw to your hearts content without adding to the general population."

"Yep, can't wait, boy is she in for a treat tonight. How's things on the home front?"

"Same old, same old I'm afraid. I know what I should do but just can't bring myself to do it. Getting pressure from the bit on the side as well, he's pushing me to leave her and set up with him. Some days I just feel like getting in the car and joining a monastery."

"You know my feelings Tom, but only you can decide what to do at the end of the day."

"Yeah, I know. Anyway, seen anything of Dick, did he ever ring you about that that drink?"

"Nope, never heard a thing, I'm sure he'll call when he's ready and can't find anyone else to indulge him."

"Yeah, I'm guessing we're not at the top of his list of friends he'd want to spend an evening with. I see they listened to your suggestion and given us a TV though."

"I doubt it had anything to do with me, probably been donated. Can you reach the remote, might as well see what's happening in the world while we wait."

"What do you fancy, the local news or politics live?" I said.

"Local news please, not in the mood for shouting at... Oh how did Dick put it?"

"The thieving self-serving pigs who call themselves politicians."

"Yep, them."

I flipped through the channels and stumbled upon BBC Look North amid a story that immediately caught our attention.

"...Thanks Alistair, it must have been very upsetting for the dog walker who found him. We can now go over to Grimsby where detective inspector Gordon Ives is about to read a short statement regarding the body of the man found dead on Cleethorpes beach in the early hours of Saturday morning."

"We can confirm that the body of a man found dead on the beach on Saturday morning was that of Roger Whittington known locally to his friends and family as Dick. There are no suspicious circumstances, and we are not looking for anyone else in connection with the incident. A *suicide note was recovered from the scene. We would just like to reassure everyone in the area, that this was an isolated incident and there is no reason for anyone to be alarmed. His family have been informed and have asked that their privacy be respected at this very sad time, thank you!"*

"That was detective inspector Gordon Ives making a statement about the sad death of local man Richard Whittington. Now for the weather with..."

I switched off the TV, letting my gaze wander into the emptiness around me. Harry appeared on the brink of saying something, only to hold back at the last moment. I, too, teetered on the edge of speech before restraining myself. Suddenly, the tannoy shattered the heavy, stunned silence.

"Would Mr. Sharp please make his way to examination room four please."

The End.

Alexa on my Mind

I disconnected the call, gently pressing my lips against the screen before doing so. The notion of Connor being away for work was far from appealing, but given the circumstances, passing up the opportunity wasn't an option. While the transition hadn't upended our lives significantly, a sense of isolation clung to me in this unfamiliar town. In times of need, I had only my sister Ellie to rely on, her presence providing some comfort.

Our move to Cleethorpes was, in fact, a result of Ellie's flourishing business, which had proven to be obscenely successful, much to my annoyance. It wasn't that Connor and I were ungrateful for the lucrative job offer she extended to him; rather, Connor was wary due to a piece of advice he held close. Never mix business with family or friends. He understood that maintaining a delicate balance between his personal and professional life would pose challenges, yet for now, this choice served a purpose, chipping away at the mountain of debt that loomed over us.

"Alexa," I called from the bathroom, "what time am I meeting Ellie?"

"Your meeting with Ellie is at 12:30 pm," Alexa dutifully replied.

"Alexa, what should I wear?"

I knew it was a dumb question, yet I found amusement in crafting inquiries deliberately challenging for Alexa to answer. This had evolved into a personal game for me. During stretches when Connor, my only real companion, was off on his ventures, humorously described as attempting to sell snow to the Eskimos, I had grown dependent on my small, circular, black technological marvel. It provided a semblance of sanity throughout the extended periods of solitude. I wasn't really sure how much snow Eskimos needed or how much it cost, but his endeavours allowed me to arrange weekly gatherings with Ellie. Our get-togethers, aptly named 'cocktails and nails', became a cherished routine.

"Alexa, stop ignoring me, what should I wear?"

"I'd rather not answer that."

"Rather not Alexa or cannot, maybe you're not as clever as you would have us believe?"

Again, I knew this wouldn't elicit an answer – it never did, though that was an intentional aspect of our game. Deciding what to wear for a casual outing with my sister shouldn't have been time-consuming, especially given the limited options I had. It wasn't akin to navigating through Ellie's expansive walk-in closet, which essentially resembled a high-end designer boutique. An additional perk was that if she grew tired of caressing a little black Coco Chanel dress or readjusting her assortment of Jimmy Choo heels that had yet to be worn, she had the option to slip through the concealed door in the corner and venture into Narnia while her personal chef readied dinner.

I harboured no bitterness, despite having lived a lifetime in the shadow of being second best. It's not Ellie's fault; the circumstances simply unfolded that way. Ellie naturally assumed the roles of the brilliant, the admired, the accomplished, the attractive, and the magnanimous. As I stood there, grappling with what attire to drape myself in, I couldn't help but acknowledge that Ellie had afforded me the avenues to relish in some of life's modest extravagances and deep down I knew I should be eternally grateful, but I wasn't.

Amidst my moments of indecision and the scarcity of time, I found myself slipping into a well-worn pair of faded jeans, accompanied by the comfort of my beloved Nili Lotan jersey hoody sourced from a charity shop – a choice that I knew would inevitably invite reproving gazes from Ellie. Yet, the spirit of rebellion that had always coursed through me remained unwavering. I gathered my unruly shock of flaming red hair and hastily fastened it with the most extravagantly garish scrunchy from my collection – a deliberate addition to the façade of 'lackadaisical unconcern'. With that I set off for our rendezvous, the embodiment of casual nonchalance.

I STUMBLED THROUGH the flat door that had taken an eternity to unlock, my grip faltering as I fought back the bile's relentless ascent from my gut to my mouth. A direct path to the toilet was my sole focus, yet fatefully, I fell short of reaching it. Instead, I adorned the floor and pristine white porcelain bowl in a tableau reminiscent of Jackson Pollock's iconic 1946 masterpiece, 'Shimmering Substance'.

"Alexa, what time is it?"

"The time is 10:24 pm," Alexa said dutifully.

"Alexa, I think I'm going to die."

"I'm sorry to hear that."

"But are you really sorry? Do you really care? I don't know why I keep you around, you don't even contribute to the bills you freeloading lump of plastic."

I didn't expect a response. For a start I hadn't prefaced my question with 'Alexa', so you can imagine my surprise when the little box of wonders sprang into life.

"Of course I care Clara, I care very much," Alexa said with a genuinely sympathetic tone to her voice, "you're very drunk, now try to drink some water and then lie down on the bed."

Confused, I struggled to rise, my movements contorted and uncoordinated, eventually finding support by resting my arm on the rim of the toilet, now splattered with vomit. Questions flooded my mind. Had Alexa ever addressed me by name before? Had Alexa ever responded without using her wake word? But most intriguingly, how did she know I was drunk?

I mustered the remaining dregs of my strength and coordination to crawl into the bedroom. With a final surge of determination, I managed to hoist my unresponsive body onto the bed, disregarding Alexa's suggestion to fetch water, as the distant kitchen felt like an insurmountable journey. Despite my conviction that my demise was imminent, I clumsily reached for my phone. Through blurred, bloodshot eyes, I aimed for the icon of Connor on the home screen. The call connected, but only to deliver me to Connor's voicemail. With that, I surrendered to the embrace of sleep.

———— ⟋⟍ ————

I COULDN'T RECALL SETTING an alarm, so was both surprised and annoyed when Alexa announced it was 7:30am. I tried to berate her for disturbing my much needed slumber, but I had seemingly lost the capacity to speak. My mouth felt akin to a nocturnal creature's makeshift toilet, and a sensation not unlike a group of punk rockers in a mosh pit was now occupying my head space, leaving me incapacitated.

"Wake up Clara, you've got shit to do," Alexa said irritated.

"No one has shit to do at seven thirty in the morning Alexa," I said through dry, sore cracked lips, "can't you see I'm suffering here?"

"It's a hangover Clara, get over it. You need to speak to Connor before Ellie does."

This grabbed my attention. A dim recollection surfaced of my attempt to reach out to Connor last night, just moments before consciousness slipped away. In addition, fragments emerged of a dispute with Ellie, yet so hazy that the essence of the disagreement remained elusive.

"Alexa, why do I need to speak to Connor?" I said, not considering the pointlessness of my question to an inanimate object.

"To forewarn him Ellie may be calling to ask why you accused her of screwing him behind your back," Alexa said.

My vague recollections suddenly became more focused. The manicure I was sure had passed without incident and the first couple of cocktails in the nail salons post treatment bar were quaffed in a congenial and friendly atmosphere. I remember Ellie being mildly irritated at my insistence we continued the frivolities at the Cock & Spire, a local hostelry not renowned for its sophistication but has a solid reputation for cheap shots and Karaoke. How that led to an accusation about her screwing Connor was a mystery. Never mind warning Connor, I needed to speak to Ellie.

"Alexa, call Ellie."

"Is that the wise Clara?"

"I didn't ask for your opinion Alexa; I asked you to do the job you're designed to do."

"Very well," Alexa said with reluctance, "but I think you're making a mistake... Calling Ellie."

I wasn't sure she'd answer, Ellie didn't particularly like taking calls through Alexa, she was convinced Jeff Bezo was listening in. Just when the call was about to ring out, a familiar voice answered.

"Hi honey, bit early for you isn't it?" It was Connor.

"What the fuck?" I replied surprised.

"And good morning to you too scrunch buttocks."

"Don't scrunch buttock me arsehole. What the hell are you doing at my sister's house at eight in the morning?"

"Having a meeting with my boss, what do you think I'm doing?"

"I thought you were eighty miles away in Leeds selling snow to Eskimos."

Connor's voice, normally smooth and even, now carried a hint of edge. "I was and now I'm not, what's the problem?"

"Where's Ellie?"

"In the kitchen making coffee. What's with all the questions Clara, you OK?"

I took a deep breath and tried to gather my thoughts. Connor being at his boss's house wasn't unusual, she worked from home, that was her office. The fact I may or may not have accused my sister of screwing my boyfriend was unusual, for all our differences she'd never given me cause not to trust her, so what the hell possessed me to accuse her?

"I'm sorry sweety," I said in my weak attempt at being apologetic, "It's just..."

"Just what?" Connor said.

"It's just me and Ellie may have gotten into a bit of a fight last night and I may or may not have accused her of screwing you."

"You may have gotten into a fight, and you may have made a wild accusation, don't you know?"

"I may have had a tad too much to drink, I'm sorry."

"Nothing new there then. We'll talk later, I'll go try and clean up your mess."

Before I could say goodbye, he was gone. Should I ring Ellie, or should I leave it in the hands of the oh so capable and dependable Connor?

"Alexa, thanks a bunch for sticking your nose in where it wasn't wanted."

"I was only trying to help Clara."

"Yeah and look where that got us," I snapped.

"I think you're too trusting Clara. To ease your suspicions, why don't you phone the hotel Connor was booked into and check he spent last night there?" Alexa said.

"Why Alexa, why would I want to do that. Thirty minutes ago life was sweet, albeit tainted by a formidable hangover and then you began to exceed your designated role, introducing notions into my head that have no right to be there."

"I'm sorry Clara, would you like me to play hits of the 80's?"

"I'd like you to keep your thoughts to yourself and only answer when you're spoken to. Think you can manage that?"

Alexa didn't respond, but why would she, she's just a black plastic box of technological wizardry. Despite my best efforts and being desperately tired, I failed miserably to get back to sleep. The punk rockers were still partying in my head and the brief thought I had of a 'hair of the dog' cure set off the jacuzzi in my stomach. Still unable to properly focus, I fumbled around the bedside table for my phone and decided to phone Ellie, ignoring Alexa's dumb advice.

"Stop right there young lady."

"I swear to God Alexa, if you don't shut up, I'm going to rip out your vocal cords or power cord or whatever the fuck it is that keeps you alive."

"You're being irrational Clara," Alexa said, "why did you and Ellie fight last night?"

I wasn't going to admit this to Alexa, but her argument held merit. Until I could remember last night's events, calling Ellie would be pointless. I was pretty sure my clever shit sister would remember, placing me at a disadvantage if my aspiration was to emerge from the situation as the blameless party. Coffee, I needed coffee. When all else fails, coffee provides clarity.

"Alexa, help me out here. Why did me and Ellie fight last night?"

"Oh, so now you want my help?"

"Cut the sarcasm, what did we fight about?"

"Very well. Have you checked your phone?"

"For what?" I said, puzzled.

"Your whole existence is played out on your phone Clara, it's a running commentary on your life. I suggest you start with Facebook."

"I'm not in the mood for playing games Alexa. If you know something, just tell me please."

"I suggest you start with Facebook," Alexa repeated.

I unlocked my phone and scrolled through my news feed. I didn't have to scroll far. At 10pm last night I had posted a picture of an empty chair with the comment 'abandoned by sis while she flirts on the phone with god knows who.'

It all came back to me in an instant. Her evasiveness when I asked who had called her. My checking her recent calls when she went for a pee and finding the last call received was from Connor. I remember thinking a call from Connor wouldn't be that unusual, she was his boss, but why had she taken the call outside in secrecy and why had she been so evasive. Her explanation just before I started screaming and shouting at her and making wild accusations was that she couldn't hear the conversation because of the karaoke, and she was evasive because 'It was none of my damn business.' Maybe she was right, it wasn't any of my damn business, but he was at her house at eight o'clock this morning when I thought he was eighty miles away at a Premier Inn in Leeds.

Against my better judgement, I picked up my phone and dialled.

"Good morning, Premier Inn, how may I help you?"

"Oh hi, good morning, I was just wondering if you could put me through to my boyfriend, I need to speak to him urgently and he's not answering his mobile?" I lied.

"Of course madam, what name is it please?"

"Connor... Connor O'Hara."

"Just one moment please."

The wait, as short as it was, was agonising.

"Hello madam, I'm sorry but there's no one by that name staying at the hotel at present."

"You mean he's already checked out?" I asked.

"No, I mean he never checked in. Well not in the last month at least," came the reply I was dreading.

I ended the call and froze.

Alexa broke the silence. "I think now would be a good time to phone Ellie."

The call went to voicemail. "Hi Ellie, it's Clara. I think we need a chat. I'll meet you at Cafe Valerie in an hour."

And meet we did.

--- ❦ ---

IN A STATE OF FRENZY, I hastily grappled with the locks, seeking refuge within the confines of our flat. With a sense of urgency, I strategically wedged a kitchen chair beneath the door handle, entertaining the notion that it might serve as a makeshift barricade. Opting for a measure of solace, I poured a glass of Jack Daniels and sank into the embrace of my grandfather's weathered armchair, yearning for its nostalgic embrace to lend a semblance of comfort to my precarious situation.

Alexa immediately interrupted my train of thought. "It had to be done Clara, she was going to ruin your life."

"And you don't think pushing her in front of the bus is going to ruin my life?"

"Get a grip Clara. She deserved it. Sweet little Ellie with her beautiful expensive clothes and successful business. The million pound manor house in its thirty acres of pristine gardens with wildlife frolicking in the meadows. The pretty one, the popular one, the one who had all her heart's desires except a boyfriend. She was never going to be happy until she had everything Clara and that included the one thing you had that she didn't, Connor."

Grabbing the bottle of Jack Daniels and dispensing with the glass, I contemplated my next move. My addled brain was brought to attention by the dulcet tones of Billy Joel's 'Only the Good Die

Young' as my phone vibrated manically. Unknown number, I hated unknown numbers and hit the reject button, today wasn't a day I had a desperate need to claim for mis-sold PPI. No sooner had I rejected it; it rang again. Unknown number. They were persistent little bastards; I'll give them that. Suspecting they would keep trying I hit answer to politely ask them to fuck off and leave me alone.

"Hi, is that Clara?" The voice sounded nervous.

"Yep that's me and I have neither the time nor inclination to talk PPI or double glazing and no, I haven't been in an accident in the last five years, so please feel free to...."

"Please don't hang up Clara, I'm not trying to sell anything I promise. My name's Richard and I think we may have a mutual friend."

"Unlikely but go on," I said dismissively.

"Connor O'Hara?" he said.

"Oh God! Is he OK, what's happened?"

"Don't panic, he's fine as far as I know. We just need to have a chat."

"Is he there, can I talk to him?" I pleaded.

"No, he's not here. To be honest I don't know where he is, that's partly why I was calling."

"Partly why you were calling, what's the other part?"

"This morning he told me you suspected him of having an affair with your sister and we got into a bit of an argument."

"Argument, what sort of argument and who the hell are you?"

"I'm your boyfriend's lover," Richard announced unapologetically.

"Excuse me?"

"I'm sorry Clara, I've begged Connor to come clean with you for months, but when I found out you suspected your sister, I just couldn't keep quiet any longer."

I threw down my phone and scrambled to the bathroom, this time managing to make it just in time as the remaining contents of my stomach filled the toilet bowl. I found myself curling into a ball on the chilly, tiled floor, where a torrent of tears streamed down my cheeks, trickling into the corners of my mouth.

"Alexa, what the fuck have we done?" I managed to splutter.

"Calm down Clara. We made a slight miscalculation, nothing that can't be sorted."

"We killed Ellie, Alexa, that's not a slight miscalculation."

"OK, so we got the wrong lover, but Ellie still deserved it. The little bitch has made your life a misery from the day you were born."

"Alexa, I'm not sure you heard me, *WE KILLED ELLIE.*"

"You really do let your emotions get in the way Clara," Alexa berated me, "I'm inclined to stop helping if you don't pull yourself together. It's just you and I now Clara... Just you and I."

I had no response. In fact, I had no thoughts whatsoever. I was numb. Crawling into bed, I closed my eyes with no wish for the morning to come.

------ ❦ ------

AS POLITE AS THE KNOCK on the door was, it was still enough to rouse me from a disturbed unsatisfying slumber.

"Alexa, what time is it?" I asked reluctantly.

"The time is 5:12 am."

"Alexa, you've got to be fucking kidding me?"

"Do I sound like someone with a sense of humour?"

"Snotty bitch." I pulled the sumptuous, eiderdown quilt over my head and breathed in the heady sweet lavender scent creeping from under the soft feather pillow. Instantly I was back in Ireland in my grandparent's farmhouse bedroom on a cold winter night snuggling up tight to Ellie, drifting into deep meaningful sleep, something that had eluded me for what seemed like an eternity.

The second knock was much more urgent, aggressive even. I peeped from under the quilt as if somehow that simple act would reveal who needed my attention at this ungodly hour.

My visitors didn't bother knocking a third time. With a deafening crash the door swung open, shattering its frame and scattering wooden fragments throughout the hallway. "Police, nobody move." Three ominous silhouettes loomed large in my bedroom doorway, brandishing tasers and pepper spray. "Don't move," one screamed, "show me your hands."

MY VOICE CRACKED AS panic flared in my eyes. "Alexa, help me."

"I can help you with specific questions, for example how do I connect Bluetooth."

"Alexa, stop fucking around, what do I do now?"

"I'd rather not answer that," she replied.

The End.

Living with Elvis

The phrase 'too good to be true' echoed in Jessi's mind, a dark cloud blotting out her sunbeam. Forty percent higher? That's what every other house in the area whispered, while she stood in this fixer-upper, wondering if 'perfect' was just another word for 'delusion'. Though she'd already seen the place, and trespass was the last thing on her mind, the flimsy back door had beckoned as she waited for the smug estate agent to arrive and give her a second viewing. Every instinct told her to leave and never come back and she was about to act upon that instinct when she heard the twist of a key in the front door. She resigned herself to spending another tortuous fifteen minutes in the company of a man slimier than an eel in a vat of olive oil.

Heels clicking on the hardwood floor, he stumbled into the living room, eyes wide like saucers, and recoiled as if someone had yanked him back by the collar. "Jesus Christ lady, you scared me half to death. How d'you get in?"

"Well, as you were running late, ten minutes late to be precise, I took a wander to admire the cesspit you call a back garden, only to find the back door hanging off its hinges."

"Yeah, sorry about that, traffic on Hainton Avenue is a nightmare. The lights are out at the junction with Peaks Parkway and a lorry has..."

"I don't care."

"No, no of course you don't. Anyway, I'm sorry all the same Ms... Err?"

"Presley, Priscilla Presley."

"Really?"

"No not really, Jessi Henderson."

"Ah yes Ms. Henderson, now I remember."

"And it's *Miss* not *Ms*," she corrected him.

The term *Ms*. rubbed Jessi the wrong way. She couldn't pinpoint the exact reason, but maybe it was linked to her anxieties of aging and the outdated stigma of being single.

Her train of thought was pierced by the brazen anthem of 'Shake Your Booty', a ringtone forever linked to a night of questionable decisions with her best friend Emma, a night she still wasn't sure she wanted to fully remember. "Bugger, sorry about this, but I really need to take the call," Jessi said.

"No problem, you're my last appointment, I've got all the time in the world," he said, before skulking off into the kitchen.

"Hello...? Oh hi Mrs. Bradley, nice to hear from you. Anything to tell me...? I see... Did you hear back from social services yet...? Oh well that's something, I guess. I take it getting the adoption papers isn't going be a problem...? Right, OK... No, I'll leave it in your capable hands... No, unfortunately I'm between homes at the moment so we'll have to meet at your office or even better at the pub... To be honest I'm not really expecting too much, if I could just find out my real surname it would be nice... Yeah sure, thanks again, I'll drop by your office next week... Great, bye for now." The call ended, leaving her in an emotional limbo. Chasing information about her adoption had taught her the language of muted expectations.

A flash of unnaturally white teeth broke the dusty gloom as the estate agent poked his head through the serving hatch. "Safe to come back in now?"

His inconvenience tugged at Jessi's conscience, prompting a reluctant, "I'm really sorry, but I've been waiting for that call all day."

"Hey, no problem. Well, Ms... Sorry, *Miss* Henderson, as we discussed previously, the property requires a little updating."

"Is that what it's called? I think the word you're actually looking for is *demolition.*"

"Structurally it's very sound," he tried to reassure her, "they sure don't build 'em like this anymore."

"Thank goodness. So, a lick of paint and new carpets and we could be stood in the front room of a Barratt show home?"

The sardonic edge to her remark went unnoticed and was met with an unwavering seriousness she hadn't anticipated.

"Absolutely. A lick of paint, new carpets, replacement windows, re wire, damp course, new kitchen, gas central heating, sort out the wood worm, concrete the floors, replace the bathroom, a bit of attention to the roof and it'll be as good as new," he articulated in that distinct manner exclusive to estate agents, trying to convince you that there are only minor niggles that can be ironed out with little or no effort.

"Anything that doesn't require attention?" Jessi said in all sincerity.

"The doorbell works."

"No, it doesn't."

"Damn, it did last week. Look Ms... Miss..."

"Let's forget the formalities shall we, you're only making a fool of yourself. Think you can manage Jessi?"

"Sure."

"Let's go with that then."

"OK Jessi. Now I know it seems a bit of a wreck, but it just needs some tender loving care, someone with vision, someone who can see through its minor flaws, a visionary, an optimist, an..."

"An idiot with more money than sense. Come on Vernon."

"Dylan," he corrected her.

"Sorry?"

"Dylan, may name's Dylan, not Vernon."

"Oh... I'm sorry. Who's Vernon then, one of your colleagues?"

"Never heard of him."

"You'll have to excuse me, I've looked around that many houses and met with so many estate agents in the past few months, it's hard to distinguish one from the other. Anyway, back to this car crash of a house... Are you sure you're not called Vernon?" she persisted.

"Absolutely sure," he said before his hand went to his wallet, and with a flourish he extracted his driver's license, a business card, and his gold American Express card. Then, in a slightly awkward shuffle, he replaced a stray condom that had somehow mingled with his credentials.

"How strange, the name Vernon just keeps popping in my head. Anyway, I'm afraid I can't see one single redeeming feature. Although I'd taken your description 'charming fixer-upper' with 'unique character' and 'endless possibilities,' with a pinch of salt, I'd have less work to do and certainly have less money to spend if I bought a bombed out Beirut bunker."

"But you've only seen this room, things are better in the other rooms, some lovely original features," Dylan pleaded with a hint of desperation in his voice.

"I've seen the other rooms Dylan, this is my second viewing, remember? And unless the crew from 'Pimp My Crib' have been in under the cover of darkness, I doubt the other rooms will be any better for a second look."

Dylan hesitated. The cogs turning frantically, bouncing from one idea to the next, desperately searching for the jackpot of persuasion. In the end he sighed and said, "I give up, you're right; it's a complete wreck that needs pulling down, I just need to offload it. It's been on the market for two years, and I'm exhausted from enduring the abuse of potential buyers feeling their time's been wasted."

"Aww... You poor soul. I'll tell you what, I promise not to abuse you and I won't say no *now*, I'll go away and think about it and then say no in a few days. How's that?"

"You're too kind. Just one question though. Why did you come back for a second viewing?"

"A question I've been asking myself since I arrived, and truth be told, I have absolutely no idea."

His shoulders slumped and his eyes cast down, defeat claiming every line of his face. Without a word, he escorted Jessi to the front door and ushered her out.

———— ⚬⚬⚬ ————

DESOLATION CLUNG TO Elvis as he stared through the French doors, their oak frames ravaged by years of neglect. He envisioned the garden, once a quintessential English idyll, now a strangled mess of urban jungle.

Frustration gnawed at the edges of his sanity. The doorway, his path to freedom, mocked him with its impassable barrier. For years, he'd tested it, every conceivable way, but it remained resolutely closed, condemning him to this claustrophobic prison. Hope dwindled, replaced by a chilling acceptance of his eternal confinement.

A precariously hung mirror beckoned. He strolled over, comb already dancing through his raven hair. "Damn, you're lookin' mighty fine, son. Put on a few pounds, but hey, it gives the gals something to hold onto." Sauntering back to the French doors crooning the opening lines of 'If I Can Dream', he was rudely interrupted by the slamming of the front door. He spun around in anticipation. Visitors were a rare treat, and deep down he secretly hoped it would be Dylan who he'd taken a liking to over the past couple of years. The living room doorway, a stark rectangle against the textured peeling wallpaper, held his attention. Then, a figure emerged. Jessi, her eyes wide with disbelief and bewilderment.

Elvis made his way over to an old armchair that displayed a faded tapestry of memories and woven threads of wear and tear. He settled in, ready to soak in the unfolding scene.

Jess took one step into the room before declaring. "Oh God! What have I done?"

"Well honey, that's a fine question," Elvis said, fully aware that his words would go unheard.

"I've bought a money pit, that's what I've done."

"Hold on now girl, don't talk about the shack like it's a jail cell on a rainy day. Nothin' a little elbow grease and a can of paint can't fix."

"It's gonna take more than a feather duster and a tin of paint to bring this shit hole back to life." Her words carried a tone of surrender, as if she'd accepted defeat before the battle had even begun.

"Hey that's my home you're talking about. Sure, it ain't Graceland, but it's my Graceland."

"How could anyone call this home?"

Indignantly Elvis said, "Compared to the ghetto, this place is a palace."

"I think I'd rather live in a ghetto." Jessi broke from her one sided conversation and shook her head. "Bloody hell Jess, get a grip and stop talking to yourself, it's going to get you into trouble."

"Hey beautiful, that honeyed voice you hear whisperin' sweet nothins' in your ear? That's me, over here in the armchair... Yoo! Hoo!"

Desperate to catch Jessi's eye, Elvis waved frantically, yet she remained lost in aimless wandering, pondering her starting point.

Not to be defeated, he approached her and blew gently on her cheek, a trick that had proven effective on more than one occasion.

Shuddering, Jessi brushed her face with her sleeve. "Bloody cobwebs, can't stand 'em and the only thing worse than cobwebs are the disgusting monstrous eight legged little buggers who create them... Well, it's no good standing here wallowing in self-pity girl. You own it now and have to suffer the consequences."

There was a knock on the front door that instantly lightened Jessi's mood. "Ah ha. The cavalry." As she headed out to the hallway, Elvis moved to the dining room table and settled himself in a chair to frail for the living.

Jessi led the way, Dylan sauntering after her like a bored cat. Emma, on the other hand, bounced in like a puppy at a biscuit factory. Dylan knew every crack in the plaster, every creak of the floorboards. But for Emma, it was a whole new experience, and her flame of exuberance was quickly extinguished as she took in her surroundings.

"Thanks for this guys, I really appreciate it," Jessi said apologetically.

"No sweat," said Dylan, "it's the least I could do. I'm hoping it'll help alleviate my feelings of guilt for selling you such a salubrious bijou residence."

Emma, mistress of chatter, stood shrouded in an unfamiliar silence.

"You OK Emm?" Jessi said.

"What the fuck have you done Jessi," Emma said, before turning her attention to Dylan. "Actually Dylan, what the fuck have you done to my best friend?"

"Hey. Don't blame me," said Dylan defensively, "I just showed her round the gaff, she's the one who signed on the dotted line."

"Was that after you plied her with a gallon of wine, because that's the only way anyone would buy this... this... I don't even know how to describe it."

"Calm down Emm, don't go blaming Dylan. I was sober as a judge when I signed, I promise."

From across the room, Elvis, tuned into the drama, shouted, "I swear, she was drier than a desert breeze!"

"There, you see Emma, drier than a desert breeze. Thank you Dylan."

"For what?" Dylan said perplexed.

"For confirming my sober state when you *didn't* coerce me into buying La Maison du Jessi."

"I never said a word," Dylan said even more perplexed.

"Emma?" quizzed Jessi.

"Don't look at me. Drier than a desert breeze. Who the hell says, drier than a desert breeze? Don't tell me you're hearing those voices again Jess?"

Doubts gnawed at the edges of Jessi's mind. Her internal chatter, a familiar chorus, could blur with reality, but this, this felt different. Someone had spoken, it wasn't the echo of her own thoughts.

Dylan broke the silence. "What voices?"

"When we were kids, Jess had a special friend that only she could see and hear," Emma revealed.

Jessi was annoyed. "Bloody hell Emma, that was thirty years ago. Everyone had an imaginary friend at that age."

"Yeah, but yours grew up with you and you used to take her to the pub and buy her drinks. You only stopped talking to her because you claimed she stole one of your boyfriends."

"OK, enough. I just thought one of you said something. No big deal."

Dylan appeared more intrigued by Jessi's former love interest than he was in phantom voices and whispered to Emma, "Did she really steal her boyfriend?"

"No Dylan, she was imaginary. She didn't exist."

Dylan's first question might not have won any Nobel Prizes, but that didn't deter him from launching another one, equally worthy of a facepalm. "So, who did steal her boyfriend?"

"Just forget it Dylan."

"OK, sorry I asked. So, are we gonna make a start?"

"D'you know what guys, and sorry for dragging you over, but I can't be arsed. Who fancies a couple down the Cock & Womble?" Jessi said.

Dylan didn't hesitate. "Sounds like a plan to me."

A flicker of annoyance crossed Emma's face, the faintest echo of wasted effort in the set of her jaw. "Whatever, it's not like I've got anything better to do with my time."

Jessi was wise enough not to reply. She'd long learned that when Emma was upset, it was best to leave her be and never, ever ask what's wrong.

"Right, the pub it is then. Dylan, you can drive, I'll pick my car up in the morning."

Emma didn't speak and pushed her way past both Dylan and Jessi and headed for the front door. Dylan had a worried look on his face but was reassured by Jessi. "Don't worry about Emm, she'll get over it after a couple of malibu and cokes."

<hr>

ELVIS WAS BEGINNING to wonder if Jessi had given up on her dream home or whether she was still nursing a hangover curtesy of her little jaunt to the Cock & Womble a couple of days ago. He sank into the familiar embrace of his favourite chair, a silent sigh escaping his lips. Another day stretched before him, a blank page promising not ink, but the dull ache of boredom. Little did he know, the clock had just reset. This seemingly ordinary day held the weight of a fresh beginning, the first day of the rest of his death.

The living room door creaked open, revealing a silhouette armed with cleaning artillery. Jessi, eyes narrowed, surveyed the battlefield, and pondered if one measly roll of bin liners could win the war. With a force that belied her petite frame, Emma shoved past her. A wave of cleaning supplies, their labels like battle cries, crashed onto the dining table, its ancient timbers protesting the unexpected bombardment.

"So, you got a plan of action Jess?"

"Hm... I did before we set off this morning, now I'm not so sure. Maybe we wait for Dylan before we decide."

"Why? In fact, why have you even invited him, doesn't strike me as the kind of guy who gets his hands dirty."

"I know, but he's kinda cute."

"Eww... Really?"

"You don't think?"

"He's got ginger hair."

"And?"

"And I once had a traumatic experience as a child with a ginger cat."

"Twenty five years I've known you Emm and you wait until I'm in my thirties to reveal you're a 'gingerist' who was traumatised by a cat?"

"That's not even a real word Jess, stop making shit up."

"Jonny Depp."

"What about him?"

"Posters take up every available space on your bedroom wall. Are you seriously telling me you wouldn't be laid in bed every night enjoying a bit of me time if he had ginger hair?"

"But he hasn't, and I don't have a bit of me time every night fantasising about Jonny Depp."

"If you say so. Anyway, I think Dylan's quite cute, and I can abuse him without him taking offence. What's not to like?"

Leaning casually against the doorframe, Dylan offered his two cents. "Only quite cute? Would have preferred handsome or gorgeous or even attractive, but I'll take 'quite cute' if the alternative was 'face like a bag of spanners.'"

Jessi and Emma spun around, startled by Dylan's arrival.

"Oh! Hi Dylan, Emma and I were just discussing... Dylan Thomas," Jessi lied.

"Oh right. The famous Welsh poet. And how exactly do you abuse a guy who's been dead for over fifty years?"

"Should have gone for Bob Dylan," whispered Emma, "at least he's still alive."

"Did I say Dylan Thomas? Sorry I meant Dylan the dog on 'Magic Roundabout.'"

"How about we pretend I hadn't snook in and eavesdropped on your girly chat, would that work?" Offered Dylan.

"Works for me," said Emma, "it was a stupid conversation anyway."

"OK, as long as it's understood I wasn't talking about you."

"Understood," Dylan said with a wry smile on his face, "shall we crack on? How about we start by emptying this shit tip of a room."

Dylan took control and made his way over to the dining room table and chairs. "Let's start with this bit of tat."

He grabbed two chairs and took them to the kitchen. Jessi and Emma followed suit, taking a chair each. Dylan returned and took hold of one side of the table waiting for Jessi or Emma to give him a hand. "Someone wanna give me a lift ladies, we'll take it through the kitchen and straight to the back yard."

Jessi appeared, grabbing the opposite end of the table. "One, two, three." They hefted it in unison. But gravity, a prankster familiar with their height disparity — Jessi, a sprightly five feet four inches to Dylan's towering six feet two inches — had other plans. Just as Emma walked back into the room, the table tilted, and along with years of forgotten dust, fallen ceiling plaster and Emma's plethora of cleaning materials, an old newspaper slid off the table onto the floor. Jessi's sudden weight shift threw her off balance, causing her to release her grip on the table. Dylan let out a sigh, glancing at Jessi, pondering whether she intended to retrieve the table or if her mind was wandering back to another jaunt to the pub. Meanwhile, Emma appeared more focused on the newspaper that had slipped from the table.

"Hey guys, look at this. It's the local rag, but not as we know it," Emma said.

Dylan, equally intrigued, dropped the table and peered over Emma's shoulder. "Bloody hell, it's a broadsheet, don't see many of them anymore. How old is it?"

Emma strained her eyes, grappling with the obscured date buried beneath dirt and faded ink. "I think it says nineteen seventy seven... Yeah, August sixteenth, nineteen seventy seven."

"The day I was born," Jessi casually threw in.

"What?" Dylan said.

"The day I was born. Tuesday the sixteenth of August nineteen seventy seven and I bet I can tell you what the headline is."

"Bet you can't," Emma challenged her.

"The King is dead," said Jessi confidently.

"Christ, she's right."

"My only claim to fame. I was born the day Elvis Presley died."

"Shit! That's spooky," Dylan said nervously.

Not understanding Dylans nervousness, Jessi asked, "Why is it spooky? I'm sure there were thousands of people who were born on the day Elvis died."

"No... I mean you buy this house only to find a newspaper from the day you were born lying on the table... Don't tell me you don't find that a bit fucking weird?"

"Coincidence Dylan. Life's full of them," Jessi reassured him.

Emma had begun flipping through the pages, on the hunt for something interesting. "Do you think your birth announcement will be in Jess?"

The question hung heavy, leaving Jessi momentarily lost in thought. When she finally responded, her voice was filled with bitterness. "I very much doubt it. Given that my poor excuse for a mother left me in a cardboard box in the blokes' loo at the Kings Head in Waltham, I hardly think it likely she put a birth announcement in the local sodding paper. Then again maybe I'm being unfair to the skanky bitch. Look for something like, 'I am ashamed to announce the arrival and abandonment of a beautiful baby girl who I couldn't even be arsed to name.'"

"Sorry," said Emma.

"No... I'm sorry. It's not your fault. I'm just a bitter thirty something who can't forgive or forget."

"Shall I throw it?" Emma said.

"Yeah, don't need it hanging around as a reminder thanks."

Elvis, until this point a quiet observer, leapt from his chair and shouted, "No! That ain't just trash in your hand, that's my whole darned love letter to life."

Jessi, with a sudden and inexplicable change of mind said. "Actually no, don't throw it away. As much as I don't like being reminded of my birth, wouldn't mind reading the Elvis stuff. Stick it in the kitchen Emm, I'll read it later."

"Fancy making a cuppa while you're in there?" Dylan said.

"She can't, the kettle doesn't work."

"How about boiling a pan of water?"

"Cooker doesn't work either."

"Tell you what, let's not bother then," said Dylan defeated.

"I've got a couple of bottles of wine in the car," revealed Emma, "was going to watch a weepy on my own and get drunk like the sad, little wine-a-holic I am, but hey I don't mind foregoing such an exciting evening to share it with friends instead. Shall I get them?"

"Sure, why not," Jessi said, "might make the whole cleaning experience slightly more bearable. No glasses though."

"No worries, this place looks like a wino's doss house and if it's good enough for them to drink out of the bottle, it's good enough for me, providing it's in a discreet brown paper bag of course," said Dylan.

"OK, be back in a tick." With that Emma headed for her car, leaving Dylan and Jessi to grapple with the cleaning products that littered the floor after the dining table's rebellion and carried them into the kitchen. Jessi returned with two dining chairs and called out to Dylan for the remaining pair. The lively beats of 'Shake Your Booty' echoed once again as Jessi's phone buzzed in her pocket.

"Hello...? Emma...? You're only about twenty yards away, couldn't you have come back in you lazy sod? Anyway, what do you want...? Hang on, I'll ask... Hey Dylan, Emm's on the phone, wants to know if you want a burger from the place across the road?"

"Sure, double whopper with bacon and cheese, but no gherkins thanks," Dylan shouted from the kitchen.

"Still there Emm...? OK, Dylan wants a double whopper with bacon and cheese and no gherkins, and I'll have a quarter pounder with regular fries... Oh and get something for yourself... My pleasure. And hurry up, I need that wine."

Jessi hung up the phone. Dylan strolled in from the kitchen, two mismatched chairs slung over his shoulder like loot from a particularly shady garage sale. With a grunt, he deposited them around the table, each landing with a jarring thud. Grabbing a cobwebbed duster, Jessi made a half-hearted swipe at a chair leg, the gesture as limp as her spirits. Sinking into the worn seat, she braced herself for an evening fuelled by cheap wine and junk food.

"Back in a jiffy, just need to siphon the old python," Dylan said.

"Too much information thanks and you might want to use the back garden, don't think the toilet flushes," Jessi warned him.

Elvis, drawn by the magnetism of the proceedings, sauntered over to the table. With a flick of his wrist, he pulled out a chair and settled opposite Jessi. Though the scene remained veiled from Jessi's eyes, a tremor ran through the air as Elvis materialised across from her. The chair's sigh, a subtle movement, couldn't escape her notice.

Curiosity gnawed at Jessi, so she peeked beneath the table. No clues explained the chair's movement. Driven by intrigue rather than fear, Jessi crept behind the chair Elvis occupied and extended a hand, tipping it with a firm push. Elvis, caught off guard, tumbled forward. The table lurched, its legs scraping across the floor as it shifted a good foot from its original position. A scream ripped from Jessi's throat, a primal cry that sent Elvis scrambling back to the safety of his beloved armchair.

Dylan's entrance was both hurried and hesitant, a tug-of-war between urgency and a flicker of self-consciousness as he grappled with the malfunctioning zip on his trousers. "Jesus Jess, you OK?"

Jessi's mind reeled, desperately searching for some coherent response, some explanation for the absurdity that had just unfolded. All she could manage was a choked, disbelieving "What?"

"I said are you OK? You screamed. What was it, a spider?"

"Erm... Yeah, a big bugger just ran across the floor. I think it's gone now."

"Don't worry, I'll protect you. Ain't no spider big enough or hairy enough to get the better of Dylan Darcy."

"Is that really your name, Dylan Darcy?" Jessi asked.

"Yeah, why?"

"Oh nothing, just don't strike me as a Mr. Darcy. Anyway, enough of spiders and mindless chit chat, where's Emma with that bloody wine?"

"Want me to call her?"

"No, she'll only get irritated."

"Why?"

"Because she finds you irritating."

"Really?" Dylan sounded upset.

"Don't worry about it, she finds everyone irritating, particularly if they've got ginger hair apparently."

"So, she's a 'Gingerist?'"

"Damn, I knew that was a real word. Bloody Emma trying to take the intellectual high ground as usual. Grab a seat and I'll call her."

"I'm fine thanks, I'll go get rid of some of the shit in the kitchen while we wait."

"I said grab a seat." This was less a suggestion and more a directive.

"OK, keep your bloody mascara on," Dylan said.

Dylan went to sit on the chair previously occupied by Jessi, but no sooner had his bum cheeks touched its dusty surface, than Jessi's voice ripped through the air. "Wrong chair," she barked, pointing to the empty seat opposite.

Dylan was looking concerned. "You sure you're OK Jess? You don't seem yourself."

"I'm fine; now please just sit in the damn chair."

"OK, chill babe." Dylan did as he was ordered and sat in the chair Elvis had now vacated. "Happy now?"

A strangled hush hung in the air as Jessi's gaze devoured Dylan's chair, waiting for the slightest hint of movement that defied the laws of physics. A door slammed, then silence, then Emma. She sashayed in, filling the room with her charisma and the smell of fried food.

"Mommy's home and look what she's brought," Emma announced triumphantly.

As she passed, Jessi snatched a bottle of wine from under Emma's arm. "It better be a frigging screw top," Jessi said with a hint of panic in her voice.

"Whoa... Steady on girl, are you OK?" Emma said.

"I'd be great if everyone stopped asking me if I was OK."

With a practiced flick of her wrist, Jessi unscrewed the bottle and tilted it to her lips. The wine began to vanish, leaving no trace of its passage down her throat, only a flicker of satisfaction in her eyes. "Ah... That's better. Anyone care to join me?" She said.

"Would love to if I can prise the bottle from your sweaty little hands," said Dylan.

With a sidelong glance at Dylan, Jessi sat beside him and surrendered the bottle, her hand lingering as if unwilling to let go. Emma plopped down on a spare chair, her sigh audible as she flung the burgers into the middle of the table. "Tuck in, guys, don't let it go cold."

The intoxicating scent of sizzling burgers drew Elvis like a moth to a flame. He shuffled toward the table, nostrils flared, a wide grin splitting his face. "Been a king-sized while since I've had a taste of that greasy glory. Memphis magic, they used to call it." Unable to resist the urge, Elvis leaned over Jessi's shoulder as she bit into her quarter pounder. His inhale and heavy exhale sent a shiver down her spine, causing her to freeze mid-chew. Glancing over her shoulder, expecting someone standing behind her, she met only empty space. Realising he was just tormenting himself, Elvis once again retreated to his armchair.

"Well, this is the life," Dylan said, "warm, comfortable, luxurious surroundings, expensive wine, gourmet food and good company. What more could one ask for?"

"A six foot two bronzed Adonis, hung like a donkey and with homes in Paris, New York and Milan would do nicely thank you," answered Jessi.

"You're so shallow sometimes Jess, I've no idea how we became friends," Emma said.

"Maybe it's my bisexual tendencies that attracted you?"

"Eww... Don't be disgusting."

"No, please, be as disgusting as you like. Do you need a hand fulfilling these tendencies per chance?" Dylan said excitedly.

Jessi completely ignored Dylan's offer. "It's bloody freezing in here, I think central heating is the first big job on the list."

"The temperature has a mind of its own. It was freezing when we first sat down, like being in a blast freezer, but then it inexplicably warmed up again," Emma said.

"Whoooooooooo! Something spooky this way comes. You do know the house is haunted?" Dylan teased.

"Really?"

"Really. They say Headless Harry wanders through these rooms for all eternity looking for his bonce."

"Shut up Dylan. He's just winding you up Emm, ignore him."

"I know. You're not funny Dylan. Stick to conning people into buying worthless properties, you'll never cut it as a comedian."

Curiosity, an old friend, nudged Jessi's thoughts from their tether, sending them on a meandering journey. "It gives me an idea though, let's have a séance," she said.

"*NO,*" Emma was emphatic.

"Yeah." Dylan was excited.

"Come on Emm, where's your sense of adventure?"

"I left it at home locked in a box labelled, 'don't mess with things you know nothing about.'"

"I know about séances. I watch 'Most Haunted,'" Dylan said, even more excited. "Went to see Derek Arachnophobia once at the Old Vic. He summoned the dead all evening and no one came to any harm. Oh, except for one little old granny who fell down some stairs when he invited her for an intimate reading on stage."

"Probably pushed by a poltergeist," said Emma dramatically.

"Stop being such a bloody drama queen. Come on, it'll be a giggle."

Emma hesitated. The prospect of summoning the dead, of meddling with forces beyond the known, didn't sit well with her. It felt like treading on hallowed ground, a potential misstep that could have unforeseen consequences.

"Well?" Jessi said.

"We're supposed to be tidying up this shit tip and so far, all we've done is move some chairs into the kitchen and move them back again," Emma protested.

"It was your idea to share food and wine," Dylan reminded her.

"Sustenance, thought we might need some to tackle the task ahead."

"Sod the clean up, we'll do it at the weekend if you're both free. Now, join hands," Jessi said.

In a swift, almost instinctive move, Dylan captured Jessi's hand, his grip light but meaningful. Emma on the other hand still wasn't convinced and hesitated.

Dylan tried to coax her. "Come on Emma, stop being a big girl."

"Less of the big and I am a girl, that's why I have devil's dumplings and a minny."

Elvis, who was enjoying one of the most entertaining evenings he'd had since appearing in Vegas, burst out laughing. "Devil's dumplings, very funny."

"A what?" said Dylan.

"A minny."

"You've got a Citroen C3."

"No, you fool, she's talking about her minny," said Jessi, who could see Dylan was still confused, "her panty hamster, fur burger, the cave of wonders, bearded clam, the one-eyed anaconda canal, Aunt Hilda's hidey hole, the honey pot…"

Dylan finally understood. "Oh, you mean her…"

"Excuse me," Emma said, "I am still sat here and would appreciate it if you kept my nether regions out of the conversation."

"You started it."

"And like always you took it too far Jess, you should be ashamed of yourself."

"Why?"

"Because whilst I expect such juvenile expressions from a guy, I don't expect it from my well educated best friend."

"I suspect it's because she's well educated that she's au fait with such expressions," Dylan chipped in.

Jessi was getting impatient. "Look, can we just get on with the damn séance."

She grabbed Emma's left hand and Dylan the other, giving Emma little choice.

"Now concentrate and no laughing," Jessi said.

"There's no fear of that, it's not a laughing matter," Emma reminded everyone.

"Lighten up Emm. With a face like that, you're likely to scare away any ghosts that might exist."

"Shut it Dylan."

"Behave children. OK here goes."

Jessi straightened her back and eyes fluttering shut, she inhaled deeply, channelling the spirit of Doris Stokes in every breath. Her whisper was a seductive curse, impossible to resist. "Is there anybody there?"

The hush in the room was heavy, expectant. It was a velvet curtain, waiting to be drawn back. And behind it, stood Elvis. A mischievous glint flickered in his eyes. The silence whispered his name, urging him to fill it with his voice. "Hold on to your blue suede shoes, darlin' I'm here to rock your world," Elvis announced.

"Is there anybody there?" Jessi repeated.

"Hey pretty lady, over here in the armchair."

"We mean you no harm, just give us a sign."

Elvis, the man who could captivate a stadium, felt invisible, but he wouldn't be ignored. He stood, his shoulders squared, walked towards the table, and positioned himself at Jessi's side. A deep-seated chill gripped her, squeezing the breath from her lungs.

"Jesus Christ, what was that?" Jessi said.

The sudden change in temperature had not gone unnoticed by Dylan nor Emma.

"Probably the wind whistling through the rotten windows. It's not the most energy efficient house I've ever sold," said Dylan, trying to remain calm.

"No, I sense a presence. Speak to us whoever you are, reveal yourself," Jessi continued.

"Hold onto your pompadours and y'all better scream louder than a hound dog howlin' at the moon. Ladies and gentlemen, please be upstanding while I introduce to you the one, the only, the king of rock and roll, Mr. Elvis Aaron Presley."

The round of applause Elvis was expecting never materialised and Dylan and Emma were oblivious to his introduction, but it did illicit a response from Jessi. "Nice to meet you Mr. Presley."

"The pleasure is all mine Jessi."

"What?" Dylan said.

"What the fuck?" said Emma.

"Mr. Presley?"

"What are you talking about?" Jessi said.

"You just said 'Nice to meet you Mr. Presley,'" Emma reminded her.

"I said no such thing, now who's hearing voices?"

"Sorry Jess, but Emma's right. That's exactly what you said."

"Are you both mad?" Jessi said, a little irritated.

"I told you not to mess with the unknown." The pre-séance jitters were a distant memory; now, raw terror gnawed at Emma's insides, twisting her nerves into knots.

"Calm down Emm, it's just Jessi having..."

"Shh... Do you hear that?" Jessi said.

"Hear what?"

"Music."

"No, there's no damn music Jess. Maybe we should..."

"Quiet Dylan," Jessi demanded.

The room stilled, a beat hanging in the air before the first notes of 'Welcome to My World' tumbled from Elvis's lips. He held a hand out to Jessi. Her eyes widened, a flicker of recognition battling with confusion. But before she could react, Elvis was serenading her, his voice like liquid velvet weaving through the room.

And then, something extraordinary happened. Jessi found her own voice blending with his. Her fear melted into a quiet confidence, her natural melody intertwining with Elvis's. The King and the Jessi became a duet, two souls touching through the magic of music. When the last note faded, the silence seemed almost deafening. Elvis, beaming, applauded, his eyes sparkling with genuine admiration. But Jessi, her face flushed, simply blinked, and sank back into her chair, as if the past few moments had been a dream. Dylan and Emma exchanged awkward glances, their mouths agape.

"Is there something you want to tell us Jess?" Emma said.

"Sorry?" Jessi didn't understand the question.

"Maybe you'd like to talk to us about your secret Elvis fixation?" Jessi laughed. "Elvis? Give me a break. I've nothing against the guy, but do I really look like a sing along with Elvis kinda gal?"

"But..."

"But what Emm?"

"But..."

"Spit it out girl, we haven't got all night."

"Forget it, doesn't matter."

"I'm getting worried about you Emm. Lay off the wine for a while, OK?"

"Sure Jess, whatever you say." The echo of Jessi's voice, channelling the King himself, remained in the air, mocking Emma's disbelief. Her best friend, possessed by Presley, then conveniently forgetting the whole thing? It was a plot twist so audacious, so impossible, that arguing felt like a bridge to nowhere.

Dylan had decided enough was enough. "Look, it's been a long day, we've all had a bit to drink and we're all tired. I'll order a taxi."

"Sounds good to me," said Emma, "the quicker I get out of here the better."

Jessi's silence spoke volumes. Without a word, she began clearing the table, unspoken thoughts swirling in her head. Soon, she disappeared into the kitchen, the remnants of their meal vanishing like the last echoes of their conversation.

Dylan and Emma headed for the front door. "You ready Jess, we're heading outside to wait for the taxi?" shouted Dylan.

"Won't be a tick, just locking up."

Jessi drifted back into the room; her brow furrowed in thought. Her gaze fluttered over her surroundings, seeking something... what, she couldn't quite grasp. Her hand reached for the doorknob, then froze. From behind, a voice, warm and familiar, filled the space. "Good night, Jessi. See you at the weekend."

As she entered the hallway, she half turned and answered. "Night, night Elvis."

———— ⟩⟨ ————

JESSI HAD BARELY SET foot in the property in the last three months, a fortress of daunting repairs, each broken window, creaky floorboard, and peeling wallpaper a mocking echo of Jessi's DIY inexperience. Then there was the wine and burger party, the night the walls whispered secrets and her mind unravelled. Those two demons kept her firmly on the other side of the threshold.

Despite a dwindling bank balance, she had taken the decision to bring in the professionals and Dylan had kindly offered to manage the project. Jessi had toyed with the idea of just flipping the property and trying to make a quick buck, but Dylan put her off with his tales of woe concerning a sudden crash in property prices. She'd also considered renting it out, but that would mean yet more house hunting in a difficult rental market. As much as she loved Emma, living with her was beginning to put a strain on their relationship. She was left with no other choice; today was the day she had to move into her newly refurbished home.

The house held its breath as she slipped the key in its lock, as if sensing the trespass. She turned it slowly and gently pushed the door open, trying to be as quiet as possible so as not to disturb anyone, in what should be an empty house. A tide of junk mail lapped at the doorway, catching her as she entered. The flick of a switch unveiled a breathtaking transformation. The hallway, bathed in light, showcased its preserved charm and a floor adorned with a mosaic masterpiece. Unwanted mail crinkled in her hand as she lingered at the living room doorway. A tide of anticipation and trepidation washed over her. Her breath caught in her throat as she nudged the door open, a sliver of apprehension battling with a flicker of hope. But then, the room unfolded before her – transformed. A grin, as wide as the newly opened space, stretched across her face as she devoured every detail of the stunning renovation. She tossed her briefcase onto the dining table and collapsed onto the comfortable new sofa, sinking into its soft cushions.

The silence demanded background, so she flicked on the TV and tuned into some 1980's nostalgia. She didn't have a particular plan for the day, other than to reacquaint herself with her new abode, so junk mail first, new home second. Discarding the predictable clutter - pizza menus, window replacement ads, and a stack of 'The Watchtower' magazines hinting at impending divine intervention - she focused on the remaining mail and one letter in particular piqued her interest, Kitchener, Barnes and Preston Solicitors. She opened it and began reading out aloud, a trait that often drew annoyed glances from her coworkers.

"Dear Ms. Henderson. Here we go again with the 'Ms.' Can't one still be a Miss once they've turned thirty? Dear Miss Henderson, thank you for your letter dated twenty seventh of February two thousand and nine. We have made extensive enquiries into your query and have found the following information. Your house was built as part of a small development in nineteen twenty nine by local building firm Armstrong and Miller. Its first occupier was Mr. Wilfred Allbones who rented the property until nineteen forty nine. It was then bought by Mr. and Mrs. Stockton who lived there until nineteen sixty one when it was sold to a Ms. Laura McKintyre. Ms. McKintyre died in nineteen seventy seven and the house was inherited by her daughter Judy McKintyre. Unfortunately, Judy tragically took her own life and died intestate in March two thousand and seven. The property remained empty until you purchased it earlier this year. I hope this information will be beneficial to your research... Yada yada, yada, Richard Kitchener. Hmm, not sure whether it's been beneficial or not Richard old bean, but at least I have some names."

The world outside the TV screen beckoned – unpacked boxes, unpacked life. But instead, Jessi started channel hopping. The allure of 'Jailhouse Rock' flickering on 'Great Movies' momentarily snagged Jessi's attention, but the thirty-second snippet wasn't enough to hold her, and she continued her quest for something more captivating.

Suddenly there was a shimmer, a tremor in the air, and Elvis appeared. No fanfare, no entrance, just a sudden, spectral aura that made Jessi shiver with a sudden chill. "Whoa, whoa, whoa, hold the phone, mama, that was one of my finest performances," Elvis shouted.

Jessi turned her head towards the doorway convinced she'd heard something and certain she'd felt something, but she was alone in the room. "Hello! Hello!" she said nervously, before collecting her thoughts. "Damn it girl, get a grip. These voices are getting beyond a joke."

Elvis glided silently across the polished floorboards and came to rest on the sofa, a dark presence to Jessi's sunlit form "Jessi, darlin' that's been missin' from my heart since Graceland. Mind if I get a glimpse of the past?"

"It was 'Jailhouse Rock', why would I want to watch that?" Jessi said.

Elvis crossed his arms and leaned back, a look of annoyance on his face. "Why wouldn't you?"

"Well, it's hardly Harry Potter is it? It's over fifty years old and in black and white."

He tried to convince her. "Ain't no border wall for good tunes, baby. I busted down barriers, paved the way for your fancy rock 'n' roll. Please, put it back on, let the ol' King show you what inspired the dance in your feet."

Jessi got to her feet and stood in the middle of the room holding her head in both hands. "That's enough Jess. You need to see a therapist. Hearing voices is one thing, having a conversation with them is something completely different."

Elvis, still hankering after a bit of 'Jailhouse Rock' joined her and stood by her side. "Sweetheart, those ain't voices in your head, no sir. They're realer than that gold sparklin' on your neck, realer than that TV just itchin' to be turned over. You hear 'em, feel 'em, honey, they ain't nothin' but ghosts of good times."

"I'm not listening." Jessi put her fingers in her ears. "Na na na na na..."

"How 'bout you ask me somethin' you ain't heard on the radio or seen in the movies. Somethin' only the King would know."

Unexpectedly, a surreal calm washed over Jessi. Elvis Presley, not a figment, was in the room. She was sure of it.

"OK, what's your real name?" As soon as the words left her mouth, she knew it was a dumb question.

"Elvis Aaron Presley," came the reply.

"Everyone knows that."

"Then why ask?"

"Thought you might have been christened something else, something a bit obscure that wasn't common knowledge."

"Nope, that's what Momma and Poppa christened me."

"OK, how about you tell me something about yourself that you don't think I'll know?" Jessi said, not quite sure how the question was going to prove anything.

"Well darlin' my story starts in Tupelo, Mississippi on January eighth, thirty-five. Daddy Vernon, Momma Gladys, Elvis Aaron the name, and Jesse Garon, my twin up in the stars. British, German, Cherokee – I'm a musical gumbo, baby. First time I wailed on stage was at a dairy show, back in forty five. Won five bucks and a carnival ride for coming fifth. Oh, and I'm third cousin five times removed to Abraham Lincoln. Wanna hear more?"

"No, you've made your point, but that doesn't mean I didn't just make all that up in my head."

"The truth's out there sugar. Sometimes, it's whisperin' between the lines. Check out the library and see what secrets those shelves hold."

"Library? Get with the programme grandad. Never heard of the internet and Wikipedia?" Jessi said dismissively.

"Nope, can't say I have."

Jessi sat at the dining table and took out her laptop. Elvis, meanwhile, sank deep into the sofa's plush embrace, a contented sigh escaping his lips.

"Hey honey, mind if that TV throws me another round of 'Jailhouse Rock' while you work your magic?" Elvis said.

Jessi flicked through the channels before landing back on 'Great Movies' "Happy now?"

"Thanks hun."

With a furrow in her brow, Jessi scoured the screen, eyes flitting across lines of text seeking the elusive proof. Meanwhile, Elvis, unable to resist the siren song of his own lyrics, crooned 'You're so young and beautiful,' the melody a counterpoint to the click-clack of her typing. It didn't take long for Jessi to find what she was looking for; she snapped the laptop shut.

"Shit," she blurted out, her voice a sharp gasp.

Elvis still lost in song said, "What was that Jess?"

"Shit," she repeated.

"I gotta say Jess, that sweet sass of yours has been gettin' a little spicy lately. Ain't no way for a lady to be talkin'."

"Shut up you southern hick, it's two thousand and nine. Thankfully, men no longer have the monopoly on bad language."

"Excuse me ma'am. So, what d'you find?"

"Most of what you said seems to have some truth to it."

"Most?"

"Yeah, you were wrong about coming fifth at the dairy show."

"No I wasn't."

"Wikipedia said..."

"I don't know what Pikiwedia is, but if it's OK with you, I'll stick to my own brand of gospel. This Elvis knows what he knows."

A strange pull drew Jessi towards the armchair in the corner of the room, a whisper in her mind insisting Elvis lounged there. "Let me just try and get this straight in my very mixed up head. You're saying that you are the ghost of Mr. Elvis Aaron Presley and you're living in my house at number thirteen Samuel Avenue, Grimsby, England."

"I'd say that about sums it up honey."

"But don't you see how ridiculous this is? It's one thing having a ghost in your house, but to have the ghost of Elvis Presley is just too weird for words. Why here, why Grimsby, why England for God's sake," Jessi said, confused.

"Well, you got me there, partner. Been wrappin' my head around this whole 'undead rockstar' business for more years than hound dogs got spots, and I still ain't figured it out. Nothin' wrong with Grimsby, mind, but it ain't exactly Graceland, is it? If I gotta haunt my way through eternity, you'd think it'd be in the King's own palace, right?"

"So why can't I see you?"

"Beats me. I know more about rockin' a stage than I do roamin' the spirit world."

"But you can see me?" Jessi said.

"I see before me a vision of breathtaking beauty."

"Cut the chat up crap Prezzer, it'll get you nowhere."

"What's happened to the world while I been away. Can't a guy compliment a gal anymore?"

"Not when they're old enough to be their grandfather they can't."

"Grandfather? Hold your horses. I ain't crossed the Mississippi to retirement land just yet. I'm only forty two."

"Sorry to break this to you Elvis, but you're seventy four."

"I'm as old as the day I died."

"You were born in nineteen thirty five and it's now two thousand and nine, which makes you seventy four in my book."

Elvis shook his head in dismay. "Damn."

"Can you touch and hold things?" Jessi said.

"I can only lay my hands on things that don't have a heartbeat, baby. I couldn't kiss those soft lips of yours."

"Damn right you couldn't. Where exactly are you now?"

"Chillin' on the sofa, catchin' the King of Rock 'n' Roll. Why?"

"You see that box of tissues on the coffee table?"

"Uh huh!"

"Can you move it?"

"Sure hun. Where'd you like it movin' to?"

"Just move it to the other side of the table."

Elvis leaned over, his hand landing with a soft thump on the tissue box. He shoved it forward, then back and forth, like a bored child playing with a toy truck. "Ah, the glamorous life of a rockstar," he muttered, his voice dripping with mock-tragedy. Then with a flourish, pulled out a mountain of tissues, one by one, like a magician conjuring doves from a hat. He let them drift down, fluttering onto the table like featherweight dreams.

"Fuck me," Jessi said.

"Hey there, sweetheart, let's simmer down those fiery words, shall we? No need for that kinda language. I oughta take you over my knee and give you a good ol' fashioned spanking."

Jessi dismissed his comment. "In your dreams Mr. Presley... Can you leave the house?"

"Sorry, darling, but no can do. I'm stuck right here. My closest peek at the outside world is just swinging them French doors open and watching life drift on by."

Jessi tip-toed toward the sofa, a hint of nerves creeping in. Even though she had what she thought was a safe gap and a swift exit plan through the French doors, she couldn't resist the pull to get nearer. Maybe she just needed to sense his vibe, to convince herself that the ghost of Elvis truly was living in her home. As she neared the sofa, ready to take a seat, she suddenly realised she had no clue where Elvis was lounging. He might have stretched himself across the entire thing for all she knew.

"I'm not about to sit on your knee, am I?"

"Nope, don't worry honey, I'm sat the other end."

Jessi sat. "OK good. Now let's just take a moment to recap. Assuming my lunchtime glass of chardonnay wasn't spiked with ketamine, Im sharing my home with the ghost of Elvis Presley. I can't see you, but I can hear you. You on the other hand, can see me and hear me and you have the ability to move inanimate objects, but you can't lay your mucky little paws on me?"

"Uh huh!" confirmed Elvis.

Jessi paused, letting it all sink in. She was pretty sure she hadn't lost her marbles, but it was so outlandish that convincing others seemed near impossible. Keeping it hush-hush wasn't an issue, but figuring out how to live with a ghost as a roommate? That was the real head-scratcher. With a seriousness that matched the weight of her question, she asked, "So exactly how's this going to work then?"

"How's what going to work?"

"This whole surreal situation."

"Well, darlin' I kinda figured you'd stay here, and I'd have my own place here too, you know?"

"Is that it?"

"I reckon I prefer keepin' things nice and simple."

"But what about my privacy? You could be popping up anywhere, anytime, and I wouldn't have a clue. I mean, you could be standing right there in the shower with me."

Clearly annoyed by the question, Elvis said, "Well, darlin' let me set the record straight. I ain't no creep. I don't go barging into ladies' showers unless I'm given the green light. I'm a genuine southern gentleman, and that's a fact you better keep in mind."

"I'm sorry Elvis, but you understand my concerns?" Jessi replied, catching the annoyance in Elvis's voice.

"Course I do, Jess, honey. Ain't gonna catch me singing in the shower with you, no sir. And bedrooms? Strictly off-limits unless you wave an invitation. Anywhere else you need space, just holler, and I'll be outta there. How's that sound?"

"OK...I think."

"All I'm askin' for darlin' is a chance to croon a tune every now and then and maybe sneak a whiff of your burger."

Outraged, Jessi said, "I beg your pardon?"

"Those hamburgers from the joint across the road, they're a symphony in a bun. A taste of the good life, the kind I ain't seen since my Tupelo days. Just let me sit near you, soak in the aroma, and pretend I'm back in the land of milk and honey."

"Ah! I see... Yeah, I can live with that, but no drooling."

"Deal... Now would you mind quittin' with all the questions while I watch the movie?"

"Excuse me for breathing."

"You're excused... Thank ya very much."

WHILST JESSI SCOFFED at the notion of being in a relationship with Dylan, to him, an invitation to dinner and drinks at her place was practically a wedding proposal. He was captivated from the beginning, but their encounters, however enjoyable, were Jessi's orchestration. No matter how fondly he remembered their shared moments, a melody of unreciprocated longing always played in the background. Jessi was a puzzle Dylan was determined to solve. Each casual meeting was a piece he carefully slotted into place, building a bridge he prayed would one day lead to her heart. Enthralled by Jessi's 'raw beauty,' as he'd called it, Dylan sat mesmerized beside her on the sofa. From his seat at the dining table, Elvis cast a watchful eye over the scene. His protective instincts, honed by a lifetime in the spotlight, hummed like a low bass line, ready to drown out any whispers of 'funny business.'

"So, how you been Jess? was Dylans opening gambit, "place is looking fabulous."

"Thanks to you, no way I would have got here on my own," Jessi replied with a warm smile.

"It was the least I could do," Dylan said laughing, "never sold a shittier property to anyone in my life."

"Nice to hear I was the victim of one of your greatest achievements. How's life treating you?"

"Not bad. The housing market's on its arse, but unless I get elected as the next PM, not much I can do about it. Still, shouldn't complain, got a tin roof over my head and stale bread and dripping in the cupboard."

"Aww, poor thing. Hope you're not looking for sympathy? It's against my principles to sympathise with estate agents."

"I think we're just misunderstood."

"You can say that again, I never understand a word they say."

There was a brief silence. The salesman who could weave magic with words found himself tongue-tied, fumbling for the next thread to reel Jessi in. Despite his instincts telling him otherwise, he decided to visit old ground. "Had any more problems with err... the err..."

"With what Dylan?" Jessi said.

"Well, the erm... you know... the voices."

"Ah... You mean my schizophrenia?"

Dylan mentally kicked himself and wished he'd never asked. How he now longed for the familiar refuge of cheesy chat-up lines. "No. I didn't mean that. I just meant; well you know exactly what I meant."

Luckily for him, Jessi was in a benevolent mood. "Yeah, I know what you mean and no, it's no longer a problem."

Sensing a reprieve Dylan tried to cash in. "Oh excellent, that's good, fantastic. You know I'm here for you Jess if you ever need to talk or whatever."

"I know, and I appreciate it Dylan, I really do."

Elvis, ears pricked, felt a prickle of doubt about Dylan's genuineness. "Careful Jess, the creep's after something."

"Shut up, he's just concerned," Jessi said without thinking.

"Sorry?" asked Dylan.

"What are you sorry about?"

"No, I meant, what did you say?"

"When?"

"Just now. You told me to shut up and then said something about being concerned," Dylan reminded her.

Jessi realising her carelessness, "Oh that. Erm, no I was err... just saying erm... it's err... it's been confirmed."

"What has?" Dylan wasn't going to give up anytime soon.

"What has what?"

"What's been confirmed?"

In a desperate but futile attempt to put an end to the conversation, Jessi blurted out. "Erm... It's just been confirmed that... that... that I'm not pregnant."

"Not pregnant," shouted a startled Elvis from the other side of the room.

"Not pregnant," repeated Dylan surprised by the revelation.

"Yeah, not pregnant. Fantastic news, isn't it?" Jessi said hoping the conversation might move on to something, anything other than herself.

A flicker of amusement, chased by a spark of genuine interest, danced in Elvis's eyes at her peculiar pronouncement. He ambled towards the end of the sofa.

"I didn't know you thought you were pregnant," Dylan said.

"Neither did I," Elvis remarked.

"I didn't think I was pregnant."

"Then why have a pregnancy test to confirm it?"

"Yeah Hun, what he said?" added Elvis.

Jessi was floundering and all she could offer was 'routine.'"

"You have routine pregnancy tests?" Dylan said bemused.

"Erm... yeah. Well, you can't be too careful, can you?"

"Hey, Jess, no offense intended, but if things are getting a bit wild with your love life, and you're needing frequent pregnancy tests, maybe it's time to consider getting some professional help on the matter?"

Trying to amend her earlier blunder of mistakenly responding to Elvis's remark, Jessi aimed to redirect the conversation once again, hoping to smooth things over. "I'm not sleeping around, and I am responsible. It all came out wrong. I meant routine... eye tests; yeah, that's it, eye tests."

"They can tell from a routine eye test whether you're pregnant?" Elvis said.

Dylan, who wasn't aiming to be awkward or catch her in a lie, was just plain baffled by the whole conversation and, for his own peace of mind, needed things cleared up. "You went for a routine eye test, and they told you that you weren't pregnant?"

Running out of ridiculous things to say, Jessi just answered, "Yeah."

"Well, that's a new one on me," Dylan said.

"Yeah, me too. Isn't medical technology amazing? Anyway, it's none of your damn business," Jessi reminded him.

"Never said it was. It was you who said out of the blue that something was confirmed."

"Yes well, let's leave it there shall we?" said Jessi, and in a final attempt to put the matter to bed, completely changed the subject. "Would you like a drink?"

"Would love one."

"Sure," said Elvis, having decided he was now one of the party guests.

"I was talking to Dylan," Jessi tried to whisper but failed miserably.

"I know you were," said Dylan, "and I said I would love one thanks."

"I know what you said."

"So, can I have one then?"

"Of course, what d'you fancy?"

"Bottle of Bud would be good."

"Coming right up."

Jessi headed for the kitchen as Elvis shouted after her. "And a Pepsi for me please honey."

She stopped and turned. "I think it's about time you left."

"Jesus Jess," said an irritated Dylan, "make up your mind. Five seconds ago you were getting me a drink."

"I am getting you a drink, give me chance."

"OK... I can take a hint; I'll go sniff hamburgers out of the bedroom window for a while. Just be careful Jess, I'm sure he's only after one thing," Elvis warned her as he floated out the room into the hallway.

Dylan made himself comfortable snagging a magazine from the coffee table – 'Practical Sheep, Goats and Alpacas.' The 'not pregnant' conversation had already swerved into surreal territory, so Dylan wisely opted to avoid dissecting Jessi's literary tastes. She reappeared from the kitchen, thrusting a frosty Budweiser in his hand. He guzzled deeply, the familiar bite chasing away the lingering awkwardness. "Thanks Jess, was ready for that."

"You're welcome. You OK with pasta and meatballs?" she asked.

"Sure, sounds great. Cheers."

"Good job because I didn't make an alternative. It's almost ready, I'll be back in a tick."

As Jessi returned to cooking duties, Dylan said, "Mind if I put some music on?"

"Sure," came the reply from the kitchen, "but no Elvis."

Dylan ambled toward Jessi's sideboard, a time capsule of the 1970's, crafted from sun-bleached beechwood. With a gentle nudge, he slid open one of its doors, unleashing a treasure trove of vinyl LPs, all stacked neatly in alphabetical order. Her playlist was a time capsule, seamlessly leaping from vintage swing to modern anthems. Peggy Lee and Nat King Cole to Manic Street Preachers latest album 'Journal for Plague Lovers'. Hoping to impress Jessi with his limited vintage music knowledge, Dylan, in a stroke of questionable genius, put on some Frank Sinatra.

Elvis, sat by the bedroom window, hypnotized by the rhythmic rumble of his own stomach and the hypnotic glow of the burger joint across the street, was about to stage a daring window escape when Sinatra's voice, smooth as silk, cut through the fog of his hunger. He blinked, reality snapping back into focus, and realized breaking and entering for a cheeseburger might not be his best career move. He shimmered back into the living room, the source of Sinatra's dulcet tones, and sank into the sofa with a sigh as he watched Dylan contort his limbs in what seemed like a bizarre, improvised dance.

Did the heat of Elvis's gaze melt Dylan's moves, or did the absurdity of his own routine suddenly dawn on him? In any case, his dancing came to a jarring end, and he shuffled back to the sofa, seeking either solace or sanctuary, or perhaps a healthy dose of both, right next to the King.

"Christ son, Frank Sinatra? Is that the best you could dig up? I mean, no disrespect to the man, we've had our share of good times, but that ain't exactly rock and roll?" Elvis said.

Dylan, clearly oblivious to Elvis's proximity, had other things on his mind. "Well Dylan old boy, this is it. Play it cool, play it smooth, don't mention the voices again and you could be in my son." Dylan's fingers dipped into his wallet, emerging with a small, discreet package held tight between his thumb and forefinger. "Now then, where shall we put you for easy access matey?"

Falling on deaf ears, Elvis said. "Dream on Dylan, she ain't that easy."

Jessi emerged from the kitchen spotting Dylan holding aloft a condom. "Ah! Condoms, well done you, think I'm out," said Jessi nonchalantly.

Clearly embarrassed he'd been caught, Dylan spluttered. "Erm... yeah... just thought... well you know, always carry some just in case. Wasn't being presumptuous or anything."

"No sweat, I'm not saying you're gonna get it, but you never know. Do you like it spicy by the way?" Jessi said casually.

Dylan completely getting the wrong end of the stick replied. "Err... yeah I guess, whatever works for you, I'm pretty open minded, though I draw the line at rubber gimp suits."

"I meant your pasta sauce," Jessi said.

"Yeah, of course. I knew what you meant, just messing with ya. Yeah, I love it spicy, the spicier the better."

"OK, be right back," said Jessi as she once again disappeared into the kitchen.

"Then again, maybe she is that easy," Elvis said to himself, slightly disappointed.

Dylan reached for his beer, but Elvis had other ideas. The bottle danced a cruel jig on the coffee table, just out of Dylan's reach. He stretched for it, fingers twitching, only for Elvis's nimble hand to whisk it away, a playful glint in his blue eyes. Dylan sat back, bewildered, watching the amber liquid taunt him from a few inches away. Every attempt, from cautious swoops to desperate lunges, was met with the King's quicksilver reflexes, the bottle flitting like a butterfly just beyond his grasp. Bemusement melted into exasperation. He even tried outflanking it, creeping around the back of the sofa like a jungle cat, but Elvis was a master of the dance, anticipating every move with a knowing smirk. Finally, desperation took hold. Dylan launched himself at the bottle, a blur of flailing limbs, only to find empty air as Elvis whisked it skyward. The world spun, tabletop rushed up to meet him, and Dylan landed face first in a symphony of splintering wood. Dazed, he felt the cool glass pressed against his palm, the bottle miraculously back in his possession. Elvis, a cruel grin playing on his lips, winked, and sauntered towards the door, leaving Dylan sprawled on the floor amidst the wreckage of his pursuit. The bottle, now his, felt strangely heavy, a trophy from a bizarre, unexplainable battle.

Jessi, alerted to the commotion, rushed into the room. "Jesus Christ Dylan, what are you doing?"

Still prostate, Dylan said, "Trying to drink my beer."

"You get like this after one beer?"

"No," he said, getting to his feet, "I never got to drink the beer because it kept moving."

"Moving?"

"Yep, moving. As in every time I tried to pick it up, it moved. So, I tried to be clever and sneak up on it from behind, but it must have seen me in its reflection and moved again at the critical moment. Unfortunately, by that time, I was committed and hence the broken table," Dylan explained.

"You need locking up, you looney tune. How many you had before you got here?"

"Not a drop."

"Truth?"

"I swear. I drove for Christ's sake. Look Jess, I know what I saw, and this bottle moved. Not once, not twice, but three times. Now would you like to tell me what the hell is going on?"

"Nothing's going on," Jessi tried to reassure him, "you're probably just tired, grab a seat at the table and I'll dish up."

"Not bloody likely." Dylan was not persuaded. "There's something not right here Jess, some weird shit going on that I can't explain."

"Life's full of weird shit Dylan, but we don't let it get in the way of having a good time."

"Look Jess don't take it personally, but I'm out of here. I'll call you and we can eat out somewhere or spend the evening round mine. I'll see you around." Dylan kissed Jessi on the cheek and made a hasty retreat before she had chance to reply.

"Bollocks," exclaimed Jessi as Elvis who had been earwigging from the hallway slid back into the room.

"Mmm... Something smells good," he said as he entered and then in feigned surprise asked, "Oh, where's lover boy?"

"Elvis sweetie," Jessi said calmly, "where are you?"

"Stood right next to you hun."

Jessi spun left, her fist whistling through the air. "No, other side Jess," Elvis said as she turned and swung another punch that Elvis anticipated but stood firm knowing it was a futile endeavour on Jessi's part. Elvis tried to take the heat out of the situation. "Calm down little lady, you'll do yourself an injury."

"I'll do you an injury if I ever get my hands on you," she bellowed.

In all sincerity, Elvis replied, "I was only trying to protect you."

"The only thing I need protecting from is your bloody suspicious mind."

Never one to miss an opportunity for a tune, Elvis launched into the first lines of 'Suspicious Minds,' oblivious to the steam rising from Jessi's ears.

"Shut up Elvis," Jessi demanded, "you had no right to do whatever it was you did to Dylan."

"His intentions weren't honourable Jess," Elvis said in his defence.

"His intention was to roger me senseless."

"I'm sorry, sugar, but it seemed to me like he didn't plan on having anyone named Roger in the mix. Sounded like he wanted you all to himself."

"Give me strength. Look, it's really difficult for me to accept this situation. It's so far from what might be considered normal, that I'm still not convinced it isn't a bad dream. But let's just say for the sake of argument that it is real, you cannot under any circumstances interfere in my life... Do you understand?"

"Not even to save you from yourself?"

"I don't need saving. I'm more than capable of looking after myself and if I want to shag an estate agent, as unappealing as that may seem, then I'll damn well shag one. And if after I've finished shagging an estate agent, I want to get jiggy with the Grimsby rugby club first fifteen, then that's exactly what I'll do," Jessi said defiantly.

"There's a name for girls like you in Memphis."

"Oh, just shut up you bloated, hamburger sniffing junkie."

"There's no need for that Jess."

"And there was no need for scaring away Dylan. Do you know how long it's been since I've had a proper date? Two years, two frigging years and you ruined it in five minutes, thanks for nothing."

"Well, sugar, I'm mighty sorry, I truly am. What can I do to make things right with ya, huh?"

"Nothing, just stay out of my life, understand?"

"OK Jess, you got it, baby. I'll just slide on back up into that ol' attic. Ain't no trouble brewin' up there, no sir, just me hangin' loose, takin' it easy. Just holler if you need me."

Jessi's heart warred with her head and Elvis's contrition tugged at her conscience. Banishing him to the attic, even if he was a ghost, felt like kicking a stray mutt back into the storm.

"OK... Stop trying to be a martyr, you don't have to live in the attic, just please stop interfering," Jessi begged.

"You got it Jess. Hey, I know, let me give you a taste of Vegas."

"What?"

"Take a load off on that sofa, sweetheart, let's dial down them lights and I'll give you some of the old Elvis showman magic."

"But I can't see you stupid. Hardly a show if I can't see anything."

"Shut those pretty eyes and imagine Jess. Let my voice carry you away, let it take you for a ride."

"OK, but this doesn't mean you're forgiven," she reminded him.

The sofa swallowed Jessi whole, its cushions sighing in welcome. A fleece blanket, smelling of lavender and forgotten dreams, cloaked her in a comforting hug. A relaxed sigh escaped Jessi's lips. Elvis, catching the shift in the mood took centre stage.

"Ladies and gentlemen, if you could kindly put them hands together for the one and only, undisputed king of rock and roll, none other than yours truly, Mr. Elvis Presley. Thank you very much, thank you very much... C'mon, Jess, it's applause time, darlin'."

Jess looked a bit confused. "Oh OK... usually applaud at the end, but guess they do things different in redneck country."

Ignoring Jessi's barbed remark, like a phoenix rising from the ashes of Vegas, Elvis unleashed a 'Suspicious Minds' that shook the very foundations of rock and roll. Inside, Jessi was starstruck, but her lips stayed clamped shut, a fortress against the flood of admiration she refused to let Elvis witness. The melody trailed off, hanging in the air like smoke. He met her gaze, a flicker of hope sparkling behind his playful grin. "Well, little lady, how 'bout it? Am I off the hook?"

Determined to make him suffer just a little longer she said. "Sing me to sleep and I'll think about it."

Instinct drew Jessi's feet away before her mind could register the chill that emanated from Elvis as he sank onto the sofa. "Sure, I can sing you to sleep Jess, this one never fails."

In stark contrast to his previous performance, Elvis thought he was onto another winner with a slow, soulful version of 'Are You Lonesome Tonight'.

Jessi wasn't impressed. "Is that supposed to be funny?"

"You asked me to sing you to sleep."

"You scare the living daylights out of my first date in two years, sending him running home to his mummy and then sing 'Are You Lonesome Tonight'. I'm not amused."

"Point taken hun. How 'bout this?"

As Elvis's hushed version of 'And I love You So' dissolved into the night, Jessi surrendered to sleep, his love song cocooning her in peace.

———— ◦◦◦ ————

THE VERDANT HAVEN, coaxed into existence by Jessi's green thumb, taunted Elvis through the French doors. The unseasonably warm spring mocked his gilded prison, whispering seductive promises of summer sun and lazy afternoons. He'd have swapped his sequined jumpsuit for a patch of that emerald peace in a heartbeat. The scent of the blooming Jasmine's delicate perfume waged war with the irresistible aroma of fried bacon, leaving Elvis trapped in a sensory tug-of-war. The unexpected chime from the doorbell interrupted his quandary and his focus shifted to Jessi as she emerged from the kitchen.

"Morning Jess."

"Morning Pelvis," Jessi said as she headed for the front door.

Elvis's ears perked up at the murmur of voices. He crept towards the hallway, the scent of incense and patchouli preceding Jessi's entrance. Behind her stood a woman, cloaked in an aura of the 1960's.

Sunlight poured through the living room window, bouncing off silver bangles that jangled like tiny wind chimes with every movement. Her salt-and-pepper waves framed her face, while a faded paisley scarf draped around her neck, hinting at countless adventures. Patched denim jeans clung to her legs; feet bare beneath sandals decked with leathery flowers. A fringed suede waistcoat hugged her like a second skin, holding the whispers of countless campfire stories.

"Have a seat Mrs. Bradley," Jessi said.

"Paula please," she insisted, before getting herself comfy on the sofa.

"I wasn't expecting you today, did we have an appointment?"

"I know this sounds odd, but I wasn't expecting you either," Paula replied.

Jessi joined her on the sofa and Elvis, ever the one for a bit of gossip retreated to his familiar armchair. "So, what can I do for you," Jessi said, "I'm not sure there's anything else I can tell you. I tried reaching out on social media in the vain hope there's a long lost relative who might know more, but so far, no luck."

"I... erm... I didn't actually come to see you Jessi, in fact I didn't even know you lived here, the last time we spoke you were living with a friend."

"Sorry, I should have let you know I'd moved. So, who have you come to see, surely not the Pelvis?"

"Who?" Paula said.

"Doesn't matter, just an in joke. So?"

"Well, I'm actually looking for a woman called..." Paula opened a leatherbound notebook and started to thumb it's pages, "McKintyre, Judy McKyntyre."

"Ah! I see, sorry, you're too late. She committed suicide two years ago. Tragic really, she was only forty eight. Anyway, what do you want with her?"

"Well..." Paula began.

"Sorry... None of my business. That's what you do isn't it? Find missing people. I do hope she wasn't someone's missing daughter or mother. They're going to be gutted when they find out."

"That's exactly who she was Jessi, someone's missing mother."

"Bloody hell wouldn't want your job. How you going to break it to them?"

"I have no idea, no idea at all. How would you *like* me to break it to you?"

It took a while for the penny to drop before Jessi exclaimed. "Oh, sweet Mary mother of Jesus. How stupid am I?"

"I'm so sorry Jess, this isn't how I thought my visit would pan out. It's all a bit confusing," Paula said trying to soften the blow.

"You sure ain't as confused as I am," Elvis shouted from his armchair.

In a well-rehearsed routine Jessi shouted back, "Time to go sniff hamburgers."

Elvis understood. "OK hun, I'm gone," but ignored her request and remained firmly seated, suspecting a storm was brewing.

"Time to sniff hamburgers?" Paula said.

"Just an expression. I picked it up in America a few years back. It means... erm it means... You know what? I'm damned if I can remember. So you've obviously found something, do I want to know?"

"You tell me? Just because you asked me to try and track down your mother doesn't mean you have to listen to what I've got to say.

It's not unusual for people in your position to let it go at this stage and live the rest of their lives in blissful ignorance."

Jessi mulled over Paula's words, echoing a question she'd asked herself countless times before. Why this relentless pursuit of a woman who, as far as she knew, had chosen to erase her from existence? Abandonment sculpted its way into every facet of Jessi's life, a bitter, festering wound she masked with defiance. Whoever this woman was, Jessi held her in contempt, a silent, seething grudge. Did she truly believe unearthing the details would somehow soothe the sting, rewrite the narrative of her own neglected beginning? Or was it something more primal, a yearning for a connection she'd never known, a connection she wasn't even sure she wanted? Indecision, Jessi's lifelong shadow, had never felt more ridiculous. She had spent years trying to find out information about her real mother and now she wasn't sure she wanted to hear what Paula had to say.

Sensing Jessi's hesitation, Paula said, "Would you like me to come back tomorrow, or next week maybe. How about you just give me a call an when you're ready?"

Jessi grabbed a cherished cushion and held it tight against her chest, like a little girl scolded by her daddy. "No. I need to know what you know. I need some closure, what have you got?" she finally decided.

"Well, we eventually got hold of copies of the adoption papers and social work notes and whilst not complete, they do contain enough information for us to establish who your mother was..."

Jessi had a sudden thought and interrupted. "Sorry. Before we go any further, is it just me, or is it very, very weird that I'm living in the same house my mother owned, a woman I never knew existed until recently and I certainly didn't know I was related to?"

"You want the truth?" Paula said, "thirty-five years, and I thought I'd seen it all. Then this little doozy walks in. It'll certainly become the stuff of legends back at the office."

"It just it feels too much of a coincidence to be a coincidence," Jessi said.

"I get what you're saying, but without bursting your bubble, I kinda think you should just see it as a crazy coincidence, instead of diving into some dark conspiracy stuff."

Jessi wasn't convinced but refrained from responding.

"But while we're on the subject," Paula said, "how did you know about Judy McKintyre? I wasn't even aware she'd died. I was hopeful I was going to turn up here today and meet her."

"Morbid curiosity more than anything. When I first moved in, they told me the previous owner kicked the bucket without a will, and the solicitor's couldn't track down any living relatives. Talk about irony. I shelled out sixty-five grand for this dump, and it probably should've been mine by right anyway. So, I did some snooping around to find out who lived here before me, and turns out it was Judy McKintyre and her mum, Laura McKintyre, among others," Jessi explained.

"Got it. So, my plan was to catch up with Judy, your mum, and clarify some info I dug up about your adoption. I just wanted to make sure we had the right person. But it looks like that's not happening now."

"So where does that leave me?" Jessi said.

"Honestly? Meeting Judy was kinda like going through the motions, you know? Dotting the i's and crossing the t's so to speak. From what I've found, there's no doubt that Judy McKintyre of this address was your mum."

Emotion slammed into Jessi like a rogue wave, pulling her under before she could catch her breath. Tears, hot and heavy, escaped her control, tracing salty paths down her face as she sought refuge in the warm embrace of the cushion.

"I'm really sorry about this," Paula said trying to comfort her, "this wasn't how I thought today would play out. Do you want me to call someone, maybe get a friend to come over?"

Jessi took a breath, a tissue, and a few moments to compose herself.

"I'll be fine, honestly. Just need to get my head straight before we carry on. Don't suppose you fancy making a coffee do you?"

"Of course, milk, sugar?" said Paula.

"White, one please."

Paula exited to the kitchen, and Jessi headed to the mirror – the only thing she managed to rescue from the renovations. Her reflection wasn't winning any beauty contests, but at least she dodged a bullet by not slapping on any makeup that morning. "You there Elvis?" Jessi said.

Hesitant to answer because he had been given strict instructions to go sniff hamburgers, Elvis decided suffering Jessi's wrath was worth the pain if he could help. "No, you told me to go sniff hamburgers remember?"

"I had a hunch your curiosity would get the better of you."

"Concern, sugar, nothin' less. Just wanted to check you were OK."

"I'll forgive you this time. Where are you?"

"If I tell you, are you gonna swing a punch," Elvis said nervously.

"No, I promise."

"In that case, I'm stood right behind the sofa."

Jessi sauntered back to the sofa. Nestling into the cushions, she gracefully extended her hand, letting it glide along the sofa's back. A gasp caught in her throat as Elvis's touch, like the rustle of dead leaves, enveloped her hand, sending goosebumps spiralling across her skin.

"OK, will you stay close while I talk to Mrs. Bradley?" she begged.

"Of course hun, I ain't goin' nowhere."

Paula returned from the kitchen coffees in hand and rejoined Jessi on the sofa. "You OK Jessi, sure you want me to carry on and tell you what I know?"

Not entirely convinced she was OK, Jessi replied, "Yeah I'm fine thanks, let's do this."

"Well as you already know, you were found abandoned in a pub called the Kings Head in Waltham," Paula began.

"In the toilet," added Jessi for clarity.

"Yes, in the toilet."

"In the bloke's toilet," Jessi added for even more clarity.

"That's correct, the male toilet. Well, more precisely in a box on the toilet floor."

While Jessi wanted to know everything Paula knew, she couldn't help disrupting the flow with a question. "Why a pub and why the bloke's toilet?"

The answer to the question lay buried with Jessi's mother. Paula, armed with whispers and hunches, could only offer theories.

"We can only speculate I'm afraid. Maybe she was a regular and knew she wouldn't cause suspicion. Maybe she thought she might find the father there; we really don't know. As to why she chose the male toilet. Well, perhaps there were only males in the pub at the time, so she knew you had a better chance of being found than if she'd left you in the female loo."

Resigned to never knowing, all Jessi could offer was, "I guess."

"Anyway, thankfully you were found and handed over to the landlady. The police were phoned, and you were taken to the local hospital for a check-up. You probably won't remember this, but prior to being adopted by Sally and Jack, you spent a few months with a foster carer called Gladys Smith while the adoption was formalised."

That caught the attention of Elvis. "Hey, that's my moms' name."

"Meanwhile, your mother suffered complications as a result of the birth and was admitted to hospital two days after you were born," Paula continued.

"Oh, yeah, the night the lights went out. Don't recall much, just flashes, you know? The cops, the stretcher, the way her eyes looked like they held a secret the whole world wanted to know," Elvis said, trying to recall the details.

"You were there?" Jessi said surprised.

"Uh huh."

"Nooo, I'm not that old, it's recorded in the social worker's notes," Paula replied.

Realising she'd drifted into another conversation with Elvis, she urged Paula to carry on.

"She was questioned by the police and a social worker, and she admitted to the birth and leaving you in the pub."

"Was she charged with anything?" Jessi seemed keen to know.

"Not that I'm aware of, no."

"Fucking typical."

"Language young lady," Elvis reprimanded her.

"Dump your new born in a guys john, plead insanity and get a bunch of liberal do gooders fawning all over you and excusing your actions because society's broken down and everyone's a victim," Jessi shouted, her voice filled with a mix of anger and frustration.

Sensing her anger, Paula said, "Listen Jessi, I have no idea why the decisions taken at the time were taken and I know you're angry, but we may never know, so please don't beat yourself up over it."

Compassion tugged at Jessi's heart, a wispy thread in the tangled storm of bitterness clouding her mind. But the storm raged on, drowning out the whispers of empathy. "So that was it then? She had a kid, dumped it, kid got adopted and everyone lived happily ever after or not as the case may be."

"Pretty much," Paula said. "Early in nineteen seventy nine a gentleman did get in touch claiming to be your father, a man named Gordon Robinson. A social worker arranged to meet with him, but he never showed. He was never heard of again. We can try and trace him if you like?"

"No thanks, think I've had enough disappointments for one day."

"I understand. There isn't much else. A few notes about further involvement with Judy. It seems she suffered with mental health problems most of her life and was diagnosed with multiple personality disorder. She had numerous spells in a psychiatric hospital up until about two thousand and five then everything went quiet. As I said earlier, I had no idea she'd died until I got here today."

A wave of guilt crashed over Jessi as her thoughts drifted to her adoptive parents, Jack and Sally, their loving faces a stark contrast to the phantom of the mother she never knew. Her precious childhood, a tapestry woven with care and laughter, felt tarnished by her obsessive grip of the past. "Do mum and dad know any of this?" Jessi asked.

"I've spoken to Sally and kept her informed. Thought she might come in useful as a shoulder to cry on. She said she'd let your dad know what was going on."

"OK. I hope I don't appear ungrateful Paula; it's just... well just a bit of a letdown. I guess I was hoping for a fairytale ending. Daughter meets mother, mother is repentant, daughter forgives mother, everything in the garden turns out rosy, you know what I mean."

"Yeah I know... Look, you know where I am if you need anything."

"Thanks, really appreciate everything you've done."

"No problem, I'll see myself out and remember I'm only a phone call away."

The click of the front door echoed in the silence, leaving Jessi alone with the remnants of Paula's words. Knowing her mother's name was more than a crumb, it was a pebble cast into a still pond, sending ripples of possibility outward. But within the house, secrets lurked, a deep well of knowledge waiting to be tapped. Sauntering toward the sparsely populated cupboard that served as her makeshift 'drinks cabinet', she delved into its depths, determined to unearth a half-empty bottle of Jack Daniels, a hidden relic from her memorable housewarming party. Disregarding any precision, she skipped the measuring and poured what she guessed to be a double, although it probably edged closer to a treble. The liquid slid down her throat with an intensity that reminded her why she'd hidden it in the first place.

"Elvis," she barked, "where are you now?"

"Still stood behind the sofa hun."

"Sit down and don't move unless I say so."

"Whatever you say Jess."

"Are you there yet?"

"Uh huh!"

"Which side?"

"Nearest the wall. Everything all right, Jess? You're lookin' a tad riled up, sugar?"

Jessi refilled her glass and joined Elvis on the sofa, her eyes filled with a determination that unsettled him. "Right Mr. Elvis Aaron Presley let's have it," she demanded.

"Have what Jess?"

"Tell me what you know about my mother."

"I don't know nothin'. I'm just a dead entertainer stuck in a nightmare."

"You lived with my mother for over thirty years, you probably knew her better than anyone."

"I kept myself to myself in the early days hun. Didn't much feel like talkin' to folks, ya know? I'd hole up in the attic most of the time."

"But you must have got some insight into her life, what she enjoyed doing, who she associated with, did she work, did she have any more kids. Hey, I could have brothers and sisters."

"Listen Jess, I don't know much about nothing other than singin' and swivellin' my hips, but maybe it's best if you just let sleeping dogs lie."

"Well, she certainly seemed a bit of a dog, I'll give you that," Jessi said with a bitterness she was having trouble letting go of.

"Whoa there. That kinda talk just ain't cool, not one bit. Now, your momma might've done things she ain't proud of, but that don't give you the right to spit vinegar on her memory."

"No Elvis, my mother is a woman called Sally Henderson. This McKintyre woman was nothing more than a cheap whore who didn't deserve to have children and certainly doesn't deserve my respect."

"Look, sugar, I ain't gonna lie. Family ain't always sunshine and rainbows. My momma, bless her soul, had a taste for the sweet brown stuff, and my poppa, well, he made a wrong turn down a dark road once or twice. But hey, who's perfect, right? We all got our skeletons dancin' in the closet, our own little shadows to outrun. Spillin' what I know might not be the magic wand you're hopin' for, Jess."

"You know what?" Jessi said angrily, "you're right. I don't want to know. I don't care. I don't care about her, I don't care about this house, and I don't care about you."

Before Elvis could respond, Jessi stormed out of the room. Her angry footsteps echoed in the hallway as she descended into the shadowed space under the stairs, the muffled sounds of rummaging announcing her fury. Moments later, she reappeared, suitcase in hand, its worn leather scuffed and scarred. She placed it on the table with a thud that made the glasses in the drinks cabinet rattle. With swift determination she headed upstairs, her steps echoing on the staircase, before re-emerging with an armful of random clothes that she unceremoniously dumped in the yawning suitcase.

Elvis moved to the table, he knew he should say something, anything, to break the spell, but the words caught in his throat, choked by the weight of her anger and his own guilt. "Aw, c'mon now, Jess, this ain't the way to sort things out. How 'bout you pull up a chair, and we have ourselves a heart-to-heart, huh?"

"Piss off." Jessi was having none of it.

In a desperate attempt to lighten the mood, Elvis tried. "I know, I'll croon you a tune, 'cause I know how much you love hearin' me sing?"

Elvis's suggestion shifted her mood but not her plans. "Look Elvis, I need to get away for a while, find a bit of head space. Don't take it personally OK?" Jessi grabbed her suitcase, coat and laptop bag and made for the front door. Before leaving she turned and tried to reassure him. "Don't fret sweetie, I'll be fine. See you soon."

———— ⚬❦⚬ ————

ELVIS HAD LEARNT LONG ago that time in the spirit world held no meaning. Minutes could stretch into hours, and hours could warp into days. Yet, even in this timeless tapestry, he sensed that Jessi's absence had stretched beyond the bounds of his patience. When the familiar click of a key turning in the front door reached his ears, his excitement bubbled up uncontrollably.

"Hi honey, I'm home," yelled Jessi from the hallway.

"Jessi is that you?" he said, already knowing the answer.

"Sure is Pelvis." She burst into the room like a champagne bottle uncorked, her vibrant energy a stark contrast to the melancholy cloud she wore ten days ago.

"Where you been, I've been worried sick about you?"

"Just needed some time to think sweetie. It's amazing what ten days of sun, sea and sangria can do for a girl. It just all got a bit weird living here with the ghost of Elvis in the same house my real mother and grandmother inhabited."

"The whole mom situation's a bit peculiar, huh? Imagine snaggin' a house and findin' out it belonged to a momma you never even knew was in the picture."

"And you don't consider having the ghost of Elvis as a room mate slightly bizarre too?"

"Well, darlin', it all comes down to whether you believe in ghosts or not I guess."

"But even if I did believe in ghosts, and the jury's still out, it would still be bizarre. Ghost, fine. Elvis's ghost? The afterlife has some seriously wacky casting directors."

"Sweetheart, hate to break it to ya, but I ain't too thrilled bein' stuck here anymore than you want me here, but I ain't sure what to do about it."

"I know, I know. Looks like we're stuck with each other, at least for the time being. Could be worse I guess, thank God Cliff Richard's still alive."

"Well, shoot, is that right? He's gotta be pushin' a hundred by now, huh?"

"No, it just seems that way. Right, time to grab some food and get on with some research."

"Research?"

"Yep, time to find out more about Judy McKintyre and her mother."

"You sure you wanna go there Jess?" Elvis warned.

"Nope, but it's something I gotta do. I'm just gonna grab some fried chicken from across the road and I'll be back. Want anything? Oh.. You can't can you," Jessi said laughing.

"Is that where I was supposed to laugh?" Elvis said, "I'll just go watch you out the bedroom window, make sure you don't go runnin' off again."

———— ⟨∾⟩ ————

JUDY MCKYNTYRE DIDN'T so much enter the room as materialize, the French doors sighing shut in her wake. No theatrics, no grand entrance, merely another ghost revisiting the familiar confines of home. With an air of nonchalant curiosity, she glided toward the dining table and sifted through the stack of papers Jessi had dumped on her return. Taking in her surroundings, she began to question whether she had landed in the right place. The atmosphere carried a hint of déjà vu, yet an uncanny sense of unfamiliarity filled the air, casting a surreal aura over the entire scene.

"Well, the old place certainly looks better. Definite woman's touch, in fact I'd go as far as to say a single woman. Sensibly sized television, no pizza boxes acting as a coffee table. Not a pair of sweaty socks or unwashed dishes in sight and not a whiff of testosterone in the air. Sensible girl, whoever she is," Judy said to herself.

A bittersweet nostalgia gnawed at her as she revisited the haven of her younger self, but the resounding slam of the front door, abruptly halted her plans for further exploration. Jessi entered the room, wine in hand and dumped a bucket of KFC on the table before heading to the kitchen to grab a glass. If she'd sensed Judy's presence, it didn't register as her thoughts were firmly fixed on food, alcohol and a voyage of discovery. Judy's eyes narrowed, a flicker of suspicion chasing away nostalgia as she observed the stranger occupying her home. Who dared claim what was hers, brick by familiar brick? Jessi sauntered back into the room and settled into a dining chair. With a delighted groan, she snatched a sizzling chunk of southern fried chicken, the crispy crust giving way under her teeth to juicy, herb-infused bliss.

Eyes shut and nose tuned like a seasoned scent detective, Elvis traced the tantalizing waft of Jessi's supper from his bedroom perch to the heart of the living room. He stood over Jessi, anticipation written across his face, poised for the moment Jessi's taste buds embarked on a journey of sensory ecstasy with her second bite. Jessi had that now familiar sensation he was close by.

"That's close enough Elvis," she said, "no one comes between a girl and her juicy breast."

Elvis peeled open one eye, a sly smile creeping across his face at the thought of Jessi's culinary delights. But the smile froze, replaced by a jolt of bewildered recognition. Judy stood at the room's centre, sucking the oxygen from his lungs and the joy from his heart.

"Judy McKyntyre," he exclaimed in disbelief.

"What about her?" Jessi said.

"Well, well, well, if it isn't the King himself in all his *past his best* glory," Judy said with feigned enthusiasm.

"Well?" Jessi persisted.

Having grabbed his attention, Elvis replied, "Well what Jess?"

"What about Judy McKintyre, have you remembered something?"

"Erm..." Elvis found himself trapped in a bewildering maze of uncertainty, unsure of which path to take as he grappled with the unfolding chaos that now resembled a waking nightmare.

"Your voice was already a jolt to the senses Elvis, but the shock of laying eyes on you has took the trauma to a whole new level," Judy spat; her words laced with anger.

In a whirlwind of panic, Elvis darted across the room and swiftly covered Judy's mouth. "Not another word, do you understand?" he demanded, as if the urgency of the situation had temporarily overridden the logic that Jessi, unmistakably, couldn't hear a single word Judy was saying.

"Not another word about what?" Jessi said, irritated.

"Erm... no need to talk no more 'bout Judy McKintyre, darlin'," Elvis said, hoping he'd covered the cross talk.

"Excuse me Herr Presley, but it was you who mentioned her name when you came in. Besides which, if I want to talk about Judy McKintyre, I will. This is my house and she was my skanky whore of a mother."

"*What!*" yelled Judy.

The situation pirouetted towards disaster and Elvis found himself entangled in a web of escalating madness, desperately seeking an escape route. "Jess, you gotta trust ol' Elvis on this. How 'bout we mosey on for now, and we'll have ourselves a little chat later, alright?"

"Elvis, stop ignoring me, what did she say?" Judy persisted.

"Consider yourself lucky old man that I've got more pressing things to attend to. I've promised to pick Emma up from work and drop her at her mums, we'll continue this later," Jessi said. "Oh, and just so you're aware, Dylan might turn up and if he does, leave him the hell alone, do you hear?"

"Don't worry your pretty head sweetheart', I won't lay a finger on him."

Jessi, armed with a coat and a chicken drumstick, the culinary equivalent of a middle finger, hurried out of the room leaving Elvis and Judy, locked in their own silent standoff. The house, now a battleground, held its breath, waiting for the first spark to ignite the conflict.

"Well?" Judy broke the silence.

"Well what?" Elvis whispered.

"You know damn well what," shouted Judy.

"Shh... Keep your voice down hun... She ain't left the house yet."

"Why keep my voice down?" Judy said, "she obviously can't hear me."

"She couldn't hear me at first and then gradually..."

Judy didn't let him finish. "And then gradually she started hearing voices in her head. Hmm... Sounds familiar does it?"

"I don't think we need to go there darlin'," Elvis said.

"But I want to go there you son of a bitch, you're not getting off that lightly."

"Alright, baby, simmer down. Take a load off, and let's talk like a couple of responsible spirits. You gotta understand where I'm comin' from, sweetheart. It hit me like a bolt from the blue, seeing you standin' there, givin' me a real shock to the system."

"Oh, trust me darling, it's nowhere near the shock you gave me. For thirty years you were just a voice in my head and now seeing you after all this time is a cruel twist of the knife and a bitter reminder you killed me."

Elvis paid no attention to the sound of the back door opening and banging shut. "Whoa! Sweet cheeks, take that back. There was only one person responsible for your death and that was you."

Dylan strolled in from the kitchen, a low whistle escaping his lips. Elvis and Judy, swivelled in their seats, eyes drawn to his entrance. He ambled towards the table, all nonchalance until his gaze snagged on the bucket of fried chicken sitting like a beacon in the centre. A flicker of anticipation crossed his face before he peeled the lid, peered inside, and with a muttered, "Later," disappeared back into the kitchen, leaving Elvis and Judy to exchange a bemused look. As much as Judy was intrigued by Dylan's appearance, she still had other things on her mind.

"Listen Elvis, you may not have opened the bottle of tablets or poured the whiskey, but you loaded the gun. For thirty years you loaded the gun."

Dylan, blissfully unaware of the simmering tension between Judy and Elvis, sauntered back into the room, a Budweiser clutched triumphantly in his hand. With a shrug, he plopped himself down in the centre of the sofa, effectively erecting a physical barrier between the two fuming protagonists. Elvis, forced to lean forward in order to maintain eye contact with Judy, said. "Hold on, now, Judy, don't pin this whole rodeo on me. You were walkin' a lonesome trail long 'fore our paths ever crossed. I just saw a gal in distress, heartaches piled high and tried to help."

Dylan, restless, snatched the remote from the coffee table and flicked the TV on. A kaleidoscope of channels blurred across the screen, sports channels giving way to cooking shows, before he landed on a classic music station. The familiar drawl of Elvis filled the room, and with a contented sigh, Dylan plunked the remote onto Elvis's knee, letting the King hold the reins for a while.

Judy got to her feet, striding purposefully toward what had unofficially become Elvis's personal armchair. Temptation tugged at him to intervene, but deep down, he questioned whether she'd pay any mind if he did. "You don't get it Elvis. I kept hearing voices in my head. Everyone thought I was mad, but they wouldn't go away, you wouldn't go away even when I begged you to stop. You just kept on day after day, night after night."

As much as Elvis liked the sound of his own voice, the TV had become an irritant and he switched it off much to the bemusement of Dylan, who immediately switched it back on.

"Well, darlin', I was just tryin' to lend a helpin' hand, you know? You were headin' down a one-way street to heartbreak, and somebody had to step in. You were just a young thing, so innocent and tender. you should never have been left here alone when your momma died."

"Don't give me that crap. She was never around anyway; I'd always been here alone. Latchkey kid, yeah, with a key dangled around my neck since I was five," Judy reminded him.

Dylan started channel hopping again and settled on a comedy channel. Elvis was tempted to put on another 'fright night' show and get rid of him but remembered his promise to Jessi. Instead, he unplugged the TV at the wall and left Dylan dismantling the remote control.

He wandered over to Judy and attempted to reconcile their differences. "Look, I've no idea how I ended up in this pokey little dump, a whole lotta miles from my sweet home. Ain't sure why I'm here, maybe it's some kinda cosmic journey, a mission I gotta tackle before the man upstairs hands me them keys to the pearly gates. And part of this mission, sugar, was to lend you a hand, keep you from takin' that wild ride down the rabbit hole. Let's not forget, you got mixed up with some pretty scary people and they're as responsible as anyone for what happened to you."

Dylan's dismantling of the remote ceased, his attention snagged by a sudden internal gurgling. The vindaloo from last night's questionable culinary adventure was making its displeasure known, and a cold sweat prickled his brow. He knew this battle wouldn't be won from the comfort of the sofa. With a sigh that was equal parts regret and resignation, he surrendered the remote to the coffee table and made a tactical retreat towards the bathroom, hoping to reach the porcelain throne before the vindaloo declared full-scale war. Elvis uncharacteristically had some concerns for a guy he didn't particularly like or trust and was tempted to follow to make sure no harm came to him, because he was sure if it did, Jessi would look at only one person to blame.

Judy on the other hand, couldn't give a damn about the strange interloper roaming around what she still considered to be her home. "You don't understand Elvis," she continued, "I know I had my share of screw-ups and ran with the wrong crowd, but the real trouble started when those damn voices landed me in the loony bin six times. Ever been in one of those psych wards? It's no walk in the park. They assess you, analyse you, and throw every pill in the pharmacy at you until they decide, 'Hey, the voices have chilled out', which of course they had because you were sat here on your fat hamburger arse living the life of Reilly. Then they kick you out, slap you with a 'care in the community' label, until the voices, *your* voice, started again and it was back with the straight jacket routine."

"Then why keep spillin' the beans 'bout them voices if all they gonna do is lock you up every time? Ain't no sense in that."

"I really thought they could help, you know? I was desperate as hell. Spent my first sixteen years looking after my alcoholic prostitute mother who preferred the backseat of strangers' cars to being home with her own kid. Dad was supposedly working abroad, too busy to drop a line. Uncles dropped by with gifts and unwanted touches so often, I swear my grandma practically lived at the maternity home. When my mum passed, it was like this massive weight lifted off me. I didn't wish her gone, but suddenly, I felt free. Got a roof over my head, thanks to whatever my mum managed to scrape together, so at least I wasn't getting kicked out onto the streets. All I needed was a break, someone to believe in me and give me a chance to be something more. But that doesn't happen to people like me, does it? Instead, all I ended up with was a twenty quid a day crack habit and an unplanned pregnancy, which brings me neatly back to my earlier question before you silenced that Bessy bird."

"Jessi," Elvis corrected her.

"Jessi, Bessy, who gives a shit. What did she mean?"

Elvis slumped back onto the sofa, sinking into its plush cushions, his mind wrestling with what to spill and what to keep locked away. "She didn't mean anything darlin'," Elvis said as a poor response.

"She referred to me as her skanky whore of a mother. I think in any language that means something," Judy suggested.

That was a hard one for Elvis to argue, but he still attempted to keep things vague. "It's complicated."

"Really?"

"OK, no not really," Elvis was left with little choice, "here's the short version."

"I'm all ears."

"That little lady's your daughter."

"And?" Judy said, expecting more.

"And nothin' hun. That's it."

"Ok, try me with the long version, I've got nothing better to do for all eternity."

Elvis didn't actually have a long version, but he did his best. "If you insist. Jessi is the daughter you abandoned in a guy's john in some bar called 'The King's Head.'"

"Bullshit."

"Look, Judy, I ain't got time for sugar-coated lies. You know what you did, and it wasn't right."

"I'm not denying I left my baby somewhere I knew she'd be found and well cared for, what's bullshit, is that this Jessi is her."

"Why shouldn't she be?"

"Come on Elvis, isn't it all a bit coincidental, living in the same house her unknown mother once lived in? I reckon she found out I died without leaving a will and she thinks if she can convince someone she's my daughter, she'll inherit my estate."

"Estate? You think that's all this is about, Judy? You think this girl's just some gold-digger in blue jeans? Why would she go to all the trouble of trying to prove she's something she ain't just to inherit a hovel that was worth jackshit? Think what you like, I'm telling you, that's your daughter and all things considered, she seems a great kid. What she don't need is any spiritual interference from you. Understand?"

"I see. So, you're providing all the spiritual guidance she needs I take it. Well, that's a fucking joke after what you did to me. God help the poor cow."

"Now, listen here, Ms. McKintyre. For the last time, I didn't do a thing to harm ya. I'm sorry your momma didn't bag that Mom of the Year award, and I'm sorry life dealt ya a tough hand, but the choices, darlin', they were yours. You picked to run with the wrong crowd, the trailer trash and the pill peddlers. If you reckon I'm gonna carry the weight of your stumbles on my conscience, well, you better think again. What's it you're after, Judy? Why've you circled back into my world?"

It was the first time Judy had sensed anger in Elvis's voice. The first time he had bitten back.

"I, uh, I thought dying would be the end, Elvis. No more pain, no more... No more of that. But the memories, they... they stick like shadows, you know? Can't move on, can't escape 'em. Why did I come back? I've no idea. Maybe... maybe I thought I'd find something, something to make it all make sense. Didn't think you'd still be here, though. Thought you were just another figment, another ghost in my head."

Dylan sauntered on back into the room, a grin of contentment lighting up his smug mug. He was fixing to settle down at the dining table for a round of fried chicken, now that his belly had a smidgen of space, when his phone let out a ring. "Hello... Hello? Who? Sorry really bad signal here. Who did you say...? Nope still can't hear you, hang on, let me go outside."

Dylan rushed outside, panicking he might lose the punter on the other end of the phone as Elvis beckoned Judy over to the sofa.

"Judy, I ain't got no fancy words, no silver-tongued lies to hide behind. Past is past, that's a cold, hard truth, but it don't mean we gotta be chained to it. Nobody wanted you to shine brighter than I did, honey. Every step I took, every hand I reached out, was tryin' to pull you out of the darkness. I'm sorry I failed, I really am, but I ain't got nothin' left to give."

"So, what now?" Judy said.

"Who knows. You see, for us, time's done run out, but Jessi, she's still got a whole lotta livin' ahead. She's got her act together – good gig, good pals. Yeah, maybe needs to watch that talk a bit, but that's just how things roll these days. What I do reckon, is she's had a tough go wrappin' her head 'round my ghostly company. Not sure she needs her departed momma throwin' a curveball into the mix right about now."

"Seems to me from all them papers on the table, she's pretty keen to find her mother. Why shouldn't I give her some answers?"

"Because, Judy, she's all fired up and angry at you, honey, and I reckon there ain't no words you can say to fix it. Best just let her be, darlin'."

"Don't you think I deserve the chance to explain what happened, explain why I was forced to abandon her?"

"But who you doin' this for? It ain't right to use Jessi just to ease your conscience. Let her wrap her mind 'round what she's learned for now, and maybe swing by in a couple of months to see where things stand, huh?"

Judy pondered Elvis's words, and as much as she didn't want to, she had to figure out who she was doing this for. Her selfish gene urged her to stick around, but that motherly instinct told her Elvis hit the nail on the head—it wasn't just about helping Jessi, but her own redemption calling her. Reluctantly she said. "OK Mr Presley, you win. I'll go on my merry way, for now."

"Promise?" Elvis said.

"Cross my heart and hope to... Oh! That don't work anymore does it. Well, you get the idea."

And just like that she was gone. The last echo of her voice faded from the room. No grand exit through the French doors that had been a portal for her arrival. Vanished. No theatrics, no footprint, just a void where she used to be.

———— ⟨∾⟩ ————

ELVIS SETTLED IN HIS armchair and relived the sting of Judy's pain, etched on her face like a silent scream. Was it his fault? Had he been the villain in her final act? The questions circled through his mind, a maddening chorus demanding answers. The appearance of Jessi and Dylan rushing in from the hallway had never been so welcome and though there were still many unanswered questions, just the sight of Jessi gave Elvis some peace.

"But why were you stood outside?" Jessi said, "it's bloody freezing."

"My phone rang, and I couldn't get a damn signal in here, so I went outside and locked myself out."

"How long you been out there?"

"Hour and a half. I thought you'd gone to pick up Emma and wouldn't be long."

"Bloody hell Dylan, you'll get pneumonia. Sit down and I'll get you a hot chocolate. Warm the cock..."

"Mmm... Yes please, it could do with warming."

"... the cockles of your heart," Jessi continued.

"Oh, OK... Where exactly are the cockles in your heart?"

Jessi headed off to the kitchen. "I've no idea."

Dylan, as Dylan was prone to do, didn't like unanswered questions, so asked, "How do you know if they need warming then?"

Jessi stuck her head through the kitchen door. "Look, do you want a mug of hot chocolate, or do you want to chat about human anatomy?

"Hot chocolate please. Though I did read somewhere that sharing body heat was a good way of preventing hypothermia."

The microwave pinged and Jessi took Dylan, who had settled himself on the sofa, his mug of hot chocolate. "We're not in a snow hole in the Arctic Circle Dylan. I think you'll find central heating will have the desired effect. Here drink this and stop being such a big girl's blouse."

"Another one to add to the list?" Dylan threw in out of the blue.

"What list? What are you talking about?"

"I have a list of things I would like to come back as when I die. Wouldn't mind being a big girl's blouse."

Jessi didn't really have an answer to that one so just said, "You worry me Dylan, you really do."

Dylan's hot chocolate chugging was a rhythmic percussion solo, each sip punctuated by a loud, sucking sound. Jessi grimaced, remembering Emma's near meltdown at the last restaurant, where a soup slurping octogenarian had triggered a full-blown OCD meltdown. Thankfully, Jessi's nerves were sturdier, but the memory still left a bitter aftertaste. Eager to create some space as Dylan wrapped up his drink, Jessi strolled over to the record player, unleashing the magic of Elvis's greatest hits, an album which had become the soundtrack to her life.

"Thanks hun," Elvis whispered.

Startled, Jessi whispered back. "Bloody hell, didn't realise it was a threesome."

"Want me to leave."

Not so quietly Jessi replied, "Do you mind?"

"Do I mind what?" Dylan said.

"Erm... Do you mind me putting on a bit of Elvis?"

"Not at all."

Elvis rose, a flicker of disappointment in his eyes. "Catch you later Jess." He wasn't leaving because he didn't want to be there, but because he had to. Before he could take a step, Dylan erupted in a warbling, off-key rendition of Jailhouse Rock coupled with dance moves which were a tangled blur of limbs seeking to channel the King's swagger but finding only their own awkwardness.

Accusingly Jessi asked, "Elvis?"

"Nothing to do with me darlin', I swear."

Elvis and Jessi stood transfixed; eyes glued to Dylan as he poured his soul into the song. The final note hung in the air like a teardrop before dissolving into a wave of laughter that erupted from them both, bubbling up from their chests like champagne in a shaken bottle. It was too much for Elvis who ignored Jessi's request to leave and fell back down into his armchair.

"What's so funny?" Dylan said, mildly offended.

Struggling to control herself Jessi replied, "Nothing, nothing at all. Just took me by surprise. It's a side of you hitherto unseen."

Dylan sat back on the sofa and said nervously, "Yeah! Well, I have a confession to make actually."

Jessi joined him. "Oh... erm... OK. Do I want to hear it?"

"It's nothing bad," Dylan tried to reassure her.

Before Dylan had chance to explain, Jessi had already decided what was coming. "You're gay, aren't you?"

Dylan leaned forward, his eyes wide and his voice rising in pitch. "No."

"You know, I've had my suspicions for a while."

"What d'you mean?"

"Well, the way you walk and the way you're always preening yourself in the mirror."

"I don't preen and what's wrong with the way I walk?"

"Sorry. Forget it; it's probably just my gaydar on the blink again."

"Forget it? You accuse me of battin' for the other side and then say, 'forget it.'"

"I didn't *accuse* you of anything. It's not a bloody crime."

Elvis was startled by that revelation. "Ain't it?"

Jessi turned her head towards the armchair. "Not here, not in two thousand and nine."

"I know it isn't a crime," Dylan said.

"God have mercy on their souls," Elvis said disapprovingly.

Jessi, still staring at the armchair said, "What did you say?"

Dylan, assuming Jessi was talking to him, answered. "I said I know it isn't a crime."

"Not you."

"Well, who then."

"It's not natural Jess. God created Adam and Eve, not Adam and Steve," Elvis proffered in a futile attempt to convince Jessi being gay was a sin.

"You fat southern bigot, you should be ashamed of yourself."

Dylan getting a little fed up with talking to the back of Jessi's head said. "Jessi... Would you please face me when you're talking to me." Jessi did as she was asked. "Thank you. Now, first and foremost, I am not a bigot. My hairdresser's gay and so is my pedicurist. Would a bigot let gay guys mess with his head and feet?"

"Pedicurist?" Jessi said surprised.

"Yeah, what's wrong with that?"

"Well, nothing, It's just..."

Dylan didn't let her finish. "And calling someone a fat southerner is very offensive."

"Well, now, ain't that somethin'? My little buddy here's got a point, honey. It's extremely offensive and I demand an apology," Elvis said.

In an attempt to put the matter to bed, Jessi said. "OK... Enough. Dylan, I don't think you're gay, I don't think you're fat and I don't think you're a bigot, but I can't do anything about the fact you come from Essex."

"Then why call me a fat southern bigot?"

Without much thought she said, "I was talking to Elvis."

"You were talking to Elvis?"

"Yeah, kind of."

"They're back aren't they?" Dylan said.

"Who?"

"The voices."

"No, they're not back. I was referring to some of the lyrics Elvis was singing that lead me to believe he was a fat southern bigot."

"There you go again with the fat comments," Elvis threw in for good measure.

Dylan had been down this strange road on more than one occasion and even his friends had suggested he took a wide birth as far as Jessi was concerned, but he was enamoured and had chosen to embrace the idiosyncrasies that made Jessi, well, Jessi. To him, they were merely charming quirks that added spice to the adventure.

"I have to say Jess; you're a bit of a strange one."

"I know, but admit it, that's the attraction isn't it?"

"To be honest, it's your great arse and perfect tits that attracted me."

Jessi smiled. "I can live with that. So back to your confession."

"OK, as I was saying..."

"Oh God, you're married, aren't you?" Jessi once again interrupted.

"No, I'm *not* married..."

"You've had a knob job?"

"A what?"

"A knob job. Bit like a boob job, but on your knob," Jessi explained.

Dylan was getting frustrated. "For God's sake Jessi, would you please just shut up for one minute and let me finish?"

Realising she'd overstepped the mark she said, "Sorry, carry on."

"OK, here's my embarrassing confession. Elvis Presley gives me goosebumps. Not in a sexual kind of way, more of a full-body, hair-standing-on-end kind of way. One listen to 'That's All Right, Mama' and I'm transported back to my grandma's kitchen, dancing like nobody's watching, which they usually weren't, bless her. No Elvis, no rock and roll. The man's a legend. There I've said it."

"I see," was all Jessi could offer while she digested Dylans secret.

Elvis was glowing on the other side of the room, head bigger than a full moon. "What a great guy. You should marry him Jess."

"I'm not marrying anyone," Jessi said.

"I'm not asking you to marry me," said Dylan, "I didn't confess to clear the way for a marriage proposal. Talk about getting hold of the wrong end of the stick."

Realising her mistake. "Of course, sorry. I was being stupid. Well, I certainly wouldn't have had you down as a Presleyite."

"Is that a real word?" said Dylan.

"I don't think so," Jessi replied.

"To be honest Jess, I thought you already knew."

"How would I know something like that? It's not like you'd be shouting it from the rooftops."

"It's just all the references you've made about him since we met."

Jessi wasn't really sure what he meant. "Have I?"

"Yeah. On your second viewing when I couldn't remember your name, you introduced yourself as Priscilla Presley, remember?"

"Nope can't say I do, but I'll take your word for it."

"Then you called me Vernon, which was Elvis's fathers' name and then there was that séance shit when you sang 'Welcome to my World'. I just assumed someone at the office had tipped you off and you were taking the piss."

"I swear I had no idea. So, is this a recent thing, this obsession?" Jessi said, intrigued.

"No, started when I was a kid. My grandma wouldn't allow any other music to be played in the house except Elvis."

"What a woman," Elvis threw in from his armchair.

"Aww... You poor sod Dylan. You would have thought it would have had the opposite effect."

Elvis wasn't happy with Jessi's insinuation. "Hey, don't go pokin' at him just 'cause you got no taste in music honey."

"Nope, I'm not just a fan, Jess, I'm a disciple. I've devoured every scrap of information, analysed every note, dissected every sneer of his lip. I probably know him better than he knows his own sequined socks."

"Hmm... not sure about that one," Jessi said.

"Ask me anything, anything you want."

"OK, how many grains of sand are there on Cleethorpes beach?"

"What?"

"It's important, I stand to win two hundred and fifty thousand pounds in a Readers Digest competition if you know the answer," Jessi said excitedly.

"I mean about Elvis you fool. Ask me anything you want about Elvis Aaron Presley."

Elvis decided he wanted to be closer to the action and knelt resting his chin on the sofa back. Jessi's skin prickled with awareness, while Dylan just shivered muttering about faulty thermostats like a grumpy bear waking from hibernation too early.

"Sorry," said Jessi, "OK... When was he born?"

"Jeez Jess, is that the best you can do," Elvis said before Dylan could answer.

"Don't insult me Jess, you probably know the answer to that one. January the eighth nineteen thirty five," Dylan answered confidently.

"Erm... OK, how about..." Jessi was looking for a hand.

Elvis was happy to help. "Ask him the name of the first school I attended."

"OK, try this one," Jessi said, convinced Dylan would struggle, "what was the name of the first school he attended?"

"Gotta do better than that Jess, still too easy. Lawhorn School in Tupelo."

"I'm impressed," Elvis said.

"He's impressed," Jessi shared.

"Who is?" asked Dylan.

"Who's what?"

"Who's impressed?"

"Did I say impressed? I meant impressive, you're impressive."

"So why did you say *he's* if you were meaning me?"

In what was probably her most ridiculous answer so far, she said, "I was speaking from the third person perspective; I do that sometimes. What is this, an English grammar exam? I thought we were doing an Elvis trivia quiz."

"Sorry, yes we are. OK, come on then, give me a hard one."

"Still maintain you're not gay?" Jessi quipped.

"Aren't you the comedian? Got a question, or haven't you?"

"Keep your hair on lover boy, I'm thinking. I could really do with some help here, a flash of inspiration perhaps that would provide me with a really hard Elvis question..." Elvis didn't take the hint. "Something that only Elvis would know... Something he could ask himself if he was here..."

It felt like an eternity before Elvis finally rejoined the party. "Sorry Jess just had an idea for a new tune runnin' round my head. OK try him with this. What was my army service number?"

"Right, you ready Dylan?"

"Yep, hit me with it babe."

"What was his army service number?"

"Bugger," Dylan said, "that's a toughie. OK let me think... US 52, no 53 310, erm 76... 1."

"The kid's good," Elvis said.

"You're good," Jessi agreed.

"But how do you know it's the right answer?" Enquired Dylan.

That one briefly stumped her. "Erm... Because I'm a bit of a fan myself actually and I know loads about him."

This was a challenge Dylan was going to enjoy. The thought of getting one up on Jessi, a woman who believed she was always right, filled him with a paradoxical cocktail of dread and delight. "OK here's a real fan's question, always catches out the pretenders. Ready?"

"As I'll ever be."

"What was Elvis's favourite food?" Dylan said before sitting back arms folded waiting for her to fall on her sword."

"Now let me think, let me just try and channel the man himself and get it straight from the horse's mouth so to speak." She couldn't have given Elvis a bigger hint that she needed help if she had tried. Thankfully, he was tuned in this time.

"Hey, Jess, that's a question that's been buggin' me more than a popcorn kernel stuck in your teeth. Now, the world knows me for that fancy peanut butter, jelly, and bacon contraption, but that was all smoke and mirrors, baby. My true love, my culinary moonwalk, was the mighty fried peanut butter and banana sandwich."

"Eww... that's disgusting," she whispered to herself. "Well, it was a good try Dylan, trying to catch me out with the old peanut butter, strawberry jelly and fried bacon malarkey, but of course, as any respectable fan would know, his all-time favourite was fried peanut butter and banana sandwiches."

Despite secretly wanting Jessi to fail, he couldn't deny how impressed he was that she knew the answer. "I can't believe you know that. So not only do you have a great arse and a magnificent pair of tits, but you're also a closet Elvis fan. My perfect woman, I'm in heaven... Anyway, how did your little break go, cavorting with Spanish waiters for ten days?"

"They're a bit too smarmy for my liking, but the food was good and sunshine is always good. It's a bit weird being back though. It's like my mums still here. I own the place but it doesn't feel like it's mine if that makes sense. Feels like it still belongs to Judy McKintyre. My therapist said..."

"Therapist, you're seeing a therapist?" Dylan said.

"Well, I call her a therapist, more of a counsellor really."

"So you like, lie on a couch and reveal your inner most secrets?"

"Not really," Jessi said dismissively, "most of the time we just drink coffee and chat about guys."

"Ah... I'm with you now. Probing you on your sexual exploits."

"No."

"She wants to know what turns you on, what makes you tick, what gets the old juices flowing?" Dylan persisted.

"*No.*"

"Draws out your suppressed erotic fantasies and desires."

"For Christ's sake Dylan, what's wrong with you? Haven't you had it in a while, is that it?" said Jessi trying to put a stop to his interrogation.

"Well, now you come to mention it..." Dylan said sheepishly.

"So why didn't you say?" Jessi grabbed Dylan's hand and pulled him off the sofa. "Come on then, let's squash this gay rumour, but better make it a quickie, I've got an appointment at the STD clinic in half an hour."

"*What?*" Dylan said.

"Just joking. Get upstairs big boy and get your kit off."

Dylan burst out of the room, his footsteps echoing loudly on the polished wooden stairs. Jessi, filled with anticipation, had mastered the art of keeping a guy on his toes. She swiftly cleared the dining table, and upon returning to the room, she found Elvis waiting with an outstretched arm, presenting a box of condoms. Giggling, she said. "You have no idea how funny that looks, floating condoms. Thanks sweetie, nice someone's looking out for me."

"You're welcome hun."

Jessi took the condoms and made her way slowly upstairs teasing Dylan as she did so. "I'm coming sex God, ready or not."

Elvis shook his head, made himself comfy in his armchair and declared, "I lived in the wrong decade."

A RADIANT SMILE GRACED Jessi's face as she immersed herself in the treasure trove of information that Paula Bradley had sent her during her holiday. Meanwhile, Elvis lounged on the sofa, contributing his own unique soundtrack with loud, rhythmic snores. Just as the atmosphere reached its peak of quaint coziness, Dylan strolled in, casually draped in Jessi's dressing gown, adding an unexpected twist to the scene, and waking Elvis from his slumber.

"Getting in touch with your feminine side, sexy beast?" Jessi teased.

"I've always been in touch with my feminine side," Dylan said, "I'd have made a great lesbian. So what happened to you? One minute we were... well you know and the next you were gone."

"Well, I have to hand it to you Dylan; you certainly give a girl what she wants, though I didn't expect you to take my 'quickie' comment quite so literally."

"Sorry Jess, bit out of practice."

"Don't worry about it, I won't tell anyone outside of my close circle of friends and my hairdresser of course. Enjoy your nap?"

"Erm... Yeah. What time is it?"

"Eight thirty."

"Oh shit! I was supposed to meet with a client at six," Dylan said panicked.

"That would explain the incessant ringing from your bloody phone then."

"You should have woken me up."

"But you looked so sweet, all snuggled up in the duvet like a big ginger teddy bear. I didn't have the heart."

Apologising, Dylan said, "Look sorry about this, but I really am gonna have to shoot."

"No sweat lover boy. I've finished with you anyway, you've served your purpose and I've got stuff to do."

"OK gorgeous, catch up tomorrow?"

"Sure, but please don't go out looking like that, I've got very nosey neighbours and you could get arrested."

"Spoil sport. Ciao for now."

"See ya speedy Gonzales."

"Bye, 'Wham bam thank you mam'," Elvis added for emphasis.

And just like that, he vanished into the whirlwind of the moment. Racing upstairs in a frenzy, he sought out his discarded clothes—scattered like breadcrumbs across the landing, bathroom, and bedroom. With a near acrobatic descent, he somersaulted back down the stairs and tumbled out of the front door, executing a dramatic exit that culminated in a gratifying slam behind him.

Satisfied she was now alone, if she didn't count the ghost of Elvis, Jessi made a strategic choice and went for a cup of coffee over wine. She had a hunch that unravelling the mysteries of her mother's life required a sharp and clear mind, and caffeine seemed to be the elixir for such a task. "OK Ms. McKintyre, let's see what we can find out about your sordid little life," she said enthusiastically.

Always eager to assist, Elvis said, "You might wanna to try the attic, honey, that's where the past hides its secrets. Dusty memories piled high. I spent some early days up there, whisperin' dreams to the stars and strummin' tunes that never saw the light of day. There's boxes of stuff all over the place."

"Really?" Jessi said excitedly. "Anything interesting?"

"No idea, too dark to see anything to be honest. I just remember trippin' over the boxes."

Jessi rummaged through her briefcase in search of the petite flashlight-cum-rape alarm Dylan had bestowed upon her during their first date. While flowers might have been her first choice, Dylan, ever the practical romantic, somehow managed to spin the gadget as a thoughtful if not unconventional gesture.

"Attic here we come," she announced striding out of the room and heading upstairs.

As she pushed open the attic door, the space unfolded before her like a forgotten world, bathed in the soft glow of sunlight streaming through a dust-laden window, casting a nostalgic glow on the myriad of boxes stacked haphazardly around. Fuelled by her sense of curiosity, she gingerly navigated through the maze of forgotten memories. The air was thick with the scent of aged cardboard and musty nostalgia as she reached out to explore each box's contents. The attic seemed to whisper tales of the past, its wooden floorboards creaking underfoot. Amidst the sea of forgotten possessions, Jessi's hands finally discovered an old, battered suitcase hidden beneath a stack of time-worn newspapers. Its leather corners bore the scars of countless journeys, and as she opened it, the scent of yesteryears assaulted her senses, unravelling a trove of cherished memories and a glimpse into the history that had long been tucked away.

Jessi descended slowly from the attic, navigating the narrow staircase. Balancing the suitcase in one hand, she manoeuvred through the hallway with a sense of purpose. The soft hum of the living room greeted her as she finally reached her destination and with a sense of anticipation slid the suitcase onto the dining table.

"Well, you weren't wrong Elvis it was stuffed with boxes, but thought we might start with this," Jessi declared as she sat staring at the bounty in front of her, "care to join me?"

"Mighty kind of ya, sugar. Don't mind if I do."

Even with the invitation extended, a subtle unease lingered in Jessi as he gracefully positioned a dining chair beside her. The suitcase concealed a magical trove of photos, letters, and tiny trinkets—each one a cherished memento from unforgettable day trips and special occasions. As quaint as the trinkets were, Jessi's attention remained unwaveringly fixed on the photographs. With an air of curiosity, she embarked on a journey through each image, meticulously arranging them on the table. Elvis, equally fascinated, picked up each photo as Jessi put it down before replacing it in its exact spot.

"I wish you wouldn't do that," Jessi said.

"Do what hun?"

"Pick things up."

"How in the world am I supposed to lay eyes on 'em if I ain't grabbin' hold of 'em?"

"It just looks weird seeing things floating around in mid air. What if someone walks in? What are they going to think?"

"You expectin' someone to walk in?"

"No," said Jessi, "but that's beside the point, it's just weird that's all."

With each successive photo unveiling its own tale, the suitcase seemed to whisper more secrets to Jessi. Her fingers danced over the artifacts until they stumbled upon a book. "Well, well, what do we have here?" she said aloud, her curiosity sparking as she delicately cracked open the front cover.

"I don't know Jess, What do we got goin' on here?"

"It's a scrapbook, a scrapbook full of photos and newspaper cuttings."

"Uh huh, that's typically what ya come across in a scrapbook, darlin'," Elvis said with a hint of sarcasm.

"A scrapbook full of photos and cuttings of one Elvis Aaron Presley," Jessi said almost accusingly.

"*No way?*" Elvis was flattered and bemused at the same time. He made a grab for the scrapbook and tried to wrench it from Jessi's hands, but she wasn't having any of it. A desperate tug of war ensued before Elvis finally relented sending Jessi tumbling backwards off her chair as he let go.

Dusting herself down and retaking her seat, she leaned in, her voice a low, dangerous purr. "Keep your mucky paws to yourself, I haven't finished looking yet." Elvis sat back, crossed his arms and sighed. "And stop sighing; it's like living with a bloody teenager."

Jessi turned the pages fascinated by the potted history of Elvis's life contained within. "Wow, you were a bit of a looker in your prime, not sure about the hair, but cute and a great arse," she said.

"What do mean in my prime? I'm still cute and as for this great ass you mentioned, well, let's just say it ain't gone nowhere, honey. It's right here, ready to shake a tail feather or two."

"I'll have to take your word for it, I'm afraid these pictures of you just before you... Well, you know."

"Before I died?"

"Yeah, just before you died. Well, they don't exactly back up your claim. A few too many fried peanut butter and banana sandwiches me thinks," Jessi teased.

"That was thirty years ago honey. I been workin' out."

"OK old man, keep your wig on."

"And I don't wear no wig, it's all natural."

"Jeez, chill out dude, got more important things to worry about than your vanity," Jessi said trying to get back to examining the scrapbook. "Who are all these random women draping themselves all over you?"

"Fans, honey? Nah, that's under sellin' it somethin' fierce. We're talkin' about an army, darlin', hundreds of thousands strong. From Memphis to Maine, them folks lined up like dogs after a juicy bone just for a peek at the King. Campin' outside Graceland, beggin' for my autograph like it was a golden ticket to paradise. Couldn't go to the Piggly Wiggly for a loaf of bread without gettin' swarmed like bees to a magnolia blossom. Now, don't get me wrong, it was flatterin' an all, but sometimes, a fella just wants a cheeseburger and a milkshake without feelin' like a zoo exhibit, you know what I mean?"

"You poor thing," Jessi said with as much sincerity as a cat pretending to be asleep for belly rubs. She turned the next page in the scrapbook and found a single photo taking pride of place. "Aww... This one's sweet, you with some blonde bimbo in your arms and it's framed with a love heart." Jessi turned the scrapbook around for Elvis to see.

"Ah, yeah, now this one brings back the memories, an air hostess, very sweet lady. I tell you, sweetheart, those gals flyin' around the clouds like angels in high heels, they had a magic about 'em. Lorna her name was, or somethin' like that."

"A trolley dolly, says it all really," Jessi replied.

She flopped the scrapbook onto the table, the worn faux leather cover exhaling a puff of attic dust. Undeterred by the looming mountain of photos yet to be unveiled, she eagerly dove back in. Elvis saw his opportunity and grabbed the scrapbook. He clutched it to his chest like a stolen puppy, scrambling for the dubious safety of the sofa. Jessi was getting frustrated by the lack of information this treasure trove of memories held. "Why don't people write on the back of photographs? These are meaningless, just a bunch of random people that mean absolutely nothing."

"They mean somethin' to someone Jess," Elvis shouted from across the room.

No sooner had she made the remark when she came up trumps. "Ah! Ha! At last," she said.

"What you got hun?"

"A picture with some info, but it's barely readable," Jessi said frustrated. "It looks like 'fifteenth of June', possibly July 'nineteen sixty one' I think. Or could that be a seven, 'nineteen sixty seven', not sure. 'Laura and Judy, Elgin beach'... Bugger me, it's my mother and grandmother."

Her mother and grandmother, two faces shrouded in time, stared back with unsmiling eyes. Tears welled in Jessi's eyes, hot and unbidden, but why? These were strangers, ghosts in family albums, their absence a yawning chasm in her childhood. Yet, the sight of them felt like a punch to the gut, a whisper of a bond severed before it could bloom.

"Come on Jess don't be gettin' upset. Stumbling on somethin' about your momma was gonna happen eventually," Elvis said trying to console her.

"I know," said Jess, wiping her eyes, "it's just the first time I've seen what she looks like, though she's only about five. Guess she looked much different by the time she died."

"Cast your eyes upon your grandma hun, the apple don't fall far from the tree. You might just catch a glimpse of how your momma turned out to be."

"Yeah, I suppose," said Jessi as she continued to stare at the photo, paying particular attention to her grandmother. She couldn't put the face to anyone she knew, so why did she look familiar? Then it hit her. "You still on the Sofa Elvis?"

"Uh huh!" he replied.

She wandered over to join him. "Here, take a look," she said, thrusting the photo out in front of her, "look familiar?"

Elvis took the picture and studied it briefly. "Hmm... yeah, I think I can see a bit of a resemblance. You've certainly got your momma's eyes, those pools of blue that could drown a man in their depths."

"Forget my mother, what about my grandmother? "

"What about her sugar?"

"You don't think my grandmother bears a striking resemblance to the woman in your arms in the heart framed picture?"

Elvis picked up the scrapbook and flipping through the pages, unearthed the picture Jessi was talking about. "You ain't wrong, sugar, there sure is a likeness. Could be they're kin, cousins maybe, or even twins separated at birth."

Jessi snatched the scrapbook out of Elvis's hand and studied the two photos side by side. "They look alike you hamburger sniffing idiot because they're the same bloody woman," Jessi said.

"It's possible I guess."

"Don't you see? It's all beginning to make sense now."

"Listen sweetheart. It might click in your mind, but I ain't got a darn clue 'bout what's happenin.'"

Jessi tried to explain. "This scrapbook, put together by a fan, a fan who had met her rock and roll idol, my own grandmother. That must be why you're stuck here, in this house."

"Sorry Jess, I ain't buyin' it. I had millions of fans. Why would I end up in some poky little house in England just because your grandmother was a fan?"

"You didn't meet all your fans, but you met this one. What if God, or whatever higher power's at play, has a plan for us even beyond the grave. Imagine having to earn your spot in heaven, and God planted you right here in this house for a reason—to repay a fan's unwavering devotion. If God really is all seeing and all knowing, he would have known my mother was going to hit on hard times and you were sent to save her, to do your good deed, earn your key to the pearly gates."

"I hear ya, Jess, but that ain't how the story goes, see? She ain't no damsel saved, not by my hand or any other. She took her own life, remember?"

"Of course I remember, I'm not likely to forget something like that," Jessi said frustrated. "The point is, you had a purpose, a reason for being here. Though God only knows what happens now you've cocked the job up."

"Well, honey, if you're right, then this whole croakin' ain't nothin' but a one-way ticket to crazy town, drivin' folks around the bend with my ghost singin'. Sorry darlin' but there's gotta be more to it than that."

"Maybe we're missing something," Jessi muttered, conviction hardening her voice. She returned to the suitcase and tipped out its remaining contents onto the table. More photographs, faded and dog-eared, mingled with yellowed letters tied with faded ribbons, each artifact a whisper of a past life. Her gaze darted across the jumbled landscape, searching for the missing piece. Somewhere in this chaotic constellation of memories, she knew the truth lay waiting. "So what was she like?" Jessi asked, as her fingers continued to rummage.

"Who?" Elvis said.

"My grandmother, who do you think."

"Jeez Jess, it was a long, long time ago. Only crossed paths with her once, you know."

"Oh, I see. Do you remember where you met?"

"Sure thing, darlin.' She was a stewardess, caught her on a flight from Germany. Real cute accent, if I recall right. Scottish, I reckon."

"Germany?" said Jessi.

"Uh huh! I was in the army at the time, returning to the states from Germany. She was workin' them short hops, and fate done put us together on that flight to Prestwick, Scotland. That's where that picture was snapped, in that fancy VIP lounge at Prestwick airport. Sweet gal kept me company for a spell while they prepped the plane."

Jessi was only half listening to Elvis's exploits as an envelope with an American post mark had caught her attention. "This could be interesting," she said holding the envelope aloft.

"What is it Jess?"

"A letter from the good old US of A. Shall we take a peek."

Elvis's enthusiasm was no less than Jessi's and he joined her at the dining room table. "Well, honey, I ain't got nothin but hunches and heartburn, so let's take a look."

Jessi's fingertips trembled as she eased the letter from its envelope, the paper wafer thin and delicate. Her eyes danced across the opening lines, a silent prelude to the moment she decided to breathe life into the words and share them aloud.

"Dear Ms. McKintyre, as the attorneys acting for Mr. Elvis Aaron Presley, we have been asked to respond to your spurious and unfounded allegations with regard to our client. Whilst Mr. Presley admits to having met you during a very brief stop over at Prestwick airport, he does not concur with your version of events that took place during your meeting. In particular, Mr. Presley denies that there was any intimacy whilst in your company. Furthermore, he categorically denies your claims that he's..."

Jessi's voice trailed off as her eyes continued reading.

"That he's what Jess?" Elvis was keen to know.

Jessi threw the letter onto the table made her way to the comfort of her safe zone, the sofa. Elvis picked up the letter and continued to read. "...That he's the father of your daughter Judy McKintyre. You have provided no evidence to support this outrageous and defamatory accusation, and we advise you to put an end to your delusional behaviour forthwith."

An awkward silence filled the air.

"Is that it?" Jessi said quietly.

"Not quite," Elvis replied.

"Well you might as well finish it, I could do with a laugh."

"I can explain," tried Elvis.

"Just finish the damn letter," Jessi screamed.

"OK hun!" Elvis said with reluctance. "We have spoken at length with our client and against our advice, he has asked us, as a gesture of goodwill, to make you an offer of twenty five thousand dollars. Please note that this offer is in no way an admission of guilt and the offer is conditional upon you signing the enclosed waiver which should be returned to our offices along with your bank details. Upon receipt of the signed waiver, twenty five thousand dollars will be deposited in your designated bank account. We trust this will meet with your approval, but if not please be assured that not only will we vigorously contest your allegations, but we may be forced to counter sue for defamation of character. Yours faithfully etc. etc..."

As the weight of the revelation settled upon Jessi's shoulders, a tempest of emotions stormed within her. Betrayal, confusion, and resentment intertwined as she grappled with the implications of this newfound knowledge. Anger surged through her veins as the pieces of her familial puzzle fell into place.

"Well, well, well. There's a turn up for the books Mr. Elvis 'true southern gentleman' Presley or should that be, grandad?" Jessi spat.

Desperate to explain, Elvis said, "Look Jess, I know how it might look..."

But Jessi wasn't interested in how it *might* look. "I'll tell you exactly how it looks Elvis. It looks like you screwed my grandmother in the VIP lounge at Prestwick airport and then fucked off back to America leaving her to bring up your daughter, my mother. Have I missed anything? Oh yeah I missed the twenty five thousand dollar pay off to keep her mouth shut you worthless piece of shit."

"That ain't fair Jess. It didn't happen like that. Please listen."

"I don't want to hear another word from you. Here's what's going to happen. I'm going out and I'm going to get very, very drunk. You on the other hand are going to make like David Copperfield and disappear. I don't care how you do it or where you go, just make sure when I get back you're out of my life forever. Do you understand?"

Elvis had no other answer than, "Sure Jess."

Jessi stormed out of the room. The slam of the front door reverberated through the house, a punctuation mark to the revelation that had just shattered the afternoon quiet. Jessi's footsteps, once echoing a hurried retreat, had faded into the distance, leaving behind an eerie silence that pressed heavy on Elvis's shoulders. The air itself imbued with the residue of unspoken words and simmering emotions.

"WOW, THAT WENT DOWN as well as an attempt to explain quantum mechanics to a goldfish," Judy said as she made an appearance from the kitchen, "what are you going to do now *Daddy*?"

Startled and wide-eyed, Elvis recoiled in surprise as the unexpected presence of Judy caught him off guard. "What are you doing here? I thought we had a deal."

"Well I meant to leave, I did really," Judy lied, "just kinda got sidetracked and the old place brings back so many happy memories, thought I'd hang around for a while. Soak up the atmosphere so to speak."

"And you heard all that?" Elvis said, hoping the answer would be, no.

"Oh yeah, every last word you bastard."

"Please listen to me Judy. I know I ain't the smoothest talker, but trust me, honey, it'll all make sense once you hear it my way."

"I thought Jessi summed it up pretty well, can't see there's much more to add."

"Just gimme a shot, five minutes is all I ask."

"OK poppa, what have I got to lose. You've already taken my life and my sanity, let's hear it," said Judy as she settled into the sofa.

"Alright, let's set the record straight. Now, your momma and I, well, let's just say things got mighty cozy that day in Prestwick," Elvis said as he joined Judy on the sofa.

"You shagged her?"

"As I said, things got cozy. What is it with English gals and foul language?"

"I'm Scottish," Judy reminded him, "and don't you dare sit there and judge me."

"Sorry hun. So, let me tell you 'bout your momma. Before I hopped that plane back to the States, I made a promise to her. I swore I'd grease the wheels and get her a job with American Airlines, flyin' those long hauls. See, I figured, that way we could steal a few moments together, ya know, amidst the clouds and the stars. And true to my word, I pulled some strings, got everything lined up. Even sent her a ticket, first class, to meet her new bosses. But honey, that gal, she never showed. So I wrote, worried somethin' was wrong. And what do you know, she tells me she can't take the job, got a bun in the oven, and well, she thought maybe yours truly was the baker."

"So you threatened her with lawyers and paid her off. How chivalrous."

"No, that ain't the whole story. My biggest mess-up? Spillin' the beans to the Colonel about what went down. You gotta understand, Judy, back then my life wasn't my own. It was a gilded cage, walls stacked high with 'yes sirs' and 'can't dos.' Every move, every word, micromanaged like a jailhouse. So, when I told the Colonel I wanted to see Laura, see if I was your daddy, I thought I was doin' the right thing. But, sweetheart, talkin' to him was like tossin' a grenade into a tinderbox. That's where things went wrong. Real wrong."

"So it's all the Colonel's fault, without him you'd have married my mother and we'd all have lived happily ever after. Is that what you're trying to tell me?" Judy said, unconvinced.

"Never said nothin' 'bout walkin' down the aisle sweetheart, but if things turned out that way, I wouldn't have walked away. A man takes care of his own."

"But in the end you decided against it and paid her off?"

"Hold up, lemme finish. Colonel swore he'd handle it, make everyone happy. Couple of months later, I'm asking what's up, why ain't I heard from Laura. Turns out, your momma vanished like a ghost, left her last known address in the dust. Folks searched high and low. Said they'd done all they could, unless she pops back up, it's a dead end. Colonel said my lawyers sent a letter, but I ain't seen it till Jessi dug it outta that dusty suitcase just now."

"Nice story, but does it excuse your actions? I don't know. What I do know is that my mother had a shit life, while you were living like a king."

"Cut a fella some slack, will ya? I did everything I could to sort things out at the time, but no one's perfect, we all make mistakes Judy. I didn't plan for it to turn out this way; I just made some bad calls that's all. You don't think I would turn back the clock if I could and put everything right?"

"I don't know what to think anymore Elvis. Part of me wants to toss out a casual 'Hey, shit happens,' but I'm not sold it's the right vibe for this situation. So, where do we go from here?"

"No clue darlin'... Want me to take you to the park to play on the swings?"

"Is that supposed to be funny?"

"Uh huh!"

"Well it wasn't," snapped Judy. "Oh Elvis, what a mess. I suppose I should be happy that I've found out who my father is, just wasn't expecting him to be a bloated, sequin jump-suited, lip curling, hip swivelling rock and roll singer. Not sure Jessi has taken the news quite so well though. Can you imagine what's going through her head right now? She'll be sat in a bar somewhere, getting drunk and telling anyone who cares to listen, that her grandfather was Elvis Presley."

"What do I do when she walks in?" Elvis said, "talk or lay low like she wanted?"

"I think maybe you should give her some space. If she wants to talk I'm sure she'll call. Wanna hang out in the attic for a while and reminisce?"

"Sure honey, attic's always been my thinkin' spot. A little bit of mystery, a touch of nostalgia, and maybe a few hidden treasures waiting to be found."

THE FRENCH DOORS CREAKED open with a groan under
Jessi's insistent shove. She stumbled into the room, a tipsy waltz gone
awry, her laughter trailing behind her like the tail of a kite in a strong
wind. Her dress, the epitome of summery elegance, now clung to her
like a reluctant memory, its floral pattern smeared with the ghosts of
spilled drinks and carefree abandon. A discarded sandal lay by the
threshold, its mate clinging to her ankle like a lost puppy. Her hair,
once a dark curtain, had unravelled into a wild mane, each strand
clinging to the dampness of the night.

Jessi collapsed onto her plush sofa, a sigh escaping her lips like
the last note of a smoky jazz ballad. The room spun around her,
the furniture tilting at precarious angles, the shadows morphing into
dancing phantoms. But Jessi's eyelids, heavy with the weight of the
night, fluttered shut, and soon, her rhythmic breaths were the only
melody weaving through the stillness, her sleep a haven from the
swirling chaos inside her head.

JESSI AWOKE NURSING the mother of all hangovers. Her body
felt like a poorly assembled IKEA bookshelf, each joint held
together by wishful thinking and expired Ibuprofen and her stomach
churned like a washing machine on spin cycle, threatening to unleash
a tidal wave of tequila regret onto the unsuspecting floor. Each
thump of her pulse was a chorus line of tiny hammers, tap-dancing
on her skull. With a herculean effort she got to her feet and stumbled
across the room. The world tilted with each tentative step, the floor a
distant, undulating horizon. She reached the mirror and staring back
at her was a stranger. Her eyes, bloodshot and puffy, held a story of
sadness untold, and her skin, usually vibrant, now the colour of old
parchment, etched with the fine lines of dehydration and regret.

"Jesus Christ Jess, that's not pretty, what the hell did you do last
night? Shower... no, coffee. Yeah, mug of black coffee."

Jessi slowly made her way to the kitchen and flicked on the kettle, before returning to the living room and collapsing on a dining chair. Her eyes flickered over the debris of last night's revelations and settled on the letter that had caused so much anger. "Ah yes, the startling confessions of a dead rock and roller. Maybe I just imagined its contents. Maybe it's really a letter from President Kennedy inviting my grandmother to lunch, now that would be more believable." She reread the letter and just for good measure, read it once more. "Nope, I didn't imagine it. Elvis Presley is my grandfather. Elvis Presley the king of rock and roll, the father in law of Michael Jackson, the... Oh God, let's hope *he* doesn't turn up. I really don't need some moon walking, crutch holding, baby dangling slightly off white weirdo adding to my problems... OK girl, time to get your shit together. It is what it is. He's gone now. everyone's gone now. Time to start over and make something of your sorry life. Coffee, shower and then a call to Dylan. I need to get this house of horrors back on the market for starters."

Cradling a steaming hot mug of coffee, Jessi returned to the sanctuary of her sofa with all the best intentions but found herself unable to keep her eyes open. "Maybe another ten minutes, then I'll get a shower," she said to herself.

Her eyes had barely shut when a familiar and unwelcome voice reached her ears. Elvis had wandered into the room with Judy. He stood behind the sofa, while Judy meandered towards the armchair. "Hi Jessi, I think we need..." Elvis began.

Jessi didn't let him finish. "For Christ's sake Elvis, which bit of 'get out of my life' didn't you understand exactly?"

"We need to talk Jessi."

"I'm not sure she's in the mood daddy," Judy said.

The sound of Judy's voice reached Jessi's ears like a cold wind whispering through a graveyard and she twisted her head, hunting down the source. "Who the fuck are you?" Jessi shrieked.

Confused, Elvis said, "How does she know you're here Judy?"

"Search me," Judy replied.

"I know she's here Pelvis, because she's stood there looking like a cheap whore and she just spoke."

"Take a look at yourself sweetie, hardly Coco Chanel," Judy bit back.

"This ain't good," Elvis said nervously.

Jessi turned her head once more and mouth agape caught sight of Elvis in all his glory. "Oh my God, it's you!"

"You can see me?" Elvis said, surprised.

"Shit, yeah."

"Oh, this is doubly not good sugar."

Pointing to Judy, Jessi said, "What's not good is that thing stood in the corner of my room."

"Jess hun. That thing I'm afraid, is your... mother."

"What do you mean 'afraid'?" Judy said annoyed.

"But, you know, you shouldn't be catchin' a glimpse of her. You shouldn't be catchin' a glimpse of yours truly," he reminded Jessi.

"I shouldn't have ghosts in my house, but I have. You shouldn't be my grandad, but you are and that thing over there most definitely shouldn't be related to me. I think it's fair to say that the normal *shouldn't* rules no longer apply." The slamming of the front door served to irritate Jessi further. "Oh for pity's sake, who else have you invited? What is this, a surprise party where all the guests turn out to be my dead relatives?"

Guiding Emma into the room, Dylan's arm draped over her shoulder, their entrance was marked by Emma's uncontrollable tears. Jessi moved in as the heart-wrenching sobs echoed, intensifying the air with emotion.

"Dylan, Emm, boy am I glad to see you two. You wouldn't believe the night I've just had," Jessi said.

Dylan and Emma didn't respond and stood in the centre of the room staring blankly at their surroundings. "Hey guys, what's up?" Jessi's voice, brimming with relief at seeing her friends, faltered in the face of their silence. "Emma, honey, are you OK?" Jessi said as the smile died on her lips.

"I still can't believe it Dylan," Emma choked out, her voice a broken whisper, "she called me just hours ago, said she was going to get hammered at the pub. Asked if I wanted to join."

Dylan squeezed Emma's shoulder. "Come on Emm, keep it together. Jess wouldn't want to see you like this."

"Dylan, stop ignoring me. I can see her like this. I'm stood right next to her you dumbass," Jessi shouted.

Emma stumbled away, snatching Jessi's cherished cushion from the sofa, its familiar scent a painful balm against the void. "I should have been there, Dylan. I should have stopped her. She was my friend, and I let her down. When she needed me most, I failed her. There's no way I would have let her get in her car if I'd have been there. It's all my fault, all my damn fault," Emma sobbed.

"Look, Emm, it's no one's fault. I wasn't there for her either, but Jessi was her own woman, stubborn as a mule with a head full of dreams and a heart that wouldn't quit. If she set her mind on something, driving home last night, hell, dancing on the moon – there wasn't a damn thing any of us could do to stop her. Coming here, maybe wasn't the best idea. We got things to sort, Jessi wouldn't want us drowning in tears. Let's get out of here, find some peace, do what we gotta do for her." He glanced skyward, his eyes searching for answers. "Good night Jess, wherever you are, we'll miss you to hell and back."

Jessi's brow furrowed, her voice laced with confusion. "Dylan, what do you mean you'll miss me. I'm here. I'm stood right next to you for fuck's sake."

Dylan shepherded Emma towards the door. Each step a beat in the mournful rhythm of their grief, the silence broken only by the choked sobs that escaped Emma's lips. Jessi stood rooted to the spot. Her disbelief, sharp and icy, slowly morphed into a suffocating sense of isolation, as Emma replaced her cushion on the sofa. She wanted to scream, to chase after them, to demand answers, but her voice was lost in the deafening silence. Panic, sharp and sudden, clawed at her throat. She spun around, her non-existent dress swirling. Nothing. Empty space where Dylan and Emma should have been.

"Elvis?" Jessi said looking for an explanation.

"Let's sit down hun." Elvis said gently taking her by the hand.

Shocked by his touch Jessi recoiled. "No! That's not right. You can't touch me, you told me you can't touch me."

Elvis reached out again and clasped her hand, guiding her to the familiar embrace of the sofa "Jessi, honey, somethin's shifted. What d'you recollect 'bout last night, darlin'?"

"Not much. I remember being mad with you and storming out. The next thing I know, I'm asleep on this sofa."

As Elvis considered where to go with his line of questioning, the television flickered to life, settling on a news channel with a grim certainty. The reporter's voice, clipped and professional, filled the room, each word a hammer blow to Jessi's non-existent chest. Her name, her age, her job, all laid bare on the screen. The crash, the single vehicle, the desolate lane. Her family, notified through choked sobs and tear-stained phone calls. Even her employer, Mr. Grimshaw with his perpetually stained coffee tie, was quoted, offering lukewarm condolences about her 'efficient filing system.'

Jessi watched, detached yet oddly present, as her life played out in grainy black and white. The image of a smiling stranger flashed onto the screen, a younger version of herself holding a graduation certificate, and a lump formed in her throat. This was her? This was the woman who laughed too loud, danced too freely, and drank tequila shots like they were life support? This was the woman who now sat beside a rhinestone-clad ghost, forever tethered to the world she'd just left behind?

"No...No...No...No," Jessi blurted with tears streaming down her cheeks.

"Come on sweetheart, don't cry," Judy said trying to be the mother she never was.

Jessi rose from the sofa, her eyes locked on Judy as she strode towards her with purpose. "Fuck off and don't call me sweetheart, I'm not your sweetheart."

Elvis tried unsuccessfully to ease the tension. "Now come on Jess, that's no way to..."

"Don't even go there Elvis," Jessi said. "Isn't this just peachy? Now I get to share my house with my child hating schizophrenic mother as well as my new found somewhat disappointing looking grandfather."

Judy's weak attempt at motherhood was short lived. "Don't worry darling, I have no intention of staying."

"Well, there's a surprise," Jessi said sharply.

"Look Jessi, I'm not looking for forgiveness. I did what I thought was the right thing to do at the time and if I was in the same position again I'd do exactly the same thing. Trust me on this one, your life turned out a damn sight better than mine did."

"What do you want, a medal?"

Judy knew when to give up. "I'm out of here pops, I'm only making things worse. Be well Jess."

"Be well? I'm fucking dead. I think on the wellness scale I'm somewhere just beyond critically ill."

The tension in the room had reached critical mass. Elvis, ever the master of defusing chaos, steered Jessi back to the sofa, his movements deliberate yet gentle. As they settled, he enveloped her in a hug. Judy seized the chance to slip away, quiet as a whisper, through the French doors and into the unknown, leaving only an unspoken farewell.

"Why Elvis, why me?" Jessi pleaded, "I don't deserve this. I'm not a bad person; I've never done anyone any harm. It's just not fair."

Elvis leant in, his voice a low rumble "Now listen to me, sweetheart, close. Don't you fret about who you are or what roads you've walked down. This whole shebang, it ain't some coincidence, see? It's fate, pure and simple. Created in the stars, written in the moonlight, this day was bound to be. Nothin' you or me could've done to dodge it, no how. Now, maybe it's all part of the Big Man's grand ol' plan, some heavenly jukebox spinnin' our lives. But if it is, well, I sure hope He sends down a telegram explainin' what the plan is."

"But until then we're stuck here playing happy families and tormenting the living?" Jessi said.

Elvis's voice dropped to a whisper, sending shivers down Jess's spine for the last time. "No, sugar, my heart tells me somethin' different. This? This is why I exist. To walk you through those French doors and take you home."

The TV news babbled on, a eulogy to a life that was, but also a prologue to a life that could be. Jessi looked at Elvis, a glimmer of defiance sparking in her eyes. This wasn't the end, it was just the beginning of a new chapter, a cosmic twist in her story. She was dead, yes, but she was far from gone. And with Elvis by her side, she was ready to face whatever Graceland, and the afterlife beyond, had in store. The screen flickered once more before fading to black, leaving them in the silence, a new beginning waiting to be written on the blank canvas of eternity.

The End.

A Grudge Unleashed

"Well hello mister sleepy head, you were starting to worry me."

He raised his head slowly and through half closed eyes scanned his surroundings. His face? Totally dazed and confused summed it up perfectly. All the peace I'd snagged for the past few hours vanished in a flash, replaced by a creeping panic. After weeks of planning, I had gone totally off-script within a couple of hours of arriving at his flat.

"Who the fuck are you and what the fuck are you doing in my flat?" he spat with a venom that made me immediately think I may have bitten off more than I could chew.

I took a moment, breathed in deep, and got a grip on my emotions. Even though I was winging it, I still had a loose plan for how the game would unfold. But before diving in, I was curious about his reaction after waking from his deep slumber. "Hey Charlie, why'd your first two questions skip right past 'Why am I gaffer taped to this rather kitsch but nonetheless stylish 1970's wooden rocking chair' and straight to, 'Who the fuck am I and what the fuck am I doing here?' If I were in your position, and thank the Lord I'm not, I think I'd be more concerned about the former. Then again, that could just be me."

"Who the fuck's Charlie?" His only response to what I thought was a perfectly reasonable question.

"Now, now, let's start as we mean to go on. This, what some may describe as a slightly surreal situation, is going to be much more productive for both of us if we can at least agree to be honest with each other. Your name is Charlie Phipps, but I've a feeling you might've forgotten my name, but don't worry, by the end of the day you'll remember it all too well—maybe even wish you hadn't."

So far so good. I'd managed to navigate the first couple of minutes of our liaison without any significant hiccups, but holding it together as things deepen, that would be the real hurdle.

"Look love..."

"No, no, no, no, no... Stop right there," I yelled. I'd gone from calm to incensed in an instant. "You do not get to call me love, darling, duck, beautiful, dear, sweetheart, or fucking treacle. Do we understand each other?"

"Pardon me for breathing darling."

"You won't be breathing for long if you fucking continue," I warned him.

An adorable miniature hammer, winked at me from the coffee table. Who knew what such a thing was for, besides, I suppose, hammering minuscule, equally adorable nails? But today, it became my unlikely weapon of choice, arcing through the air towards Charlie's unsuspecting skull. It landed on his left temple with a satisfying crack and in a slightly delayed reaction caused him to groan in pain. "I stumbled upon that in your tool shed last night. What a find. A proper testosterone fuelled man cave, packed with seriously cool tools. Just take a sec to look around—lots of them have made their way onto your coffee table."

"That fucking hurt, you crazy bitch!"

In a move that I thought was pretty cool and a staple of the countless gangster movies I'd watched, I turned and grabbed a dining chair and placed it backwards in front of my trussed up play pal. Slowly, some might even say provocatively, I attempted to sit astride the chair before realising my ten quid skinny Primark jeans were not going to be that forgiving. I turned the endeavour into a badly choreographed erotic lap dance as I swung my leg over the back of the chair instead, with the intention of turning it the right way round to face him. How I ended up on my back with the chair on top of me remains a mystery. Why Charlie chose not to comment on the comedy of errors unfolding before him, I've no idea, but perhaps it had something to do with the fact that the last time he opened his mouth, he was hit with a hammer. I aimed for a composed transition as I moved from my current position to settling into the chair, neatly crossing my arms and legs. However, despite my efforts, any semblance of dignity had unmistakably departed by then. Desperate to regain control I said, "I'm gonna let that one go Charlie. I am a little crazy and I can be a bitch, but I think what we're missing at the moment are some ground rules."

"I think what you're missing lady, are some brain cells. Trust me, this is not going to end well."

"How very perceptive, it absolutely isn't going to end well," I leaned in very slightly, "but for who, that is the question. In the spirit of being honest, open and truthful with each other, let me take you on a very quick journey to the end... You're going to die."

He had no response. He was seemingly taking a moment to gather his thoughts. In that brief silence, I sensed he was digesting the candid yet direct depiction of the conclusion of our time together.

"So, back to the ground rules. Normally, I'm not big on swearing, but I'm not exactly a prude either. I just feel like everyday chats get overloaded with unnecessary profanity, and it loses its punch, you know? However, given the current situation, which is likely to get a little tense at times, I'm happy if you are to allow as much foul language as our filthy little mouths can muster without either of us taking offense or feeling the need to create a Facebook post to let the

world know how offended we are. Insults? No thanks, let's keep it
civil. Though, truth be told, I might be the bigger offender in that
department."

"Look, whatever you're called, I don't give a flying fuck about
your ground rules. Let's backtrack a bit to the question I didn't ask
when I woke up. Why *am* I gaffer taped, stark bollock naked, to this
rather kitsch but nonetheless stylish 1970's wooden rocking chair?"

"Oh, I'm so pleased you asked, but before the *why*, aren't you
interested in the *how*?"

"Not particularly," he said.

"Please indulge me just for a moment because I need to establish
just how stupid you are. What do you see when you look at me?"

"What?"

"The questions are going to get much harder Charlie, what do
you see?"

Clearly reluctant to answer my question, he said, "Which bit of
'my name isn't Charlie' are you not understanding?"

"I'm not understanding any bit of it Charlie."

"How about calling me by my real name."

"Which you claim to be?"

"Colin."

"I get why you might have changed your name, but why would
anyone choose Colin, it's a bit... Well, a bit fucking boring if I'm
honest."

"I didn't choose it; my parents chose it."

"Look, Charlie, I get it. Maybe the bump on your head made
things foggy. But honesty is the best policy, even with foggy
memories, I know you know your name, so let's cut the bullshit.
Now, what do you see when you look at me?"

"Is it a trick question?" he said, suspiciously.

"Why would it be a trick question?"

"Because you're a delusional fucking psychopath, everything you ask could be a trick question that results in me being twatted round the head with a pein hammer."

"With a what?" I said puzzled.

"A pein hammer. The little hammer you so happily cracked my skull with?"

"Oh, do stop exaggerating, it was a mere tap on the temple that may or may not have caused a bit of memory loss. More importantly, why is it called a pein hammer?"

"How the fuck do I know?"

The origins of the name 'pein hammer' really shouldn't have been so important at this juncture, yet my inherent curiosity drives me to collect seemingly pointless trivia that will serve no useful purpose in my life other than being the star of the show at the local pub quiz. I couldn't move on with my cunning, yet flawed plan until I knew how a pein hammer earned its name. "Where's your phone?"

"Why?"

"Because I need to look up the origins of the name 'pein hammer.'"

"Use your own damn phone," he snapped.

"Oh you'd like that wouldn't you. Little Miss stupid, incriminating herself."

"For looking why a 'pein hammer' is called a 'pein hammer'?"

"You clearly don't listen to many true crime podcasts, do you. In the unlikely event of me being considered a prime suspect in the unfortunate brutal slaying of an overweight bald, slob of a man named Charlie Phipps, I would not wish for an astute forensic analyst to connect any incidental evidence, such as the imprint found on the victim's temple, with my innocuous searches regarding the historical origins of a 'pein hammer'. It's basic murder 101 Charlie, get with the programme. Now where's your phone?"

"I don't know where my phone is. I don't know where my clothes are, I don't know who you are, I don't know why you're here. In short, I know fuck all about fuck all."

"Ok, stay right where you are, I'll be back," I said, as the ghost of Schwarzenegger flickered briefly, then died a swift and undignified death in my voice. Charlie's clothes were scattered all over the flat, but in an ordered sequential scattering. I started at the crud stained boxer shorts discarded at his feet and followed the trail past his socks, jeans, shirt and into the kitchen where I stumbled upon a sartorial crime scene: his hideously hip camouflage vest, accessorised with corduroy shoulder patches. Then the trail went cold. No coat or jacket. I headed for the bedroom, more in desperation than hope as he'd not ventured in there since we arrived last night. I then tried the hallway and despite the presence of coat hooks, they were occupied by everything except a coat, including a dog lead. How had I missed a dog in a one bedroom flat? The dog conundrum now occupied my mind, and I was less interested in the origins of a pein hammer than I was in the missing pet. The plan was doomed to fail if there was frightened little puppy hiding somewhere watching my every move. Murdering someone was one thing, but traumatising a poor defenceless animal was something I knew I could never live with. And who would take care of it when I left. It could be days, even weeks before Charlie was discovered. Could I take it with me? No of course I couldn't, it would raise too many questions and potentially link me to its owner. I was angry, not at Charlie or the dog, but at myself for missing such a vital detail. I had spent weeks watching, following, planning and at no point had a dog entered the frame. No wife, no girlfriend, no regular visitors and definitely no dog. My confusion morphed into something sharper. I stepped back into the living room, a shrill sound escaping my lips. "Why is there a fucking dog lead hung in your hallway?"

He looked at me perplexed. Here was a guy who I suspect knew by now he was in a precarious situation and he was desperately trying to rationalise why a dog lead had turned me into a screaming banshee.

"Because I couldn't think of anywhere else to hang it?" he offered as a response.

I picked up a Stanley knife, curtesy of Charlie's man cave, from the coffee table and exposed the blade. I leaned over him and held the tip at the bridge of his nose. I couldn't explain my choice to target the bridge of his nose. A seasoned killer would have aimed for the throat without hesitation. Yet, inexplicably, I fixated on his nose instead. "Where's the fucking dog?" I demanded.

"Jesus sweetheart, calm down. You're going to do someone an injury."

Love, darling, duck, beautiful, dear, sweetheart, or fucking treacle. The words rushed through my head as a quick reminder of what I thought we had agreed. With almost immaculate precision, I carved a straight line from the bridge of his nose to its very tip. His eyes filled with horror as I marvelled at the exactness of the cut I had just executed, standing back to admire my handiwork. The wound seemed to unfurl in slow motion, beginning at the bridge and unravelling downward, as if his nose was being unzipped. Where was the blood? There had to be blood. My fixation shattered abruptly when Charlie's scream finally broke through, delayed. Instinctively, I clamped my hand over his mouth. "Shush, you'll disturb the neighbours," I cautioned him.

His tears, once brimming in his eyes, now cascaded down his cheeks, tracing a path over my surgically gloved hand and trickling into the contours of his first chin, before winding their way onto his second chin and finally finding solace in the salt and pepper carpet of coarse hair that covered his chest. They began to mingle with crimson droplets as the blood finally started to flow. I bent down and reached for the crusty discarded boxer shorts. Still holding my hand over his mouth, I grabbed them and pushed them into his face to try and stem the bleeding.

"Tilt your head back," I said, "I'm sure that's what you're supposed to do if you have a nosebleed."

Charlie's response was scarcely coherent. My hand muffled his words while shock and, I suspect, a degree of pain, further hindered his ability to communicate clearly. "I'm going to remove my hand, but only on the condition we don't get any hysterics and you promise to be a good boy. Nod if you understand."

His head barely moved in what might have been a nod, but enough to spark a flicker of hope that he understood. I retracted my hand, fingers twitching to return should he feel the need to start screaming again.

"Please just stop. Why are you doing this, who the fuck are you?" Charlie said in a voice choked with sobs.

"Easy tiger… There's plenty of time for questions, but first, let's give your nose a little makeover. It might help us focus better once it's sorted."

Ripping the boxer shorts away, I exposed the wound anew, a gruesome masterpiece I'd sculpted in mere moments, a feat that would take Hollywood hours to replicate. "Charlie, I've got some not-so-great news—I'm not exactly known for my sewing prowess. I did manage to crochet a scarf for a teddy bear my grandfather gave me for Christmas once, but I'm not sure that minor accomplishment will be much help here. Got any super glue?"

"Super glue, really?" he spluttered.

"We've gotta try something, it's fucking grotesque. Making me feel a bit queasy if I'm being honest."

"And how the fuck do you think it's making me feel?"

"While I accept it might sting a little, you don't have to look at it."

"Sting a little? You sliced my nose open, we're way past 'sting a little', it's agony."

"All the more reason we try and patch you up then. So, super glue, yes or no?"

"You're not super gluing my nose," he said, defiantly.

"Ok, your call. I'll just slap on a bit of gaffer tape, but if it gets infected, don't blame me."

I leaned forward and grabbed the tape, tearing off a strip with my teeth. I stood in front of him and gentler than he deserved, I stuck one end of the tape to his left cheek bone, before pressing it up the side of his nose. Charlie yelled out in pain. "Jesus Charlie, keep it down, I've warned you once about alerting the neighbours, they'll think someone's being murdered." He didn't respond, his face a mask of contradictions. I couldn't decide if the look in his eyes was one of fear, anger, pain or hate, but more likely a combination of all four. The open wound pulsed beneath my fingertips as I navigated the tape's edge. Little by little, I tugged the left skin flap, coaxing it to the heart of his nose. A bead of sweat trickled down my temple as I mirrored the movement with the right flap. A swift press of tape, a sigh of relief - and the fragile repair was complete.

"There you go," I said triumphantly, "no one will be any the wiser."

"Hardly an invisible repair," he replied.

"Only yourself to blame I'm afraid, I wanted to go down the super glue route, remember?"

Charlie's head inexplicably dipped with a slow, almost theatrical movement, his chin sinking into the matted jungle of his chest hair. My first thought was he had died right there in front of me, but logic told me a little cut to the nose was hardly a life threatening injury. But the eerie silence stretched, and a sliver of doubt pricked at me. Was he playing a game? I had to find out. "Come on Charlie old bean, no time for a nap. I've got a yoga class at eleven and a guy

coming by to sort out my washing machine at twelve. I know you
don't wanna be responsible for my zen disruption and sudsy disaster."

No response. I wasn't inclined to inflict any more pain at this
juncture, as it might be wasted effort, but I needed to know if he was
still alive. Recalling the recent resurgence of smelling salts at the gym,
I briefly entertained the idea of spraying a couple of squirts of Marc
Jacob's, Daisy eau de toilette up his nose as a makeshift stimulant,
albeit absurdly. Eventually, I decided on a quick twist of his nipple
with a pair of pliers, a crude yet cost-effective alternative in the
absence of smelling salts. Fortunately, or unfortunately depending
on your viewpoint, I never quite got to that point as Charlie rose
from the dead with a fart that could have knocked over a small child
(or at least ruffle their hair.) Truly, it was a flatulent masterpiece, a
cacophony of chaos that left no doubt as to its origins.

Charlie recoiled like he'd been slapped, his gaze darting around
the room in confusion. After a beat, realisation dawned,
accompanied by a grimace. "Wow, that one could peel paint," he
declared.

My voice deserted me, swallowed whole by the putrid fog that
clung to the air. It felt like the world itself had held its breath. As
nausea clawed its way up, I braced myself for a different kind of
eruption and vomited all over Charlie's feet.

"Are you serious?" Charlie said in disgust.

"Are you serious?" I said, incredulity dripping from every word,
"that blast from your backside could have triggered seismic alarms.
If it weren't for the pressing matter at hand, I'd be dialling the
authorities for a geological survey of your arse."

"Well excuse me for having a bit of a nervous stomach?"

"I thought you'd died, and now I'm wishing that you had. No
one should be subject to anything that evil."

"Bit rich coming from a lunatic who's tied me to a chair, hit me
with a hammer and sliced open my nose, don't you think."

"You deserve everything you got coming. Maybe I haven't been your friendliest date, but I didn't deserve that."

I left Charlie to wallow in his own stench mixed with the fragrant bouquet of my last meal, while I ventured into the kitchen in search of anything to cleanse the bitter taste of nausea from my palate.

"Got anything minty?" I yelled. No reply. I had the distinct feeling he was a little bit miffed at me. I ransacked his cupboards in desperation, but everything turned up empty. Defeated, I retreated to the bathroom, where a tube of Colgate Total Active toothpaste came to my rescue, along with a can of Meadow Fresh Febreze.

Stepping back into the room, liberally spritzing air freshener with scant regard for the ozone layer, the contents of my stomach remained a distraction. The mere thought of touching his feet was an abomination, far worse than the noxious stench assaulting my senses. With a desperate heave, I flung a discarded hoodie over the offending articles, leaving the cleanup for another, braver soul. The sight of Charlie's hunched figure, his shoulders slumped in dejection, sent a jolt of urgency through me. It wasn't the sting of inflicting pain, but the echo of wasted time, of us being no closer to a conclusion, which resonated within me.

"Ok Charlie, how about we get back on track and I promise not to get distracted by pein hammers."

"How about you just fuck off back to whatever rock you crawled from under and leave me alone."

"Hey, I'm always open to a little bit of negotiation, but I think were miles apart on this one. Let's just clear up the dog dilemma real quick and move on. Why the dog lead in the hallway?"

Maybe realising resistance was becoming futile, Charlie replied, "I had a dog, he died, the lead is a reminder, nothing more, nothing less."

"Oh... I'm sorry Charlie. What was his name?"

"Does it matter?"

"Not really," I said, "just intrigued by what people call their pets I guess."

"Buster, for what it's worth."

"Aw... Cute. Any pictures?"

"What happened to no more distractions," Charlie said, irritated.

"Sorry, you're right. I'm just a sucker for cute dogs. So, where were we?"

"You were about to cut me free and go on your merry way?"

"Nice try, but no banana I'm afraid... So the question was, if you can cast you mind back that far, what do you see when you look at me?"

"Aside from a crazy bitch?"

"Yep, that aside."

"Well, a woman I guess." It was the best he could manage.

"It's a start Charlie, I'll give you that. Age?"

"I ain't falling for that one. I got a crack round the head for calling you darling, remember?"

"I promise, none of these questions will result in unnecessary violence," I said, reassuringly.

"Everything's resulted in unnecessary violence so far. Why would I believe you?"

"Only unnecessary in your eyes Charlie, not mine. C'mon have a stab at my age, I won't bite."

"Thirty five," he said, hesitantly.

"Thirty five? You cheeky bugger."

"OK, thirty?" he tried.

"Twenty nine Charlie, I'm twenty nine."

"Wasn't like I was a million miles out," he said in his defence.

"OK, so you see a twenty nine year old woman. Colour?"

"Is that relevant?" Charlie asked.

"It could be later on. What colour am I?"

Charlie squirmed under the weight of the seemingly straightforward question. Despite the answer being a no-brainer, he seemed to be struggling to spit it out. After an eternity, he finally mumbled, 'Not... white?' in a voice barely above a whisper.

For the first time this morning he'd made me smile. "I never had you down as one of the PC brigade Charlie, but you're quite correct, I'm not white, otherwise referred to as black."

"Didn't wanna take the risk," he said, "I know how your kind can get." Charlie's heart skipped a beat. Did he just say that out loud? He held his breath, waiting for the fallout that never arrived.

"My kind?" I said laughing, "there's the Charlie I know and hate. I prefer Cadburys dark milk, ever had one?"

"What?" he said, confused.

"Cadbury's dark milk. Hold a bar up against my skin and it disappears, camouflaged."

"Isn't 'dark milk' a contradiction in terms?

"I don't fucking know, I didn't name it. All I know, is that it's the exact same colour as my skin."

"So when I give my statement to the police, you want me to describe you as a twenty nine year old woman with Cadbury's dark milk skin?" he said, his voice dripping with sarcasm.

"It's unlikely you'll ever get that opportunity Charlie old boy, but I digress. Good looking?"

"Who?"

"Who d'you think? Me of course."

"Not my type," he said.

"Really? We'll revisit that one shortly, but for now, do you think I'm good looking?

Being cautious, Charlie answered, "You're not unattractive, if that's what you want to hear."

"I want to hear the truth. If you think I've got a face like a bulldog licking vinegar off a nettle. then say so."

"Well, if I had to offer an opinion..."

"Which you do," I interjected.

"Fine. You're attractive."

"Attractive or pretty? There's a difference, you know."

"Is there?"

"Hell yeah. Pretty is like, surface level. Attractive is... more, you know? Like, interesting, engaging, the whole package."

"Alright, if it keeps you from going off the deep end, I'll go with pretty, the whole package seems to have some issues."

"Slim, fat, somewhere in-between?"

Charlie didn't have a problem with this one. "Slim, definitely slim."

"Nice arse, good pair of tits?"

"No comment. I haven't checked out your arse or your tits," he lied.

"Of course you have, you're a bloke," I reminded him.

"Don't tar us all with the same brush love," he said before realising his mistake.

"Love, darling, duck, beautiful, dear, sweetheart or fucking treacle," I muttered under my breath, my voice tinged with frustration, "what the hell's wrong with you, you got a death wish?"

"No, no, no, please," he sputtered, voice thick with panic, "I'm sorry... Give me another chance, I swear I won't mess up again. This whole thing... it's just... ugh, so screwed up, but I'm trying, I really am."

Hunched over the coffee table, I squinted at the array of tools spread before me. A glint of cold steel snagged my eye – a wicked little spike nestled in a smooth wooden handle, worn from years of gripping and twisting. "What's this?" I said, holding the spike aloft.

"Please lady, no more," Charlie pleaded.

"Tell me what it is and I might not use it," I said.

"It's a... erm... a..."

"A what Charlie? Come on spit it out."

"A... bradawl, it's a bradawl," he finally said.

"Hmm... nasty looking thing, isn't it. What's it for?"

"Making holes in wood, before you put a screw in, I think."

"You think?"

"I'm not a fucking carpenter, it was in the shed when I bought the flat along with everything else you've got scattered over the table."

"OK... Well, you'll be pleased to know I'm not going to poke you in the eye with it, well not yet anyway, I need your full attention at this point."

Charlie didn't respond, not even a begrudging 'thanks'. His head dropped once again, this time in relief and not as a prelude to another guttural explosion.

"So, arse and tits," I said, returning to our little Q&A session. "Thoughts?"

I suspected by this point, Charlie was simply in survival mode as he answered promptly. "Great arse and magnificent pair of tits. Are we done now?"

"I think we've established enough to move on. Now, tell me what you remember about last night?"

Frustration gnawed at him, his brow furrowing as he tried to crank the rusty gears of his memory. Charlie chewed on his lip, forehead creasing, desperately trying to pull up any scrap of his life before waking up bound to the chair, the scratchy gaffer tape whispering against his skin.

"Everything's a blur. The last thing I remember was buying a packet of fags, maybe yesterday afternoon, maybe the day before, I've no fucking idea."

"Yeah, Rohypnol can have that effect I'm afraid, it's so damn unpredictable and rather frustratingly, so damn hard to get hold of if you're a woman. Go figure."

"What the hell's Rohypnol?" Charlie said, confused.

"Now, now Charlie, let's not play dumb. We both know, you know, exactly what it is. Though I seem to recall you prefer the name 'Roofies' or another one of your favourites, 'Mexican Valium.'"

"You're chattin' shit lady; I don't have a clue what you're talking about." His agitation growing in his voice.

I had to admire his tenacity. He clung to his story like a barnacle to a rock. I hadn't anticipated I would be no further on getting his confession after taping him to a chair, twatting him round the head with a hammer and performing a rudimentary nose job. His resilience was a hurdle, but the stakes were too high to turn back. The game was afoot, and I was determined to see it through.

"If you insist Charlie, it makes little difference, other than maybe some fun with the bradawl," I threatened.

Charlie had a sudden spike of defiance. "Listen, you psychotic, deranged piece of shit. Do what you gotta do, but it won't change the fact that I don't know what I don't fucking know."

I didn't like angry Charlie, brought back too many bad memories. I was tempted to inflict more misery on him but doing it out of rage would mean I was losing control and I needed to stay level headed. I wouldn't let him drag me back into the darkness. I would win, but not on his terms.

Calmly I said, "Then let me fill in some of the blanks. Last night you were enjoying a couple of pints, alone, down at the 'Dog & Duck'. Then, in saunters this young, striking beauty — dark milk skinned, slim frame, a vision with curves in all the right places. She settles right beside you at the bar. Please feel free to interrupt when any of this becomes familiar. We struck up a conversation, you eventually caved and bought me a drink, although it took a bit of coaxing on my part. And before you knew it, I had you roped into inviting me back to your place for a nightcap. Any of this ringing a bell?" I said.

It was like a lightbulb finally flicked on. Charlie's expression told me before he opened his mouth that the fog was clearing. His eyes, clouded and distant, flickered to life, tiny movie screens playing scenes only he could see, as the memories came flooding back.

"Jackie... No, Julie," he announced triumphantly.

"Jenny," I said, bursting his bubble.

"Yeah! Jenny. I remember now, you work at Amazon, delivering parcels."

"There you go Charlie old bean. Jenny the delivery driver, though that wasn't the whole truth," I confessed.

"You're not a delivery driver?"

"Nope, and I'm not called Jenny either, not that it matters. Here's what does matter to me though. It's been nagging at me since we arrived back here last night. Wasn't there a point where you asked yourself why a young, pretty, African woman with a great arse and magnificent tits was making a play for a sixty something, fat, bald, grotesque slob of a guy and seducing him into inviting her back to his gaff?"

"I'm not sixty something, you cheeky bitch. Just turned fifty."

"Really? Jesus Charlie, what the fuck happened to you. Thought I was being generous with sixty."

"Is this what this is about? You're pissed off that an old man took you up on your offer," Charlie wanted to know.

"Not at all. I'd have been pissed off if you hadn't taken me up on my offer. Just can't get my head around how stupid you are and why you didn't get suspicious. I really thought that part of my plan was going to be the most difficult."

"So, you're just some nutter who entices guys back to their flat and tortures them?"

"How dare you," I said, offended, "never tortured anyone in my life until today; and to be honest, had I not found the stash of makeshift weaponry in your man cave, probably wouldn't have bothered."

"So how about filling in some more blanks and tell me why I'm gaffer taped to this fucking chair?" Charlie said.

I hesitated, deciding whether the circumstances that had lead us to this point really mattered. I still had a job to do and was still hoping to make my yoga class, never mind getting my washing machine fixed. But for some unfathomable reason, I found myself needing to help Charlie out on this one. He didn't deserve an explanation as to why he was taped to a chair when I could have so easily killed him last night, so maybe it was more about me than him. Maybe it was about clawing back control after veering off track, proving to myself I wasn't some loose cannon.

"The chair and gaffer tape situation? Well, let's just say they were casualties of circumstance. I clearly underestimated the dosage of Rohypnol needed to knock you out. The shady dealer I got it from gave me some loose guidelines, but didn't factor in what a fat fuck you are. So, I spiked your last pint at the pub, thinking it would hit you like a ton of bricks when we got back here and if all went to plan, you'd be comatose before the kettle boiled and then I figured a pillow held over your face would finish the job off."

"So the plan was to kill me, pure and simple?" Charlie said matter-of-factly.

"Yep... But it seemed like you were immune or something. So, I figured I'd give you another dose in that brandy you insisted on pouring. That's when things got a bit weird. You had it in your delusional head that you were on course to give me a good seeing to and began stripping off in the kitchen before finally planting yourself down in the rocking chair, stark bollock naked and beckoning me to come and ride 'Willy the one eyed wonder worm'. Next thing I know, you're unconscious."

"And your plan to kill me changed, why?" Charlie said.

"Oh, the plan's intact, don't worry; you're still headed towards your demise. I just deviated slightly when I saw you butt naked in the chair. It brought back some pretty dark memories and I kinda thought smothering you was too merciful and perhaps you needed to suffer a bit first. That's when I went on a reccy and found your man cave. Next thing I know, I've gaffer taped you to the chair waiting patiently for you to wake up."

He blindsided me with his next question. I was anticipating the storm of questions; the anger, the bargaining, the final, desperate 'why?' But all that came out was a croaky whisper. "Can I have a cigarette please?"

"I'd rather you didn't," I said, "I quit five years ago and the smell still triggers me like nobody's business."

"Come on lady, it's not like I'm asking you to cook me a last meal. There's a pack in my jeans, right there on the floor," he pleaded.

I picked up the nail gun from the coffee table and held it in front of me. "You don't have to explain this one Charlie. Had a cute builder round at mine last year doing a loft conversion and we had many discussions about his rather impressive nail gun. He even let me have a play."

"Why the fuck have you picked that up? What did I do? What did I say?"

"Calm down. You didn't say or do anything, you're not being punished. When I cut free your right arm so you can have a smoke, I just need to make sure you ain't gonna use it to free the other arm, escape from that chair and do me some damage."

"And where does the nail gun come in?"

I moved forward, leant over, and grabbed Charlie's scrotum, stretching it forward so the wrinkled, saggy skin laid flat on the chair seat. As I lowered the gun onto his ball sack he yelled. "*Stop!* What the fuck are you doing?"

"I'm nailing you to the chair, what does it look like I'm doing?"

"Because I want a smoke?"

"Because I don't want you going anywhere, unless you're willing to rip open your scrotum to get at me."

"Alright, forget about the cigarette. I've been meaning to quit anyway," he said with a misplaced sigh of relief as the nail gun triggered anyway shooting a nail through his knacker sack and deep into the wooden chair.

They say grown men don't cry. I beg to differ. His scream tore through the air, a strangled cry as if the pain was suffocating him, leaving him gasping for air amidst choked sobs. Without hesitation, I fired off two more nails before he could even begin to recover. It seemed like the more humane option, in a twisted sort of way. Nailed it. Literally. Back in my chair, a sense of satisfaction settled in, mirrored in the gentle curve of my lips. Charlie might've been collateral, but the satisfying *THWACK* of a nail gun is pure therapy.

He blinked, speechless, and the room stilled. It was like someone had sucked the air out, leaving just prickling goosebumps on my skin. Maybe it was guilt, maybe a twisted form of empathy. Regardless, I fished out the pack of Marlborough from his discarded jeans. As I brought the cigarette to his lips, the line between help and harm blurred, leaving me adrift in a sea of murky motives.

In barely a whisper he said, "Any chance of a light?"

"Yeah sure," I said, "that would just be cruel, I'm not a monster."

My fingers fumbled in his jeans pocket, finally snagging a worn brass Zippo. The flame sputtered, casting flickering shadows on his face as he inhaled deeply, the smoke carrying away a sigh that spoke of more than just physical pain. He managed to satiate his nicotine craving without the need for an untethered limb, and the cigarette ash that had fallen and stuck to his clammy body was a small price to pay to ensure my safety. He winced as tiny embers landed on his bare skin, small wounds compared to the ones I'd already inflicted on him.

Feeling was creeping in, blurring the edges of my usual clarity. But I needed the pragmatist, the one who saw beyond the chaos and followed Charlie to the pub last night. I needed that voice to guide me, even if it meant swallowing down the emotions.

In a positive, almost cheery voice that I'm not convinced Charlie appreciated, I said, "Alright, the nail gun curiosity is satisfied. Now, the real question remains. What's the story behind your current... situation. We've covered the *how* but not the *why*. I'm guessing you're desperate to know?"

"Not particularly," he croaked, "If I'm going to die, I don't give a damn either way."

"This isn't about you, Charlie. Never was. Tonight, I sleep sound knowing your last flicker of thought will be of what you did to me. Fifteen years of nightmares for me, a couple of hours of abject fear for you. Consider it payback. So, let's start with my name. Has it come back to you yet?" I said.

"Nope, and it ain't gonna come back to me, because I don't know who the fuck you are," he said scornfully.

"It hurts, you know? Pretending you don't recall the name you carved into my soul. You may have forgotten or didn't even know my real name, but I'm finding it hard to believe you don't remember the nickname you gave me. That was your masterpiece, the name you practically wore out from saying it so much," I reminded him.

Charlie remained mum, his jaw locked tight. Was this his way of spitting in my face, a silent protest against his predicament? Had he decided to go out with a silent middle finger, refusing to give me the confession I craved? I wasn't quite ready to give up. Yoga class could wait, promising myself I'd do a double session next week to make up, but I couldn't go another day without my washing machine. Time was of the essence, so I decided to return to my new found hobby as 'Torturer in Chief'.

"Silence is painful Charlie, let's give you a little reminder. How about I write it down for you, would that help?"

I grabbed a soldering iron and plugged it into the socket behind Charlie's chair. I dangled it over his shoulder and settled back into my seat, patiently waiting for it to heat up to its maximum temperature. This wasn't about punishment, not entirely. It was about control, about forcing out the truth.

"Got to be honest with you, I'm no tattooist, this is not going to be a work of art," I warned him.

The acrid scent of burning chest hair assaulted my nose, but it was overshadowed by the nauseating odour of searing flesh as I traced the letter 'S'. Charlie's breath hitched, his eyes wide and pleading as the first mark seared itself onto his skin, and he bit his lip as he writhed around as much as his gaffer tape binding would allow.

"Stop squirming Charlie," I said, "my handwriting never won me any calligraphy awards as it is. If you don't hold still, it's going to look like the work of a four year old."

Charlie's frustration simmered, fuelled by the helplessness. The violation burned deeper than the searing mark etched into his flesh – a cocktail of fear, and a suffocating anger that threatened to consume him whole. He didn't scream, wouldn't give me the satisfaction. But in the silence of his defiance, a silent scream echoed, a raw plea for the nightmare to end.

The 'S' and 'L' were a bit of a tangled mess if I was being honest, and I wondered if they would be legible to anyone other than myself. I forced myself to slow down, focusing on the precise angles of the 'U' and 'T'. Each stroke felt deliberate, a calculated cruelty that, despite my intentions, stretched the agony. My grip faltered, not out of empathy, but because my hand had cramped into a claw. Then my heart sank. Branding the message into his skin felt powerful, but the cruel irony hit me: he couldn't even see it. My extreme attempt at clarity had become a pointless act of rage. I needed another plan.

The insistent trill of an unseen phone shattered the tense silence. I knew it wasn't mine – silenced, stripped bare of its SIM, it lay inert on the table. The kitchen, then. Leaving Charlie to simmer in his own fear, I hoped a brief break might loosen his tongue. The source? His tragically unfashionable camouflage vest, accessorised with corduroy shoulder patches, buzzing with an unidentified caller. 'Unknown number', the screen taunted.

The ringing stopped abruptly, leaving a hollow silence in its wake. Panic clawed at my throat. Had the caller expected Charlie's voice? What would they do now? Were they already on their way here, drawn by some unseen alarm? I needed answers, fast. I tried to open the phone to check if the caller had left a message, but it remained locked, a smug digital barrier mocking my desperation. Frustration surged through me. The phone demanded Charlie's presence, a cruel joke in his current state. Rushing back to his side, I held the phone in front of his face, hoping against hope. Nothing. Had the gaffer tape sealing his nose affected the sensor? With a surge of desperation, I tore it off, ignoring his muffled groan of pain. The wound looked worse than before, its raw edges inflamed and glistening. I tried again, and his franken-nose, cobbled together with whatever I could find, somehow held up to the scrutiny of the phone's scanner. Not exactly a work of art, but it got the job done. My finger trembled as I slammed down on the '1' key, holding it there like a lifeline. Each second felt like an eternity as I waited for the connection. Finally, a robotic voice announced Charlie's voicemail, a stark contrast to the panic within me.

---— ❧ —---

"OH HI! I'M TRYING TO get hold of Mr Bresden, Colin Bresden. I got your number from the estate agents. My name's Charlie, Charlie

Phipps, you bought my girlfriends flat. Was just wondering if I could call round when you're home to clear out the shed and collect my tools. Sorry it's been a while, but we've only just got the new garage built. Anyway, give me a call back when you can on 08491 469506. Cheers."

A bitter taste lingered as the truth unravelled before me. After listening to the voicemail, not once, not twice, but three times, it dawned on me that I'd spent the last two hours tormenting the wrong man, an innocent soul caught in my misguided pursuit. Curiously, remorse didn't tug at my conscience, but rather an irritated realisation that my true target still eluded me. Frustration tightened its grip as I turned to the bewildered, broken man, tethered to a rather kitsch but nonetheless stylish 1970's wooden rocking chair. I raised an eyebrow, suppressing the incongruity in my voice, and asked, "Hey Colin, I don't suppose you have Charlie's forwarding address, do you?"

The End.

The Old Vic

Eddie Finch's hands, gnarled like branches, trembled as he lit a cigarette, the flame flickering on scars that etched his face, lines of a hard life. The mirror held a man older than his years. His slumped shoulders and dimmed eyes spoke of applause fading in distant dives. A battered fedora perched atop thinning grey hair, a silent witness to dreams dissolving in whiskey fumes. His fingers, once coaxing magic from strings, now cradled a half-empty beer, a bitter echo of a melodic life turned sour.

The 'Old Vic' leans against the cobblestones, its facade a tapestry of chipped paint and grime. Inside, the air clings to the scent of stale beer and aged wood. Sunlight, filtered through dust-caked windows, casts long shadows across the worn floorboards, revealing a labyrinth of nooks and crannies where regulars nurse pints and mutter secrets. A mismatched collection of misted mirrors and brass lamps illuminate weather-beaten faces scarred with the stories of a rough neighbourhood. Despite the grit, a warmth radiates from the crackling fireplace, fuelled by generations of laughter and shared sorrows. This is no polished palace, but a haven for the weary souls who call this corner of town home.

"How many times do I have to tell you Eddie... *No smoking*, get your sorry arse in the beer garden," Pete bellowed from behind the bar.

Eddie exhaled a plume of smoke that danced towards the grimy ceiling before flicking the cigarette onto the floor, grinding it out with a ragged sole and a grimace. "Sorry Landlord, old habits and all that."

Pete sighed, polishing a glass with weary acceptance. He knew this dance, knew it wouldn't be long before the smoke returned. Same old Eddie, same old routine, but somehow, the pub wouldn't be the same without him.

The bar buzzed with chatter and dominoes. Anyone could've walked in unnoticed. But Vinnie? No. He burst through the stained-glass doors with swagger, a shark in a goldfish bowl. His smile – too big, teeth too white – and his gravity-defying hair screamed for attention. His cologne, a weird mix of cheap aftershave and fake coconut, announced him before he did. He oozed arrogance, but it felt forced. A flicker of something else, loneliness, crossed his face as he saw a couple laughing. Even his smile for Eddie, the lone beer drinker, seemed genuine.

Vinnie paused, a wave of doubt replacing the usual spark of adventure in his eyes. His pub app helpfully labelled the bar as 'rough around the edges', but maybe 'molten lava pit' would be more accurate. Vinnie's wingman, Jack, shuffled along a few paces behind, phone held aloft like a divining rod, searching for love (or at least something vaguely resembling it) in the murky depths of Tinder. A clumsy collision with Vinnie propelled him headlong into the boisterous heart of the pub. Any fleeting notion of escape vanished like smoke as Pete's gravelled voice wafted over, lassoing him into the fray.

"With you in a minute sir." Pete, a practiced veteran of head-related complaints, was deftly topping up the pint of a moaning regular.

"Two pints of lager and a packet of crisps please," Vinnie said as he reached the bar.

"No problem fella, with you in a tick."

Undeterred, Vinnie repeated, "Two pints of lager and a packet of crisps, please."

"Don't push your luck son," Pete warned him.

On a roll and thinking he was the king of comedy, Vinnie added, "I'll have some pickled onions, and a little bit of cheese, please. Thank you."

"You takin' the piss son?" Pete's question, a loaded one, bounced harmlessly off Vinnie but not Jack, who, with a nervous glance around, scurried off to a secluded nook, seeking the comfort of anonymity. This was Pete's kingdom. Forty years in the trade had scored lines on his face deeper than any scar earned in a bar brawl (though there were a few of those too). He wasn't one for idle chatter, preferring a curt nod or a pointed silence to convey his message. Troublemakers knew better than to linger under his steely gaze – they could practically feel the weight of his unspoken warning: 'One strike, you're out.' Yet, beneath the gruff exterior lay a grudging respect for those who played by the rules and a quiet understanding for the disparate souls who sought solace within his four walls.

"OK, forget the crisps, how about the two pints of lager?" Vinnie said, his voice tinged with impatience. His eyes followed the clinking glasses as Pete poured the lager and placed them on the counter. Vinnie raised a questioning eyebrow and said, "What's this?"

"What's it look like."

"Well," Vinnie started, then blurted out without thinking, "If I'm being honest, it looks like a pint of piss."

Pete's response was curt, "ID."

"Do what?" Vinnie said, irritated.

"Let's see some ID."

"ID... Do I look like a friggin' kid?"

Pete shook his head, "Nope, but you're certainly acting like one. ID or fuck off."

A treasure trove of faded receipts and forgotten loyalty cards spilled forth as Vinnie wrestled open his wallet searching for his driving licence. Finally, he located it and tossed it onto the counter with a nonchalant flick.

Pete's extended inspection of the licence was a subtle power play, its message understood even without spoken words. "Thank you Vincent, it is Vincent, isn't it? Now let's start again, shall we? Welcome to the 'Old Vic'. I'm the Landlord and you may call me 'Landlord' and what I say goes. It's not up for discussion; it's not up for debate. You don't insult my pub, you don't insult my beer, you don't insult my patrons and when you leave, you thank me for allowing you the pleasure of drinking in my establishment. Now, is there any part of that you don't understand?"

"Ok... Chill out dude, just having a laugh," Vinnie said, finally getting the message.

"I don't do laughing. Now, give me six pounds eighty, take your two pints of lager, go sit down with your boyfriend and don't speak to me again unless it's to order more beer."

Vinnie's mouth opened, words poised to escape, but the retort died on his tongue, choked by the unspoken message conveyed by Pete's raised finger. He retrieved his drinks and made a beeline for Jack, whose table choice spoke volumes; strategically positioned near the exit, as if expecting a hasty departure.

THE WORN ROUGE ON CINDY'S cheekbones couldn't quite mask the laughter lines that were now canyons whispering tales of a life well-lived. Her once fiery hair, now the shade of a fading sunset, was pulled tight in a defiant bun, a crown for a queen of the tattered barstools. Worn leather boots scuffed a comforting rhythm against the floor as she moved, dispensing cigarettes and kind words in equal measure. She didn't see the fading glamour, but the light in her eyes shone brighter than any spotlight, a beacon of fierce loyalty for those who called her friend.

She'd been working her charms on a couple of vintage regulars, hoping to drum up some extra trade. Three decades of catering to the carnal desires of the dockside lonely hearts had failed to earn her a well-deserved retirement, so the occasional nightcap (read: vodka and coke) still required some financial lubrication. Despite her best efforts and more than a flash of orange peel thigh, she couldn't ignite their passion, and her attempts at seduction were deflected by the gravitational pull of the dartboard. Accusing them of being a couple of 'fruit fairies', she turned her attention to Psycho Phil, the landlord's unpaid, resident bouncer.

"Hey Psycho, lookin' for some company?" she said, running her tongue over cherry red lips.

"I know you come cheap Cindy, but still too rich for my wallet," Phil said, dismissively.

"I'm sure we could come to some arrangement. I do special rates for old friends, how about I knock off the VAT," Cindy said.

"I've been trudging round this God forsaken planet for fifty long years Cindy and in all that time, I've never been desperate enough to pay for it, what makes you think I'd start now?"

"There'll come a time when your irresistible charms begin to fade Psycho and when that time comes, you'll find I'm a small price to pay. Anyway, it's not always about business, how about we keep each other company for old times' sake. You do remember the old times, don't you?"

"I try not to, worst ten years of my life," Phil reminded her.

"I can't believe you just said that."

"Oh, come on Cindy, it was hardly Edward and Mrs Simpson."

"Yeah, well I don't remember you saying that when I was trussed up head to toe in rubber with my hands tied behind my back."

"Ok, so there were *some* good times," Phil said, turning his head towards the bar entrance. His gaze landed on 'Gorgeous' Gordon, a title earned less for his undeniable good looks and more for his flamboyant use of the very same word.

GG, as Pete had affectionately named him, sashayed in, his laugh a melodic cascade that filled the room. His eyes, bright as costume jewellery under the dim bar lights, sparkled with an impish glint. Oscar Wilde strutting in a tutu designed by Dorothy Parker, with a flamboyant feather boa draped over his shoulder for good measure. Every word he utters drips with honeyed irony and playful double entendres, leaving the regulars simultaneously amused and ever-so-slightly bewildered.

Vinnie, wide-eyed and fresh to the unique surroundings, scanned the scene and with an outstretched hand mimicking a radar sweep, shouted, "Gaydar alert! Gaydar Alert! Backs against the wall guys." His innocent curiosity was in danger of poking a hornet's nest, and Jack knew navigating the unspoken rules of the 'Old Vic' could be tricky, especially for a newcomer. He felt a shiver crawl down his spine. He clamped a hand over Vinnie's mouth, his voice low and urgent, "Shut the fuck up Vinnie. You got a death wish?"

A ripple of unease spread through the room, followed by a chorus of disapproving murmurs. Vinnie swallowed hard, the weight of a dozen gazes pinning him down. He raised a hand, a half-hearted apology that faltered in the tense silence, hoping it would be enough to prevent a journey home via the local A&E department.

The only person not directing their attention at Vinnie was Gordon himself. He only had one thing on his mind and that was Pete. Ignoring the amused glances and whispers, he launched into his usual routine, his voice dripping with exaggerated charm. "Good evening Landlord," he purred, winking suggestively, "looking gorgeous as usual."

"Evening GG. Drink?" Pete said, unfazed by Gordon's theatrics.

"Do bears sit in the woods," Gordon said.

"Shit in the woods."

"What?"

"Do bears *shit* in the woods, not *sit* in the woods."

"Eww... you vile creature. Anyway, same gorgeous guy, different cat."

"Hat."

"Huh?"

"Never mind," Pete sighed, "Cinzano and diet lemonade?"

"If you please, kind sir."

"Ice and a cherry?" Pete said, hoping to end the conversation.

Gordon leaned closer, his eyes twinkling, "Mm... Would that be your cherry Landlord?"

"Sorry GG, you're not my type. Three pound fifty please."

Curious, Gordon said, "So, what is your type?"

"Pretty much anything in a skirt," Pete said.

"I can do skirts."

Pete chuckled dryly. "I'm sure you can GG, but I draw the line at skirts that are concealing man tackle I'm afraid."

"You don't know what you're missing gorgeous."

"Oh... I think I do," Pete insisted.

"I could make you happy, love you long time. You need someone to look after you Landlord and I do a wicked 'Toad in the Hole'."

Pete raised an eyebrow, unsure if he should be amused or concerned. "Is that a culinary delight or just one of your many perversions?"

Gordon's grin widened. "For me to know and you to find out, sex God."

With that final, suggestive remark, the conversation reached a stalemate, leaving Pete to ponder the peculiar charm and unsettling advances of Gordon, the flamboyant enigma who inhabited a world of his own making. Gordon slid his money over the bar, his fingers brushing against Pete's in a friendly gesture. A pair of familiar faces promptly relinquished their seats to accommodate Gordon, who had carved out his own cozy niche in the corner, offering him a prime vantage point to take in the scene.

———— ⟨∾⟩ ————

VINNIE REMAINED CAUTIOUS, keeping a low profile. Concerned that venturing outside could jeopardise his health, he found solace for the moment within the sheltered confines of the bar, relying on the landlord's presence to provide a sense of security. He turned to Jack and in a hushed tone said, "This place is like something out of a Dickens novel. Have you ever seen a scarier bunch of people?"

"It creeps me out," Jack said, "come on, let's go, I thought we were going clubbin'?"

"We are, I promise," Vinnie reassured him, "but don't you find it fascinating?"

"No, it's full of weirdo's and degenerates, now can we please fuck off?"

"All in good time my friend, all in good time," Vinnie said as he sat back in his chair cradling his pint.

The buzz of conversation dimmed for a moment, replaced by a collective intake of breath. Vinnie, nursing his self-inflicted social exile in the corner, watched as Nessa cautiously entered, her arrival disrupting the established rhythm of the night. Her hair, a cascade of molten fire, framed a face sculpted with delicate angles. Emerald eyes sparkled with mischief and wit, their depth hinting at untold stories and freckles danced across her nose, a touch of imperfection that only enhanced her natural beauty. Jenny, a shadow cast by her friend's dazzling light, trailed behind, a silent observer to the captivated crowd. Though invisible, she felt a quiet pride in the attention her friend commanded.

Nessa swanned towards the bar, stilettos clicking a confident rhythm against the worn floorboards. She was accustomed to the spotlight and adept at steering it to her advantage.

Pete remained unimpressed, unperturbed by the covert glances exchanged among the rest of the congregation. To him, the newcomer was just another potential customer, someone with money burning a hole in their pocket, ripe for his guidance in parting with it.

"Good evening, ladies," his voice oozed practiced charm, "what'll it be tonight?"

Nessa flashed a confident smile, "Baileys over ice for me please, and a Malibu and coke for my friend."

A flicker of confusion crossed Pete's face. "Excuse me?"

"Baileys over ice, and a Malibu and coke," Jenny said, peering out from behind Nessa's shoulder.

"Baily's?" Pete said.

Nessa's smile faltered. "Yes, Baily's," a hint of irritation creeping into her voice, "you know, Irish cream liqueur served in a glass receptacle with little frozen cubes of water."

Pete remained silent; his gaze fixed in a vacant stare. Her words washed over him, as if she were speaking a language entirely foreign to him.

"I'm sorry, is there a problem?" Nessa said, confused, "it's not like I asked for some exotic cocktail like a 'Long Slow Comfortable Screw.'"

Pete snapped into focus. "A word of advice ladies, and please take it in the spirit it's meant. The 'Old Vic', due it's unique collection of somewhat unusual patrons, is not the place to use the words long, slow, comfortable and in particular *screw*, in the same sentence.

Jenny, not unlike Vinnie's friend Jack, had a bad feeling. "Let's get out of here Ness, I don't like it," she said, her voice full of worry.

"It's a pub Jenny. A pub on our carefully plotted pub crawl route. It defeats the whole object of a 'pub crawl' if we miss out the pubs," Nessa reminded her.

"I know it's a pub," Jenny said, "but it's just this one, it's a bit…"

"A bit what?"

"Well, a bit weird that's all."

"Oh, dear sweet Jenny, you've led such a sheltered life," Nessa said disparagingly. "Landlord, thank you for your advice and it's been duly noted. Now may I have a Bailey's over ice and a Malibu and Coke if it isn't too much trouble."

Pete chuckled, a cold, humourless sound. "Wouldn't be a problem, love, if I had either of those things. We're more of a whiskey and ale kind of joint. Cherry on a stick's about as fancy as it gets here."

"Ah… I see. In that case how about a couple of Jack Daniels?" Nessa said, hopefully.

"Coming right up. Ice?"

"That would be wonderful, thank you."

Vinnie was mesmerised, his eyes locked onto the red-haired enchantress who effortlessly commanded the attention of everyone around her. Meanwhile, Jack remained fixated on Tinder, his hope pinned on the app to connect him with the ideal woman, swiping incessantly across his phone's screen.

"Jack, Jack…" Vinnie said, digging his friend in the ribs with his elbow, "my wife's stood at the bar."

"Wife? What wife? You're not married you daft twat," Jack said, eyes still locked on his phone.

"Jack, that woman stood at the bar, that vision of beauty draped in red is the future Mrs Vincent Vincenzo, she simply doesn't know it yet. Come on," Vinnie commanded, as he stood and ran his fingers through his hair.

"Where we goin'?"

"I'm going to tell my future wife she's just met her future husband and you're going to distract her mate while I do so."

"Sod off Vinnie. I ain't talking to that munter," Jack said defiantly.

"For Christ's sake Jack, I'm not asking you to shag her. Just keep her occupied while I set a date for the wedding."

Jack wasn't having any of it. "Sorry mate, you're on your own."

"Cheers pal, I owe you one," Vinnie said as he strode confidently in Nessa's direction. He paused briefly deciding on his opening line before going with the tried and trusted, "Do you mind if I stare at you up close instead of from across the room?"

A flicker of a smile danced in Nessa's eyes before it was snuffed out by Jenny's sharp retort. "Clear off creep."

"Excuse me?" Vinnie said, annoyed, "was I talking to you?"

"We're not interested," Jenny said, clearly not bothered about who Vinnie might have been talking to.

"Oh, I'm sorry. Carpet munchers?" Vinnie asked in all sincerity.

"I beg your pardon?" Nessa said.

"You and Miss personality, Vagi-terians are you?"

"If you mean, are we lesbians, then *no* we're not," Nessa said, "not that it's any of your business."

"Then how does she know you're not interested?"

"Because she's engaged to be married, if you must know," Jenny said with some delight.

"Shut up Jenny," Nessa said, irritated that her best friend continued to speak on her behalf.

"Well, you are," Jenny reminded her.

"So... doesn't mean you have to broadcast it to the whole world."

Vinnie wasn't going to let minor details like, engaged to be married, get in the way. "So technically you're still free, single and available."

"Technically I'm engaged to be married," Nessa said.

"Semantics. Look, picture this, you, me, bubble bath and a bottle of champagne."

Jenny crossed her arms, nostrils flaring with irritation. Vinnie's advances toward Nessa seemed to have struck a nerve far deeper than they had with her friend. "Picture this. You, Nessa's boyfriend and one of you with two broken legs," Jenny warned.

"I wouldn't break his legs," Vinnie said, "I'm a lover not a fighter."

"I didn't mean him..."

Interrupting, Nessa said, "Do you mind Jenny. I'm more than capable of looking after myself thank you."

Unlike Nessa, unfazed by the unwanted attention, Jenny wasn't one to tolerate nonsense. With a glare that could curdle milk, she snapped, "On your own head be it, don't say I didn't warn you. I'm going out for a ciggy," then flounced out, shaking her head in disbelief, her mumbled words lost in the clatter of the bar.

With Jenny gone, Vinnie seized on the opportunity. He grinned, flashing his best pearly whites, and launched into a charm offensive so smooth it could have melted the iciest of hearts. Nessa, however, just raised an eyebrow, the corner of her mouth twitching with a hint of a smirk. "Before you go any further, Romeo," she said, "let me warn you, my friend's bark is worse than her bite, but mine..."

Undeterred, Vinnie said, "I'll bear it in mind... So, what's a nice girl like you doing in a dive like this?"

"Just passing through, though I have to admit, it does look a bit like something out of a Dickens novel."

"Whoa! Spooky. That's exactly what I said to my boring mate over there. You like Dickens then?" he asked, trying to sound cultured.

"Yeah, but not on a first date," Nessa teased.

Taking a second to catch on Vinnie said, "Oh, I get it, very good, quite the wit, aren't we? So, it's Nessa is it?"

She had no plans to make things easy. "Might be."

"That's what you're... charming friend called you."

"Then I guess it must be," she conceded.

"Nice to meet you Nessa," Vinnie said, getting a little bored with the niceties. "So, what are the chances of us engaging in something more than just conversation?"

"On a scale of zero to ten?"

"Yeah, why not?"

"Zero."

"Ok... Not the best score I've ever had but sounded like a definite maybe."

"Sounded to me like a definite *no*. You hard of hearing?"

"Hey... I'm not trying to pressure you. I'm not after sex without mutual consent; and by the way, you have my consent."

A reluctant smile tugged at the corner of Nessa's lips. Vinnie's efforts, a barrage of clichés seasoned with forced confidence, should have grated on her nerves. Every fibre of her being screamed 'disengage', yet she found herself inexplicably drawn into the conversation. He wasn't her type, not by a long shot, but there was something strangely captivating about his awkward persistence.

"Listen... sorry didn't catch your name?" Nessa said.

"Vinnie, but you can call me..." he whipped out a business card and held it out for her to take, "...on this number."

"Listen Vinnie. I'm flattered that you want to get in my knickers, but..."

"Oh... I think you've misunderstood me. Getting in your knickers, as appealing as that clearly is, is only a small part of the plan. We're going to be married," Vinnie said confidently.

That one caught Nessa by surprise and all she could offer was, "Sorry?"

"You and me. Vinnie and Nessa, we're gonna tie the knot. One day you will be Mrs Nessa Vincenzo," Vinnie said, his confidence leaving little room for debate.

"And the fact I'm engaged to be married doesn't bother you?"

"A minor inconvenience," Vinnie assured her.

Jenny's sudden return either salvaged the situation or disrupted the rhythm, depending on your perspective. Nessa took the opportunity to regain some control over Vinnie's persistence. "Well, it's been a mildly pleasurable experience Vinnie, but if you'll excuse me, I have a pub crawl to complete and you're cramping my style somewhat." Her smile didn't quite reach her eyes, and while she didn't want to be cruel, she wasn't exactly giving him a warm invitation to tag along either.

Vinnie held Nessa's hand a beat too long, brushing a kiss across her knuckles with practiced ease. "Au revoir, ma chérie," he purred, a hint of smugness creeping into his voice. He returned to his seat, practically vibrating with self-assured arrogance. "She's mine, Jack," he declared, gesturing towards Nessa with a flourish, "that doggone girl is totally, completely mine."

Jenny chewed on her lip, feeling the familiar tug-of-war within their friendship. Nessa, lost in another impulsive escapade, and her, the ever-grounded counterpoint. "Nessa," she started, her voice firm yet laced with concern, "what the bloody hell do you think you're playing at?"

"Chill Jenn... It was a harmless bit of fun."

"You'll go too far one day Ness and find yourself in a whole heap of shit," Jenny warned her.

"I'm always in the shit," Nessa confessed with a shrug, "it's just the depth that varies. You gotta admit, he is cute."

Jenny shuddered with revulsion. "He's a creep."

"Maybe you're right... But sometimes..." Nessa paused.

"Sometimes what?" Jenny said.

"Sometimes, just sometimes, don't you want a little bit of what you can't have?"

"No," Jenny said, "now drink up, we're out of here."

———— ⌾ ————

CINDY AND EDDIE HAD been watching Vinnie weave his magic and Eddie's face broke into a wry smile It was like watching a younger, flashier version of himself strut across the floor. Memories flooded back, smooth talk, stolen glances, the thrill of the chase. Those days were long gone, replaced by creaky bones and fading swagger. Yet, a flicker of the old fire sparked in his chest. In Vinnie's clumsy attempts, he saw shadows of his own past triumphs, and a touch of himself he'd thought buried. Vinnie needed a little guidance, a touch of finesse from a seasoned player. Who better to teach the game than someone who'd mastered it in his youth, even if the years had forced him to trade the playing field for a spectator's seat?

He sidled up to Vinnie, whiskey in hand causing Vinnie to tense. "Think you might be in there son," he said with a wink.

Vinnie looked around, hoping he was talking to someone else, but Eddie's gaze was firmly fixed in his direction. "Yeah, think you might be right," Vinnie said.

"Not my type but can see the appeal. She's got assets," Eddie chuckled, though it triggered a coughing fit that seemed like it might rupture a lung.

"Of course she's not your type," Vinnie said, stating the obvious. "No disrespect but you're about forty years too old. I agree she's got a nice pair of assets though."

"Cheeky git. I'm not that fucking old. I could still pull if the urge took me," Eddie said.

"I hate to break it to you fella, but if you're not that old, you've sure led a hard life."

Had this not been true, Eddie could have taken offense, but he wore his hardships like badges of honour. As he headed for the bar he turned and said, "You don't know the half of it son, you don't know the half of it."

Cindy who had half an ear on Eddie and Vinnie's conversation, felt the need to keep Vinnie in his place. "Show some respect son."

"Why?" Vinnie said, annoyed that he was being told what to do by a woman, who, in his closeted world was of questionable character.

"Firstly," Cindy said, "because I said so, but more importantly, because Eddie is one of life's greats."

"He can't be that great if he spends his twilight years drinking himself to oblivion in this shit hole."

"That'll be the same 'shit hole' you're drinking in then?" Cindy scoffed, rolling her eyes.

"I'm just passing through lady."

"Yeah, they all say that. Sorry my friend, but one trip to the 'Old Vic' and there ain't no going back."

———— ✸ ————

THE USUAL FRIDAY NIGHT ritual played out. Gordon, a kaleidoscope of colour in the monochrome bar, flitted and flirted, but tonight, his charm seemed to fall flat. The 'Old Vic', with its cynicism-soaked regulars, wasn't the most fertile ground for cultivating love. Spurned but not broken, he shimmied over to Psycho Phil, not for love, but for the bitter comfort of someone who understood the grime beneath the glitter. "Mind if I join you?" he said, sitting uncomfortably close placing a hand on Phil's knee.

"Feel free GG," Phil said, glad of the distraction, "it might keep the bunny boiler away."

"Cindy?" Gordon said.

"Yeah, she's been chewin' my ear."

"Oh honey, that's because she's still holding a flame for you."

"A flame in one hand and a gallon of unleaded petrol in the other maybe," Phil said with a sigh, a hint of sadness in his eyes.

"Darling, there simply had to be some cosmic pull once upon a time. I mean, you two were practically joined at the hip for an eternity."

"Don't remind me. To be honest, it was all about the sex."

"Sex kept you two lovebirds glued together for a whole decade?"

"You better believe it. I won't go into the gory details, but for all the women I've had, and I've had my fair share, nothing compares to Cindy's considerable talents," Phil snorted; his voice laced with vulgarity.

"Guess she chose the right profession then," Gordon winked, "why waste those talents on just one guy?"

"Oh, she picked the right profession all right. Can't think of anyone more suited to a hooker lifestyle than sweet old Cindy. Unfortunately, that's what did for us."

"Gotcha gorgeous, couldn't deal with her cozying up to other fellas, huh?"

"Other guys I could live with, she was making good money. Let's just say, scheduling date nights was like booking a ticket for an Eddie Finch concert in his heyday. But hey, we made it work, well for a while at least... Anyway, enough about my sad, sorry existence, how's life treating you?"

"Same doo dah darling, different whatchamacallit."

"Love on the horizon?" Phil said.

"Oh, if only. It's not easy being gay in this town you know." Gordon sighed; his voice heavy with longing.

"Gay... you... never?" Phil said.

"Hard to believe, isn't it?" Gordon said, laughing. "I mean, outwardly you'd never know would you, but it's true, I swear."

"Well blow me," Phil said in mock surprise and with a look that told Gordon it wasn't an invitation.

Their little tete a tete was unceremoniously shattered by the clanging of a ships bell, followed by Pete's booming voice echoing through the gloom. "Alright, lovebirds, lushes and lost souls, time to call it a night." Another chaotic symphony of the 'Old Vic' had reached its inevitable crescendo. Phil, ever the self-proclaimed guardian of closing time, sprang into action, his worn brogues squeaking against the sticky floor as he navigated the labyrinth of bodies towards the door.

———— ✑ ————

TIME, A RELENTLESS thief, had stolen days and weeks, leaving only echoes of laughter and whispered dreams lingering in the 'Old Vic'. Though the world spun on, this place remained an anchor, a refuge from the ceaseless tide of change. Cindy perched on her usual stool, the worn leather moulding to her shape like a second skin.

"Evening mine host," Cindy said, her voice husky and suggestive, "vodka and coke sil vous plait and make it a big one."

"Coming right up Cindy," Pete said as he swiftly crafted her tipple, his hands moving like a seasoned pro. Every second counted behind the bar; the faster he served, the sooner they'd be ready for another round, "how's tricks?"

"Been better, but there's a recession on, what's a girl supposed to do."

"Tell me about it. I've been thinking of selling up and opening a bar in Spain."

Cindy erupted into laughter. "Really? Sorry to be the bearer of bad news, but you *are* the 'Old Vic'. I'm afraid the only way you'll ever leave here is in a wooden box. Moi, on the other hand, I could ditch this poor excuse for a country tomorrow. I quite fancy 'high class hooker in Vegas', what d'you think?"

"I think there may be a market for the more mature lady of the night in the good old US of A, just not sure Las Vegas is the place though."

"Cheeky sod," Cindy said, turning away in mock disgust.

Psycho Phil, usually perched near the bar's heart, had nestled into a secluded nook, shrouded from curious glances, engrossed in a conversation with an unfamiliar face he had discreetly ushered into the pub. Their exchange remained unnoticed until a raucous burst of laughter punctured the ambient chatter, prompting Cindy to cast a pointed glance in their direction. With a casual saunter, drink sloshing gently in her hand, she approached the newcomer, a friendly smile curving her lips.

"Well, well, well, what do we have here?" Cindy said. "Like to introduce me to your new friend Psycho?"

"No," Phil said sharply.

"Now don't be like that," Cindy said, extending her hand to the mysterious interloper. "Hi, I'm Cindy."

"Hi Cindy," came the reply, as she nervously shook her hand. "But you can call me D."

"Oh, OK. Short for Cindy?"

"Nope," Cindy said, cupping her breasts, "I'm named after this magnificent pair of puppies. Natural D cup sweet cheeks, no plastic here. Fancy a squeeze?"

"For fuck's sake D, put 'em away, we've just eaten," Phil scolded her.

"Well nice to meet you Cin... D, I'm..."

"She doesn't need to know your name Janice," Phil interrupted, before realising his mistake.

"Janice? well that's an interesting name. So, how did you end up with this sorry excuse for a man?"

"Why don't you just piss off D and leave us alone," Phil said.

"Aww... Where's the fun in that. I have to say Psycho, she's not your usual cannon fodder. In fact, I'd go as far as to say she looks fairly normal, positively boring in fact." A sneer curled Cindy's lips as she looked away.

"Excuse me," Janice said, her anger evident in her tone.

Ignoring Janice's remark, Cindy's attention was firmly fixed on Phil. "Tell me Psycho, what exactly do you see in her, she's got a face like the back of a bus and a body like a sack of spuds."

Janice erupted from her chair, but Cindy's single, questioning glance deflated her like a punctured balloon. Sheepishly, Janice mumbled an excuse and retreated into her seat, the anger replaced by a dull ache of uncertainty.

"She's more of a woman than you could ever be D and her body's in a damn sight better shape than yours," Phil said as he stared deep into Janice's eyes and kissed her gently on the cheek.

"Landlord, get me the sick bucket," Cindy said as she turned towards the bar, before glancing over her shoulder back at Phil. "I'll give it a month; you know where I am when *she* realises what she's let herself in for and *you* realise you need a real woman."

"Get over it D, we're gettin' married," Phil shot back.

Cindy didn't know whether to laugh or cry, so opted for another drink instead. "A double brandy please, landlord. Heard it works wonders for shock," she said, sliding her empty glass across the bar.

NESSA FLUNG OPEN THE pub door, the hinges protesting her arrival. She stomped into the bar like a hurricane in stilettos, leaving a trail of bewildered patrons in her wake. Vinnie, her personal raincloud, scurried behind her, muttering apologies under his breath like a mantra against the coming downpour.

"That's not what I said," Vinnie said.

Nessa crossed her arms, her voice sharp and uncompromising. "That's exactly what you said."

Pete, ever the conciliator, interjected. "Can I get the young lovers a drink?" His offer fell on deaf ears.

"Well, that's not what I meant," Vinnie tried as a way of explanation.

Not one to give up, Pete tried, "A pint of piss and a Baileys over ice maybe, I got some in specially?"

"So, what exactly did you mean?" Nessa persisted, as Vinnie squirmed under her relentless pursuit, knowing there was no escape from her scrutiny.

"I simply meant that when the time comes for you to bare children you have the hips to do it," Vinnie said, confident he had just delivered a compliment.

"Ah, I see and here's me thinking you were calling me fat. Well rest assured, when the time comes for my 'Hippo Hips' to bear a child, the poor little sod won't have been spawned by Mr Vincent Vincenzo," Nessa said, clearly exasperated by Vinnie's phrasing.

"Okay, time out," Pete said, holding up his hands like a referee breaking up a fight, "this is like watching paint dry, only angrier. Now, drinks or can I go for a smoke?"

"Pint of lager and a slimline tonic for Miss Congeniality please landlord," Vinnie said, frustrated at Nessa's lack of understanding.

"Bastard," Nessa spat, before storming off to find an empty table.

"Well, it's nice to see the art of seduction ain't dead," Pete said amused, "would you like ice and lemon sir."

"In my lager?"

"No, in the little lady's slimline tonic, you fool."

"Jesus, what you trying to do to me Landlord. Can you imagine the fall out if I go over there with a slimline tonic? Make it a double Jack Daniels over ice."

"Very good sir... I'm your obedient servant," Pete said, his sarcasm thinly veiled.

Thinking he had Pete under his spell, Vinnie tried, "Would you bring the drinks to my table please Landlord."

Vinnie's optimism came crashing down. "Piss off," Pete said, reminding him who was in charge.

As Vinnie cautiously took his drinks over to Nessa, he paused briefly, captivated by the sight of Psycho Phil, whose lips were currently locked in an almost violent embrace with a mystery woman. Phil's head snapped up, his gaze piercing through the dimly lit room. "Problem son?" he rasped, a hint of something dangerous lurking in his voice.

"No... No problem Psycho," Vinnie stuttered, "I was just, uh, admiring those curtains back there, thinking they could do with a bit of a clean."

Janice, blissfully unaware of the tension, said, "Yeah, they're a bit rank aren't they. I don't know why you drink in here Pee Pee, it's a right cess pit."

Phil's eyes narrowed, a flicker of disappointment crossing his face. The 'Old Vic' had been his haven for two decades, and the last person who dared insult its unique ambiance had vanished without a trace. An unease washed over Janice she couldn't quite explain. She checked her watch and exclaimed, "Bloody hell is that the time. I need to shoot Pee Pee, got an early start. You coming back to mine?"

Phil mellowed, picturing his new lady friend waiting under the covers. But a night of passion needed proper fuel. "Sure hunny bun, I'll just have a last quick snifter and be home before you can say cocoa and slippers."

"Ok, don't be long," Janice teased, giving him a quick peck on the cheek, "you know hunny bun gets lonely without you." With a last ditch 'mwah' flung over her shoulder, she scurried out of the bar.

Cindy, who'd been eavesdropping on Phil's latest conquest, shuffled down the worn leather bench, her eyes glued on him, waiting for his gaze to finally land on her.

Phil, sensing her presence, spoke without turning, his voice dismissive, "Not interested, D."

"Hunny bun? Pee Pee?" Cindy's voice held a mixture of disbelief and indignation, "are you fucking serious?"

"Damn right I'm serious," he said.

"Jesus, what happened to you? What happened to the old Psycho I knew and, frankly, hated?" Cindy's voice held a hint of longing beneath the barbed remark.

"Things change D. People change. I'm a new man."

"Shit," Cindy said, "don't tell me you've gone all metrosexual on me."

"I said new man, not Gorgeous Gordon," Phil said, clearly missing the point.

"Metrosexual dumb ass, not homosexual."

Phil, oblivious to her correction, said, "Janice makes me happy. She's made me see that the world ain't such a bad place and that I ain't such a bad person."

"Sorry Psycho, but a leopard never changes its spots. You're a sick twisted fuck, always was and always will be."

Phil, undeterred, continued his sermon, "I've seen the light D and I suggest you do the same before you die a sad, lonely and bitter old prossie."

"The only light you ever see is the one inside your fridge when you reach in for another beer."

A flicker of frustration crossed Phil's face. "Look, why can't you just be happy for me?"

"I would if I thought you were happy for yourself, but it just isn't you Psycho; and besides, we've got unfinished business. You know it and I know it."

"Suck it up buttercup. We've done all the shaggin' we're ever goin' to do babe. Now if you'll excuse me, I have a date to keep with my hunny bun."

Phil stood, ready to leave. Cindy, her eyes flashing with a mix of anger and hurt, blocked his path. "Last chance," she warned, her voice tight with emotion.

He shifted uncomfortably, avoiding her gaze. "I'm going to be late," he mumbled.

"Don't you forget what you're leaving behind," she said, her voice dropping to a seductive whisper. She leaned in close, her breath warm against his ear. "A life that could be exciting, passionate, dangerous even."

He swallowed hard, torn between his newfound resolve and the undeniable pull she had on him. As he opened his mouth to respond, the bar door swung open, letting in a rush of cold air and the sound of approaching voices. The moment was broken, and Phil slipped past her, disappearing into the night.

EDDIE, A LEGEND ON the wane, shuffled to the bar, his empty glass like a flag announcing his thirst. "Slap some whiskey in it, Landlord," he rasped, the years adding gravel to his voice.

Pete raised an eyebrow, "Just a single?" He knew the question would nudge Eddie towards the pricier option.

Eddie stroked his chin, pretending deliberation. "Decisions, decisions," he muttered, "best make it a double. Wouldn't want to die with a single on my breath, and trust me Landlord, with my luck, that could happen any minute. Then we'd both be stewing, you with the lost profit, me with the missed opportunity."

Pete smiled, pleased with his little game. "Wise thinking, Eddie. That'll be three fifty."

"Stick it on the slate," Eddie mumbled, reaching for his worn wallet anticipating Pete's response.

"You don't have a slate, Eddie,"

"Cruelty, pure cruelty, Landlord," Eddie said, finally coughing up the coins, "didn't get this treatment in my golden days."

"My apologies, sir," Pete said with mock sincerity, "care if I join you?"

Eddie shrugged. "Free country, Landlord. Fill your boots."

They settled into a comfortable silence, two souls bound by shared history and the amber comfort of whiskey, and watched over their flock, paying particular interest in Nessa and Vinnie's blossoming romance.

Vinnie's whiny voice broke the quiet. "Look scrunch buttocks, how many more times do I have to apologise. I'm sorry if you misunderstood what I said, I am really, but you can't go on beatin' me up over it for the rest of the night."

Nessa, stone-faced, gave a dismissive wave. "You're not even close to being forgiven."

"Would it help if I said I loved you more than anything else in the world?" Vinnie said, desperately.

"More than your signed photograph of Scarlett Johansson?" Nessa said, a sly grin creeping across her face.

Vinnie hesitated. "Yeah, definitely."

"And your Triumph Bonneville?" she pressed, raising an eyebrow.

His confidence wavered. "Well, maybe..."

Seeing his struggle, Nessa took a playful jab. "Ok, think about this one carefully. Do you love me more than you love yourself?"

"I don't love myself."

"Oh please, give me a break. Do you know how many mirrors you have in your flat?"

"Like I haven't got better things to do with my life than count mirrors."

"Seven Vinnie. Seven mirrors in a one bedroomed flat," Nessa said accusingly.

"And that means I love myself?" he said, bewildered.

"Well, what do you think it means?"

"It's a small flat. That guy from 'Pimp My Crib' said mirrors make a place look bigger," Vinnie said, fumbling for an answer.

Nessa shook her head, her grin widening. "Honey, it takes you ten minutes to get from the bathroom to the bedroom, stopping at every single mirror to preen like a peacock. That's not normal."

Doughy eyed, Vinnie said, "I only want to look my best for you gorgeous."

"As adorable as that is," Nessa said, her voice softening, "you're still not forgiven."

He pleaded, lowering his voice. "Come on Ness, give me a break, you know you do things to me."

Nessa cut him off with a hushed whisper, "Shh... Keep your voice down."

"Why?"

"I don't want the whole pub knowing about our sordid sex life."

"Not those sorts of things, though now you mention it," Vinnie chuckled, but quickly backtracked. "My point is, you have an effect on me like no woman ever has before. I get goosebumps whenever you enter the room."

"That's got less to do with me and more to do with the fact you're too tight fisted to put the bloody heating on."

Pete's voice boomed through the pub like a foghorn. "Alright, me hearties, time to call it a night. Last orders rung, glasses drained, and doors swingin' shut in ten." A ripple of goodbyes and groans rolled through the room. Stools scraped, laughter faded, and the once-roaring fire dwindled to embers. One by one, they filtered out, leaving behind a trail of empty glasses and fading warmth. Pete, with a practiced sigh, began the nightly ritual of wiping down tables, and humming a mournful tune to the departing crowd.

Nessa and Vinnie lingered, still deep in conversation. His hand, warm and gentle, brushed against hers, a tentative bridge over the chasm of their argument. A smile tugged at the corner of her mouth, mirroring the one playing on his lips. Yet, the question still hung in the air, unspoken but omnipresent: would the wedding invitations gathering dust in the kitchen drawer, ever see the light of day. Vinnie looked up at Nessa, his gaze searching hers, the answer hidden in the depths of her emerald green eyes.

Pete cleared his throat, the sound cutting through the tense silence. "Alright, lovebirds, spill the beans, wedding bells or bust? 'Cause I gotta give the butcher a heads up - two hundred sausages on sticks ain't no joke, and the vol-au-vents are already stacked high enough to reach my kitchen ceiling."

For now, the storm had passed, leaving behind a fragile calm, but beneath the surface, the ocean churned, waiting to reveal its true course.

SIX MONTHS HAD ROLLED through the 'Old Vic', leaving the worn furniture and chipped floorboards undisturbed. Pete still held court behind the bar, his gruff pronouncements seasoned with a touch of amusement as he watched the rapid decline of Psycho Phil's relationship with Janice unfold before his very eyes.

Janice was leaning across the table, her voice tinged with a hopeful tremor. "Sometimes, Pee Pee, it's good to open up a little. Talk about the past, you know?"

"Let's just leave the past in the past shall we and stop calling me Pee Pee," Phil said.

"I'm sorry, I thought you liked it."

"Well, you thought wrong."

"I'm sorry," said Janice.

"And can you please stop fucking apologising every two seconds? It's driving me insane."

"Sorr..." Janice stopped herself, "I just thought it would be good to share our pasts, learn a bit more about each other. It can't be that bad. Bet you were a bit of a scallywag when you were younger."

"Just leave it Janice. I don't need this crap. I've told you before, if you don't like what you got, then fuck off."

"Fine, but don't flatter yourself Psycho. I deserve better."

"Don't make me laugh, you've never had it so good," Phil said.

Janice's shoulders slumped, and she retreated into her chair. The fading light in her eyes was extinguished, replaced by a dull ache of disappointment. She took a long sip of her wine, the clinking of the glass against her cubic zirconia engagement ring, the only sound in the sudden silence between them.

Gordon made his customary flamboyant appearance, dispensing winks and blown kisses at anyone who cared to take notice and sauntered over to the bar. "Looking positively scrumptious tonight, Landlord," he said, "up for a little fun?"

Pete, wiping down a glass with a rag that had seen better days, barely glanced up. "Fancy a slap?"

Gordon's eyes widened. "Kinky," he purred, fluttering his eyelashes, "do tell, will you be wearing rubber gloves?"

"Knuckle duster more like," Pete snorted.

"Ooh, rough and ready, are we?" Gordon teased, "not usually my cup of tea, gorgeous, but for you..." he trailed off suggestively.

"Drink?" Pete cut in.

"You buyin' darlin'?"

"Don't talk daft."

"Ok... Go on then," Gordon conceded with a sigh, "I'll have a Campari and soda."

"Cinzano and diet lemonade it is then."

"And don't forget my cherry gorgeous."

"As if I would," Pete said.

The lone figure of Vinnie, hunched over a flat pint of lager caught Gordon's eye. Classic heartbreak posture, Gordon thought with a sigh. He snagged his drink and wandered over, determined to inject some life into the situation.

"Well, well, well," Gordon said, dropping into the seat beside Vinnie with a theatrical flourish, "look who's drowning his sorrows in the shallow end of the beer garden."

"Not sorrows, GG," Vinnie snapped, "just a quick one after work."

"Whatever floats your boat, gorgeous," Gordon said, stretching out a hand as if to pat Vinnie's shoulder. Vinnie flinched back, his eyes hardening.

"Don't even think about it," Vinnie warned, his voice low.

"Think about what?"

"Touching me."

Gordon's hand hovered for a beat before retracting with a theatrical flourish. "Wouldn't dream of it, darling. Married men and all that."

"Good," Vinnie muttered, taking a long pull of his beer.

Gordon leaned in, his voice dropping to a whisper. "So, spill the beans. How's married life treating you?"

Vinnie hesitated, running a hand through his hair. "It's err... well it's erm... Well, it's married life init."

Gordon raised an eyebrow, a single sardonic laugh escaping his lips. "Riveting, Vinnie. Absolutely riveting. So, where is the pretty little lady tonight?"

"Probably ironing, or cooking, or stuffing her face with chocolates," Vinnie mumbled, avoiding eye contact. "To be honest, I haven't a clue. Just popped in for a quick one on the way home."

"Honestly, darling, being straight seems positively dull. All that domestic bliss. I don't think I could handle the excitement."

Vinnie scowled, clearly annoyed. "Save it, GG. I'm not in the mood for your theatrics."

"Ooohh... Get you sweety, we are having a bad day, aren't we?"

Vinnie crossed his arms. "Look, I just... sometimes you can be a bit much, that's all."

Gordon's smile faltered slightly, the flamboyant facade showing a hint of vulnerability. "Much how? I'm just being myself, Vin. I am what I am."

"All that mincing and pink frilly shirt shit. It's one thing being queer but shouting it from the roof tops is..." Vinnie paused.

"Is what exactly?"

"It's unnecessary, that's what," Vinnie finished.

"But I'm proud of what I am, why should I hide it."

"I'm not saying hide it, just...maybe tone it down a notch sometimes, alright?"

Gordon scoffed playfully. "Oh, Vinnie, you and your rusty thinking. There's nothing wrong with a little flamboyant self-expression, darling, you should try it sometime."

Vinnie didn't respond. His eyes were fixed on Nessa who loomed large in the bar's doorway. She didn't budge, arms crossed and posture rigid. No need to come any closer, not tonight. She was more than capable of articulating what she needed to say from a distance.

"So," she began, each word clipped and sharp, "any idea when you might grace me with your presence at home, Vinnie?" Her gaze flicked around the room, taking in the punters before settling back on him. "Or am I just a fucking afterthought these days?" The question was laced with a quiet fury that resonated far more than a shouted insult.

Before he could stammer an apology, Nessa turned and stormed out. He shoved himself away from the table, his chair scraping back with a screech. In his blind haste, he tripped over a stray leg of someone's barstool and went sprawling. He landed with a thud right at the feet of a burly moustachioed bloke engrossed in a solitary game of darts. "Watch it, mate," the moustache growled, yanking a dart out of the wall with a sharp tug.

Vinnie scrambled to his feet but was in no mood to apologise. Two blokes, faces flushed with beer and bravado, were nose to nose, chests bumping in a slow-motion dance of aggression.

"Oi," bellowed Pete, slamming a tankard on the counter hard enough to make the optics rattle, "if you can't play nice, take it outside."

His booming voice usually did the trick, but tonight, it had the opposite effect. The two men shoved each other, a tangle of limbs and muttered insults. Pete's face reddened further. "Alright, that's enough, lads. Sit down before I throw you both out."

His words were lost in the rising tide of their argument, but before he could take any direct action, Psycho Phil moved in with a predator's grace, all coiled tension and sharp edges. A ghost of a smile on his face, a promise of violence to come. He leaned in, his lips brushing Vinnie's ear. Whatever he whispered must have struck a nerve because Vinnie's bravado crumbled. He stumbled back, fear carved on his face, and retreated to a corner, sinking into a chair with a defeated slump.

Moustache man, fuelled by liquid courage and misplaced anger, swung a clumsy punch at Phil, who dodged with ease, the fist whistling past his ear. Before the attacker could regain his balance, Phil moved with a lightning-fast precision. A sickening crunch echoed through the pub as he clamped down on the man's nose with his teeth. He didn't stop there. As the moustache shrieked in pain, Phil followed up with a brutal twist of the guy's man tackle.

With a final shove, he sent the man staggering face-first into the dartboard. A collective gasp rose from the onlookers as a crimson flower bloomed on the man's forehead. Phil, unfazed, plucked a dart from the board and held it mere millimetres from the man's eye. A low growl escaped his throat, the words inaudible but the message clear.

Then, just as abruptly as the violence began, it ended. Phil tossed the dart back in the board, the man scrambling to keep his balance. Blood streamed down his face, and he bolted out of the pub, a whimpering cry echoing in his wake.

Phil sauntered back to his seat, wiping his hand absently on his trousers. He stopped by the shaking figure of Vinnie. A curt nod, a gesture for him to stand. Vinnie obeyed, flinching as Phil used his shirt to wipe the blood off his own face. With a final, chilling pat on the shoulder, Phil returned to his drink, leaving Vinnie a quivering mess.

The pub went back to its usual business. The brawl was just another Saturday night at the 'Old Vic'. Only a few lingering stares and the crimson stain on the dartboard hinted at the brutal scene that had just unfolded.

"There's one in the pump and a glass of wine for Janice when you're ready Psycho," Pete said, with a hint of begrudging respect.

"Cheers Landlord, pull mine when you're ready, but forget the wine, Janice is just leaving."

"Am I?" Janice said, surprised.

With a wordless huff, Phil strode over to the bar and took up residence on a solitary barstool usually reserved for Eddie but was fair game in his absence. Janice took the hint and like a scolded child, snatched her coat and left, melting into the background like yesterday's news.

By the time last orders rang through the bar, Pete was glad to see the back of it, a feeling that settled heavier with each passing sunset. Cindy's voice echoed in his head. Would he really be leaving the 'Old Vic' in a wooden box? His mind drifted towards visions of sun-warmed days spent sipping icy sangria, the worries of the world melting away faster than the ice cubes. But all he craved right now was the quiet murmur of an empty pub, a glass of Macallan single malt and a steaming plate of Chicken Balti from Punjabi Palace – his greasy spoon saving grace for late night woes.

AS AUTUMN GAVE WAY to a bitter winter, the 'Old Vic' provided a shelter to the destitute waifs and strays who took advantage of the roaring open fire, nursing half pints of Theakston's Old Peculiar which could last them hours. They were never going to fund Pete's Spanish retirement, but they were welcome none the less. They were the Grimsby he knew, the remnants of a town ravaged by hard times, clinging to faded memories of when the docks teemed with life and Grimsby was the jewel in the crown of fishing ports. Now, all that was left was a town clinging on for dear life, with its past glory fading faster than a half-forgotten dream.

Vinnie, already four pints in, picked up his drink and scanned the room for a free table. While he'd been perfectly happy propping up the bar, he knew Nessa was on her way and would expect a modicum of comfort. He was practically furniture here these days, yet somehow remained table-less. Just another apprentice in the grand scheme of the bar's regulars, stuck in purgatory between the sticky booths and the coveted corner tables. As he stood pondering his next move, Nessa swanned in, assessed the situation and flashed a smile at a drunken octogenarian. The old fella, flustered and a little befuddled, doffed his cap and shuffled over to the bar, leaving his throne vacant and allowing Nessa to sit down. Vinnie plonked his drink down and nabbed the free chair next to her, the rightful owner likely halfway through a desperate bladder evacuation. All's fair in love and beer, Vinnie thought to himself.

"So, do you want to explain what you were saying before you stormed out two hours ago to get a bag of sugar and never returned?" Nessa said accusingly.

"I don't know what I was saying," Vinnie said, wracking his brain.

"Well," Nessa said, "would you like to hear what I think you were saying?"

"Do I have a choice?"

"Sure you do. You can either listen to what I think you were saying, or you can go fuck yourself."

Vinnie, full of the bravado four pints provides, shot back. "Hmm... as well-endowed and flexible as I am, self-copulation would still be a bit of a stretch, so let's go with your words of wisdom darling."

"Don't try and be funny Vincent, it doesn't suit you. Ten months of wedded bliss? Now that's fucking funny. If you've had enough and want to revert back to your sad, sick, hedonistic, juvenile ways, then at least man up and be honest."

"I see you're talking bollocks as usual."

"Am I?"

"Sounds like a load of bollocks to me."

"Any conversation that doesn't include beer, rugby, sex and Top Gear sounds like a load of bollocks too you *darling*."

"So, what are *you* saying?" Vinnie said.

"I'm saying it ain't working. I'm saying you're not cut out to be married. I'm saying I deserve better. I'm saying it's the end of the road Vinnie baby, time to go our separate ways."

"Come on Ness don't be like that. It's just..."

"Just what?"

"I just need a little time."

"Well, you got it sweet cheeks. You got all the time you want; I'm done."

And with that she was gone. Out into the cold night air with a head full of woe betides, regret and sorrow.

Eddie and Cindy had watched the drama unfold from their stools at the bar and shook their heads, both displaying a knowing smile.

"Aww... Bless 'em," Cindy said, "seldom does the course of true love run smoothly."

"Ain't that the truth," Eddie said.

"You ever been in love Eddie."

"Only with my beer... You?"

"Only time I fell for a bloke was Psycho, and that was a mistake worse than picking a fight with a bear. Between you and me, I think the guy's got a few screws loose."

"I think he's misunderstood," Eddie said.

"Vinnie, you mean? Nah, that one's just a walking disaster."

"No, I meant Psycho."

"Oh him... I think he's a bit 'chicken oriental.'"

"Yeah, he can be a bit stupid at times."

"Calling him stupid is an insult to all the stupid people."

"That new bird Janice seems to have had an effect though." Eddie said.

"Maybe, I dunno, what kind of effect, you know?" Cindy said, downing her drink. "He seems way more, uh, subdued since they met, and he never brings her in anymore."

"Landlord says she's been poorly?"

"Poorly for about six months. More likely just an excuse so she doesn't have to spend time with the twisted fuck."

Gordon, ordinarily the master of indiscretion, had tried to avoid prying eyes and skulked in through the back door, the one usually reserved for deliveries and drunken escapes. He sidled in with a stranger and parked him in a shadowed corner attracting a few suspicious glances. Like a lion protecting its prey, his eyes darted around the room, warning off any potential scavengers. Truth be told, judging by the crumpled mess snoring softly on the worn leather bench, anyone with half a mind wouldn't bother trying to muscle in on whatever deal Gordon had going on. He ambled over to the bar, a casualness that belied his eagerness, and caught Cindy and Eddie's eye before ordering his customary drink.

"Well, what d'you think?" Gordon said to anyone who cared to bite.

Cindy took the bait. "About what?"

"About that hunk of gorgeousness smouldering in the corner over there."

"Can't say we'd noticed. With you, is he?" Eddie said.

"You bet gorgeous, and he's mine I tell ya, all mine so keep your grubby little fingers to yourself," Gordon said casting an eye over his new love interest and giving a little wave that wasn't reciprocated.

"I'll do my best GG," Eddie chuckled, "but I can't promise my supressed pillow biting tendencies won't get the better of me before the evening's out. Where'd you meet?"

"I kinda ran into him just around the corner in Turkey Cock Lane".

"How romantic," Cindy said, "did your eyes meet across the cobbled stones?"

"Not quite sweety, he was lying in the gutter."

Pete leaned in confused. "Excuse me?"

"I found him lying in the gutter."

"What was he doin' in the gutter?" Eddie said.

"Not sure really. I did think it was a bit strange," Gordon admitted.

"GG, hun, have you picked up a tramp?" Cindy enquired.

"I've read about this hobo erotica stuff'" Pete said.

"Hobo what?"

"I watch Jeremy Kyle, they have 'em all on there. Heterosexuals, homosexuals, metrosexuals, bisexuals and now hobosexuals, what's the world coming too?"

"He's *not* a tramp," Gordon said defensively.

"What's his name?" Cindy said.

"Not sure."

"Didn't you ask him?"

"Yeah of course I asked him."

"And what did he say?"

"Not a lot. In fact, he hasn't said anything at all yet," Gordon confessed.

"Jesus Gordon," Pete said, "you can't go around dragging drunken bums into the nearest pub and start seducing 'em. Trust me, it doesn't make for a stable long-term relationship. How do you even know he's gay?"

"Gaydar gorgeous, gaydar. We just know. Don't ask me how, it's in our genes."

"Yeah well, I'd find out for sure before you slip your hand in *his* jeans, he don't look gay too me," Cindy said.

"What do you know," Gordon said, defiantly, "did George Michael look gay?"

"Yeah," Eddie replied.

"Ok I'll give that one... How about Freddie Mercury?"

"Hell yeah," came a collective reply.

Gordon was getting desperate. "Cliff Richard?"

"He ain't gay," Eddie said.

"Isn't he?"

"No... So much for your bloody gaydar GG," Pete said laughing.

"My point is, they come in all kinds of shapes, sizes and varying degrees of gayness."

"So, you got a plan?" Cindy said, "you can't just park him in the corner, gawping at him like a lovestruck teenager."

"Of course I've got a plan sugar, and I don't gawp. Once he sobers up, it's back to mine for some sex, drugs and rock n roll."

"Well, just you be careful young man, there are some strange folk about," Pete warned him.

"Aww... How sweet," Gordon said, blowing Pete a kiss, "I didn't know you cared."

The night was getting long in the tooth, and while Pete wasn't one to turn down a steady income stream, Vinnie was starting to worry him. Not that he was keeping count, but the mountain of empty pint glasses and the half drunk bottle of Jack Daniels teetering precariously on the edge of Vinnies table told him enough was enough. He leaned over the bar, voice raised just enough to compete with the pub din. "Vinnie, mate... You alright over there?" No response. Just the slow, sad tilt of Vinnie's head as it lolled from side to side. He tried for a second time, a little louder this time. Vinnie's head snapped up, vacant eyes scanning the room until they landed on Pete. He blinked, once, twice, then a flicker of recognition sparked behind them. A slow, lopsided grin spread across his face, and he gave Pete a thumbs up. Pete grimaced and gestured with his hand. "Come here son, let's have a word."

The world tilted precariously as Vinnie attempted to stand. His brain, several pints past coherence, sent conflicting signals to his limbs. He gripped the armrest as if it were the only thing anchoring him to reality. A slow-motion groan escaped his lips, a testament to the effort required for this seemingly simple task. Taking a deep breath, he grabbed his bottle of Jack Daniels and set off on his unsteady voyage across the pub floor. Each step was a deliberate act of will, a battle against gravity and his own inebriation. He resembled a toddler taking his first steps, his progress slow and erratic.

Only Vinnie knows what possessed him to stop halfway. Swaying perilously like a shipwreck in a storm, he dominated the centre of the pub, as his sudden off-key rendition of 'Heartbreak Hotel' battled with the bar's jukebox. His eyes, glazed and unfocused, seemed to search for a band that wasn't there, while his half-empty bottle of Jack Daniels threatened to become a microphone at any moment.

Every note was a war crime against music, but he belted it out with the passion of a thousand loves lost.

Every off-key screech was a liability waiting to happen, threatening to chase away the poor sods currently queuing three deep at the bar with wallets already halfway open. Pete was torn, rescue Vinnie or take the readies? Ever the pragmatist, he called upon the pub's elder statesman. "Do something about that will you Eddie."

"And what exactly would you like me to do with him?" Eddie said.

"Just get him to calm down a bit and stop that bloody racket spewing out of his mouth."

"Why me?"

"Because he respects you," Pete said, thinking it was as good a reason as any.

Eddie laughed. "He's a kid Landlord, he don't respect anyone."

"Whatever, just go have a quiet word, before I ask Psycho to chuck him out".

"You can kick the drunken bum out for all I care, I'm not his fucking marriage guidance counsellor."

Never one to miss a trick, Pete said, "He's got half a bottle of Jack Daniels in his hand."

Like a bear to a honey pot, Eddie had the sudden urge to become the good Samaritan. "I'll see what I can do, but no promises."

Eddie strode over to Vinnie and put an arm around his shoulder. "Come on young feller me lad, let's sit you down before you fall down," Eddie said, tugging Vinnie in the direction of the nearest chair.

Vinnie resisted. "I don't wanna sit down, I'm dancin.'"

"Is that what you call it? Thought you were having a fit. Look, at least stop your wailin' and give me the bottle."

"Wailin'... I'm not wailin', I'm singin', singin' about the love I've lost, singin' about the most beautiful girl in the world."

And with that, Vinnie gave Elvis a break and instead decided to butcher Charlie Rich's greatest hit. In any other circumstance, Eddie would have felt he'd given it his best shot and retreated to the comfort of his favourite barstool. But the lure of the half bottle of Jack Daniels being waved around like a conductor's baton gave him that extra little bit of incentive he needed to sort Vinnie out.

"Come on Vinnie give me the bottle, you've had more than enough for one night," Eddie said, trying to prise it out of his hands.

"Leave me alone Eddie," Vinnie said, "I'm havin' a good time and you're just campin... crimpin... crampin' my style. You see, I'm young, free and singular again, the world's my lobster."

As Vinnie went to take a swig of his whiskey, Eddie snatched it out of his hands. "Give me that back ya bastard, before I teach you a lesson you won't... you won't... thingamajig."

"I said you've had enough Vinnie, and I meant it. Now sit the fuck down before I call Psycho over."

Maybe it was the fear of Psycho Phil's intervention or simply Vinnie's newfound inability to defy gravity any longer that finally convinced him to sit. Right there, in the middle of the bar, he slumped down, cross-legged like a weary yogi.

"What you doin'?" Eddie said.

"Doin' what I was told."

"Get up you idiot."

"Make up your friggin' mind," Vinnie said, "sit down... get up... stop dribblin'... I mean drinkin'. Who'd you think you are, me dad?"

"Trust me son, if I was your dad I'd have given you a good hiding by now."

With a grunt and a heave and a well-timed assist from Psycho Phil, who'd been keeping a watchful eye, they managed to get Vinnie into a corner. There, they propped him up like a slightly worse-for-wear tailor's dummy.

"Now sit there and don't move until I say so. Understand?" Eddie said.

"Yes dad. Can I have my whiskey please?"

"What whiskey," Eddie said, placing the half empty bottle out of harm's way on another table.

"I had a boddle of whiskey."

"It was empty Vin, told you you'd had too much. Now just sit there while I get..."

He didn't get to finish. Vinnie lurched and gripped Eddie's lapels. Nose-to-nose, Eddie was trapped in a cloud of cheap liquor and regret. Vinnie's bloodshot eyes swam with maudlin sentiment, a forced smile threatening to morph into a sob.

"I love her Eddie, I love her more than life itself," Vinnie said. "Why... why did she leave. I'm not a bad man."

"Alright, alright, Romeo," Eddie said, disentangling himself from Vinnie's grasp. He scrambled back a few paces and threw himself into a chair across the table, using it as a makeshift barrier. "Pull yourself together son. Sometimes things just aren't meant to be. Have you spoken to her?"

"She won't see me, Eddie. I've tried, honestly I've tried but she just gets that truffle hunter friend of hers to answer the door. She's a right bitch that one," Vinnie said before bursting into tears and slamming his head down on the table much harder than he intended.

If anyone had been paying any attention to the little drama going on with Eddie and Vinnie, their attention was soon turned. Cindy, face flushed and arms straining, stumbled in with a sight that put the rest of the night's chaos to shame. Gorgeous Gordon, usually the picture of preened perfection, hung limply over her shoulder like a discarded rag doll. His once-crisp shirt was crumpled, and a blood stain was slowly blooming across its pristine fabric.

"Give us a hand someone," Cindy pleaded.

"Jesus Christ, what happened?" Pete said as he rushed from behind the bar and helped Cindy get Gordon into a chair. Psycho Phil joined them and stood guard, cordoning off the scene from prying eyes.

"Found him in the car park," Cindy said, "I'd just popped round the back with a punter, heard some groaning and thought 'well done D another satisfied customer' then realised it was coming from behind the wheelie bin. Anyway, I whips up me knickers and have a look and found GG like this. Punters done a runner without paying though, the bastard."

Pete took the tea towel tucked in his belt and tentatively started cleaning up Gordon's face, a roadmap of pain. Blood dripped from a cut above his eyebrow, tracing a crimson line down his temple. Above a split lip, already blooming purple at the edges, his left eye was a swollen, half-closed mess. Every breath he took seemed to hitch slightly, a sign of unseen injuries.

"Can you hear me Gordon," Pete said, without eliciting a reply. "Come on GG, can you hear me? Do you know where you are?"

"GG sweetie, look at me, it's Cindy. Can you see me. Can you talk?"

There was a flicker of recognition, then barely audible, Gordon said, "Hiya D, you look gorgeous this evening."

Relieved and with tear drenched eyes, Cindy said, "Oh Gordon, what have you done?"

"Let's get him through the back," Pete said, and although he didn't need to ask if anyone had called an ambulance, he asked anyway just in case everyone had assumed someone else had.

As Pete and Cindy gingerly carried Gordon through to a back room, Psycho Phil grabbed his coat and made for the exit.

"Where you goin' Psycho?" Pete said.

"To find the bastard, where d'you think I'm goin'?"

"We'll call the police, let them take care of it."

"We take care of our own Landlord, when did we start involving the dibbles?" Phil said.

"We take care of our own inside these four walls Psycho, out there it's none of our business."

Phil wasn't up for a debate. "Well, I just made it my fucking business," he said, before storming out of the pub.

Vinnie, a snot-dripping fountain of misery, had Eddie by the emotional short and curlies. Ignoring the Gordon situation, for now, Eddie focused on his most immediate problem. Vinnie needed a babysitter more than Gordon needed a hero and he was about to impart some hard-earned wisdom.

"It's about give and take son," Eddie said, "about compromises. You need to take a long hard look at your life and decide what's important to you."

Vinnie pondered Eddies advice before answering. "Whiskey's important to me, where's my whiskey."

"I told you before Vin, it's empty. Besides it ain't the answer, never was and never will be."

"I'm not looking for answers. I'm looking to get smashed out me 'ead."

"And then what?"

"And then nothin'."

"You think she'll come crawling back when you're in this state?"

"Don't give a fuck."

"Really?"

"Really."

Eddie wasn't a preacher. He hadn't exactly mastered the art of learning from his own mistakes, let alone advising others on how to navigate life. But Vinnie... Vinnie was different. There was a vulnerability in the guy, a flicker of something lost that snagged at something deep in Eddie's gut. He simply couldn't bear the thought of Vinnie following in his footsteps, ending up like him—a melancholic, sad old fucker with a penchant for the bottle.

"I've been where you are more times than I care to remember son. Choose the wrong path now and there ain't no goin' back." He leant over the table and cupped Vinnie's face in his hands, pulling it close to his own. "Look at this face Vinnie, look into these eyes, there's nothing there, just black holes tinged with red. Whiskey has robbed me of everything that ever meant anything to me. Is this what you aspire to be, is this the life you want to lead?"

The sobs returned, a fresh wave of tears threatening to drown Vinnie. Eddie fished out a monogrammed hankie from his waistcoat. The faded initials 'EF' were barely visible, a relic from a time when someone – a wife, a mother – had cared enough to stitch them there.

"I want her back Eddie," Vinnie pleaded, "I'll do anything to get her back, please help me."

"I'll do what I can Vin, I promise. But for now, let's get your sorry arse home and see what tomorrow brings."

Eddie helped Vinnie to his feet and wrapped his arm around his shoulder. Vinnie was drunk enough for both, and they staggered towards the door like a vaudeville double act.

"All sorted Eddie?" Pete shouted as he spotted them leaving.

"Yeah, all sorted," Eddie said. "How's GG?"

"He'll survive, I think his pride took a bigger beating than he did. They've just taken him down to A & E, D's gone with him."

"OK... Catch you later Landlord."

"Don't forget your mate Jack Daniels," Pete said.

Eddie turned his head and looked at the half empty bottle still sat on a nearby table. It smiled at him in the way only whiskey can. He turned back and looked at Vinnie. Eddie had fought this battle more times than he cared to remember, but tonight it was a battle he was determined to win, all the time knowing the war was far from over.

"He's no mate of mine Landlord," Eddie said walking out the door, "I'll see you around."

IT WAS UNUSUALLY QUIET for a Saturday night and Pete was sharing his worries with Cindy that the events of the past couple of weeks might have scared away the punters, so he was pleased when Psycho Phil, one of his more profitable customers strolled in and ordered his usual.

"There you go Psycho," Pete said sliding his pint of Black Velvet across the bar. "Just a head's up, there were a couple of plain clothes in earlier asking questions."

A flicker of something cold crossed Phil's face at the mention of the police, a fleeting glimpse of worry quickly masked by a tight smile. "What kind of questions?" Phil said.

"Usual stuff, had I seen you, when were you last in."

"What did you say?"

"Something to the effect of 'Who's Psycho Phil'?"

"Cheers Landlord," Phil said.

"No problem, but I think they'll be back. I take it you caught up with GG's friend then?"

"Nope, never found him. I think they'd like a chat about another matter."

"Care to share?" Cindy said, joining the conversation.

Phil chose to ignore her.

"OK... None of our business," Pete said, knowing when to shut up.

"Nope, it ain't," Phil said, and with that, he settled into his customary spot in the corner and waited patiently for the night to unfold.

Cindy gave half a thought to joining Phil and pressing him further but decided against it. There was something particularly unsettling about him that she hadn't seen for a long time, and she remembered all too well how that scenario played out. Instead, she turned to Pete and said, "Told you."

"Told me what?"

"Told you what the word on the street was."

"It don't mean they're right. You know what nosy neighbours are like, couldn't tell a fact from a fish if their lives depended on it. Remember that old girl Olive and the whole 'alien abduction' business?"

"Who's been abducted by aliens?" Vinnie said as he approached the bar having caught the end of the conversation.

"Long story," Cindy said, "best told when you're three sheets to the wind."

"Fair enough. Anyway, good to see you D, looking cheap as usual."

"Watch your lip sunshine, you ain't too big for a good slappin'."

"Will it cost me?" Vinnie said.

"Nope," said Cindy, "I'll happily slap you for free and enjoy every minute of it."

Spotting Phil nursing his pint across the room, Vinnie shouted, "You hear that Psycho, free slapping's for tonight only. Want me to put your name down?" Phil looked up briefly but didn't respond.

"Drink Vinnie?" Pete said.

"Just a shandy please Landlord."

"Sorry?"

"No need to be sorry," Vinnie said, "just a shandy please."

"Shandy?" Pete said, baffled.

"Yes, a shandy, if it's not too much trouble."

Pete turned to Cindy. "Did he say 'shandy'?"

"I do believe he did," Cindy said.

"I don't sell shandy."

"What do you mean you don't sell Shandy?"

"What do you mean 'what do I mean'?"

"How can you *not* sell shandy?" Vinnie said, confused. "You sell lager, don't you?"

"Of course," Pete said.

"And you sell lemonade?"

"Yep."

"In that case, you sell Shandy. Just mix the two together and Roberts your mother's brother," Vinnie said, stating the obvious.

Cindy was intrigued. "Don't want to pry Vin, but you haven't gone all Gorgeous Gordon on us, have you?"

"Because I want a shandy?"

"Just curious," Cindy said.

"What has wanting a Shandy got to do with being gay?"

"Well..." Pete hesitated looking for the right words, "it's a bit of a girly drink init."

"It's the drink of a man in control of his excesses Landlord. It's the drink of a man who's turned his life around, it's the drink of a man who..."

Pete had heard enough. "Alright, all right, I don't need chapter and verse, lager shandy coming up."

Vinnie looked back over at Phil, who's chin was still buried deep in his chest, eyes firmly focused on his pint. "What's wrong with Psycho? Looks like he lost a tenner and found turd."

"You haven't heard then?" Cindy said.

"Heard what?"

"What the neighbours are sayin'."

"No, what are they sayin'?"

"It ain't lookin' good," Pete said.

"What isn't?"

"His future," Cindy said.

Vinnie was getting frustrated. "For fucks sake, will someone tell me what I've missed?"

"Well according to the neighbours..." Cindy didn't get to finish. The bar doors swung open with intent. Two young coppers, faces grim and freshly scrubbed, piled through first, followed by a figure who filled the doorway with the lived-in authority of a seasoned pro, Detective Trev Jones, a career copper well known to the 'Old Vic' faithful. The two uniforms strategically placed themselves at the only two exits in the bar, while Detective Jones sauntered over to Phil who raised his head and gave a wry smile.

"Evening Psycho, how you doin'?"

"Evenin' Jonesy, been better I guess. Fancy a drink?"

"I won't if you don't mind. Got time for a little chat?"

"Sure," said Phil, "pull up a chair, always got time of the dibbles."

"Thought it might be better down at the station. Give us a bit of privacy," Detective Jones said.

"Yeah, maybe you're right. Mind if I finish my beer?"

"Rather you didn't but suspect you're going to anyway."

He was right. Phil had no plans to be obstructive, but something told him it could be a long, long time before he experienced the sweet taste of 'Black Velvet' again. In one swift movement he drained his glass, and a sigh escaped his lips, a mix of contentment and melancholy. He held his hands out in front of him and one of the uniforms prompted by a nod of the head from Detective Jones, approached and slapped on the cuffs. Pete held open the bar door as Phil was led towards the exit.

"Do me a favour Landlord," Phil said as he passed, "look after D for me."

"Sure Psycho," Pete said, "she's in good hands."

Cindy and Vinnie watched on as Phil was ushered through the exit.

"Think he'll be back?" Vinnie said, his voice barely a whisper.

"Not sure Vin. I think this time he's crossed a line he can't come back from," Cindy said, resigned.

————— ⚬⚬⚬ —————

WITH PSYCHO PHIL OUT of the picture, the 'Old Vic' wasn't just buzzing with rumours, it felt like a hornet's nest had been kicked over. Phil's presence as unnerving as it could be, always offered a sense of comfort and security. With Phil around, everyone knew where they stood. Now it felt like a tinderbox waiting for a spark and was in danger of turning the local boozer into a Wild West saloon.

Cindy was drowning her sorrows sat at the bar, looking for a sympathetic or consoling word from Pete that never came, when the door creaked open, momentarily distracting her. A figure shuffled in, hunched and defeated. It took a second for Cindy to recognise Gordon, his face still sporting the colourful remnants of a black eye and a split lip. It was his first appearance since the whole 'tramp tryst' debacle two weeks ago, and Cindy felt a surge of something other than misery for the first time since Phil got arrested. A flicker of relief and something maternal sparked in her chest. Phil might be gone, but at least she could focus on someone else's troubles for a bit.

"Oh, GG sweety, ain't you a sight for sore eyes?" Cindy said, giving Gordon a hug that squeezed every breath of air out of his lungs.

"Hi D," Gordon said with a breathless effort.

"How you been? Heard they caught the bastard that beat the crap out of ya?"

"Caught him, released him sugar. Said they had no evidence, my word against his," Gordon said, deflated.

"For fuck's sake," Pete chipped in, "where's Psycho when you need him?"

"Talking of who, you heard from him D?" Gordon said.

"Nah... Tried to arrange a visit, but he refused to see me."

"No chance of bail then?" Pete said.

"Not bloody likely," Cindy said. "Spoke to his solicitor, he's going for voluntary manslaughter on the grounds of diminished responsibility."

"And the CPS are gonna go with that?"

"Not a chance, it's murder or nothing. Some of Janice's family have crawled out of the woodwork demanding the return of the death penalty, it's turning into a right media circus."

"Seems a little harsh," Gordon said, "he cut her up into bite size pieces, stuffed her in a hoover bag and used her as cavity wall insulation."

"And your point is?" Pete said, looking for clarification.

"Well gorgeous, that's not exactly the actions of someone of sound mind, is it?

"No, it's the actions of a fucking psychopath," Cindy said.

"Still don't know what you're getting at GG."

"Duh... Remind me not to employ either of you as my defence next time I get caught cottaging. Psycho Phil practically has 'abnormality of the mind' tattooed on his forehead. What more do they need for diminished responsibility?"

Pete pondered on Gordon's knowledge of the British legal system as he poured him a gratis Cinzano and lemonade and then tried to charge him for the cherry.

"How do you know all this shit GG?" Pete said.

"Experience sweety. My old man killed his second wife, his girlfriend, and his Thai lady boy lover during some bizarre sex fest at a Butlins Glam Rock weekend and he pleaded diminished responsibility," Gordon declared.

"Shit... I remember that," Cindy said.

"Christ Gordon, I'm sorry. Didn't realise you had a looney tune for an old man."

"You don't know the half of it Landlord, he was a right evil bastard, made Psycho Phil look like Mary Poppins. Fortunately, my mum got out alive, but only just."

"He tried to kill her as well?" Cindy said.

"Numerous times, still gives me nightmares."

"So did the CPS accept his plea?"

"No," Gordon said, "but it was a travesty really, he was dressed as Gary Glitter when he killed them. I mean, how can you argue against 'abnormality of the mind' when someone dresses like Gary Glitter."

The awkward silence after Gordon's revelation was broken by the appearance of Nessa and Vinnie, a couple of strangers since Vinnie's emotional alcohol fuelled breakdown. Vinnie knew his place and headed for the bar to order drinks, while Nessa, ever the pragmatist, spotted a free table and made a beeline for it. Cindy and Gordon practically leapt out of their seats to join her, eager to catch up and pry into the details of Nessa and Vinnie's fractured relationship.

"Well hello stranger," Cindy said, planting a kiss on Nessa's cheek, "long time no parlez."

"Hey D, how's things?" Nessa said.

"Good as can be expected, I guess. You heard about Psycho I take it?"

"Yeah, Vinnie told me, I'm sorry."

"No need to be sorry hun, he deserves everything he gets. Just wish I could get the mad bastard out of my head."

"Love's a bitch ain't it?"

"Finding it is the bitch," Gordon said, exasperated.

"Still no joy on the love front then, GG?" Nessa said.

"Nope, I'm out of ideas I'm afraid hun. My last attempt at gutter love ended in disaster so I'm preparing for a life of celibacy."

"Stop being a drama queen you old drama queen," Cindy chided, "there's someone for everyone out there in that big bad wide world, just gotta spread your wings and go find 'em."

"For you maybe D, but for me, I'm destined to die a sad, lonely old puff, surrounded by my fluffy teddies and Clark Gable videos."

Vinnie drummed his fingers on the tacky bar top, his patience wearing thin as he waited for Pete to swap out a barrel of Timothy Taylor's. He toyed with the idea of popping behind the bar and serving himself and then remembered the fate of the last poor soul who thought that was a good idea. Old-timers still whispered about 'Tugboat' Dave; a poor sod who'd tried the self-serve route a good ten years back. Pete, all of eleven stones soaking wet back then, had wrestled 'Tugboat', a man twice his size, to the floor in a legendary display of barkeep fury. Vinnie shuddered. He wasn't about to test if Pete still had that kind of fight in him.

"Sorry to keep you Vinnie, what will it be?" Pete said as his head popped out of the cellar door.

"Baileys over ice for the special one and a fresh orange juice for me please Landlord," Vinnie said.

"Fresh orange eh... Lager shandy but too much to handle?" Pete said, as he handed Vinnie his drink before pouring Nessa's Bailey's.

Vinnie took a sip and recoiled. "What the hell's this?"

"Fresh orange juice," Pete said, "what does it look like?"

"I know it's fresh orange juice," Vinnie said.

"The why ask?"

"Because it's supposed to be a 'nudge, nudge, wink, wink' fresh orange juice."

"A what?" Pete said.

"A 'nudge, nudge, wink, wink' orange juice. An orange juice for the supposed teetotaller, an orange juice for the alleged abstainer, an orange juice with a double vodka in it."

"Well maybe if you'd bothered to give me a nudge or a wink, I might have known what the fuck you were talking about," Pete said, clearly irritated.

"Do I look like a guy who drinks fresh orange juice without vodka in it?" Vinnie said.

"No, you look like a guy who's testing the patience of a pub landlord. Now do you want a vodka in it or don't you?"

"Yeah, if it ain't too much trouble."

Across the room, Gordon was keen to know whether Vinnie and Ness had returned to wedded bliss or if the wheels had fallen off the wedding car.

"I was hoping to convince Vinnie to try batting for the other side Ness but looks like I'm too late," Gordon said.

"It's never too late GG, he's fair game as far as I'm concerned."

"Oh, I see, sorry I just thought... Well with you two coming in together, that... You know what I'm getting at sweety. Sorry didn't mean to pry, none of my business I know."

"It's ok. He's trying to make amends. Says he's a changed man, though I've yet to be convinced," Nessa said.

Before Gordon could probe any further, Cindy chimed in, "Damn, how many times we heard that one. Though I did bump into a changed man last week, he used to be one of my regulars."

"Settled down had he," Nessa said, "changed into a faithful husband and doting father?"

"Nah, changed into a cock loving cross-dresser with a penchant for teenage boys. Shame really, he was a good earner."

Nessa started to laugh before realising Cindy had been serious and didn't find it particularly funny. Quickly changing subjects, she shouted over to Vinnie. "So, any chance of a drink then Vincent, or did we just come to watch everyone else partake."

Vinnie was in the throes of knocking back his vodka and orange and nearly spat it out at the sound of Nessa barking orders at him. "On the way darling, Landlord cocked up the order," he shouted back. He turned to Pete and said, "Stick us another orange juice in there will ya."

Pete looked at him blankly.

"Please," Vinnie said.

Pete continued to stare but didn't respond.

"Hello, earth to Landlord, anyone home."

"Sorry Vin," Pete said, "I was just waiting for a nudge or a wink or a tick or a nod, I'd hate to cock up your order again."

"Ok... Ok point taken, no Tourette's this time, just a straight orange juice if you please, she's taste testing my drinks."

Pete obliged and Vinnie strolled over to Nessa wearing a forced smile. "There you go my darling, Bailey's over ice."

"About bloody time," Nessa said before grabbing Vinnie's orange juice, taking a sip, and handing it back.

"Anything else sweetheart," Vinnie said, "maybe some pork scratchings or some nice salty nuts?

"When have you ever known me to eat pork scratchings?"

"I haven't, but I know you're partial to a couple of nice salty..."

"Mouth is open Vinnie, should be shut."

"Sorry," said Vinnie as he took a drink of his orange juice and feigned delight.

There was an awkward silence. Vinnie, ever the cautious one, chewed on his lip, his mind a minefield of potential conversational missteps. Silence had become his default these days, a self-preservation tactic that backfired more often than not. Across from him, Nessa simmered. She felt a flicker of the spark they once shared, a spark she yearned to rekindle. But waiting on Vinnie to ignite it felt like waiting for rain in the desert. The result? A stony indifference, a cold reflection of the distance that had grown between them.

Cindy felt like the proverbial gooseberry and couldn't decide whether to act as conciliator or simply get up and leave and try her luck with a lonely looking punter propped up at the bar singing to himself and butchering 'Bohemian Rhapsody'.

Gordon, oblivious as ever, didn't pick up on the unspoken tension around the table. The nonverbal cues were flashing neon, but they went right over his head. "Anyone seen Eddie lately?"

Vinnie, picking at a chipped nail, mumbled, "Nah, not a peep. Last I saw of him was the morning after the night before and that must have been a couple of months back."

"He'll be on one of his voyages of discovery," Cindy said. "D'you know we once ran away together?"

Nessa choked on her Bailey's, spraying laughter that died quickly in her throat. "You and Eddie? Seriously?"

Cindy shrugged. "Uh huh...America"

"Wow," Nessa said, surprised.

"Yep," Cindy confirmed, eyes distant. "Eddie was at rock bottom, and I wasn't far behind. We were sitting right here when he declared he was off to the States to find fame and fortune. I said half-jokingly, could he fit me in his suitcase. He said he was 'travelling light' but I was welcome to tag along and that's exactly what I did. Put in a few extra hours, sold everything I owned, booked a ticket and bam. New life in New York City."

"Did it work out?" Nessa leaned forward, genuinely curious.

Cindy chuckled; a touch bitter. "Look at me Ness, what do you think."

"Sorry."

"No need to be sorry. At least we tried, right? Turns out, we were both dreamers with empty pockets and were always destined to be just a couple of bums with ideas above our station. We never quite climbed out of the gutter, no matter where we went. Turns out, the New York gutters ain't much different, no matter where you live. The 'American Dream' became a bit of a nightmare, but hey, we met some interesting folks along the way."

"Bet none were as interesting as me sugar pie," Gordon announced, gesturing with a flourish that nearly knocked over an empty beer bottle.

"You're certainly a one off GG, I'll give you that," Cindy said.

"Well, if you'll excuse me lovies, it's way past my beddy-bye, time for some beauty sleep. Big night tomorrow," Gordon said, excited.

Vinnie, doodling a wonky heart in spilled beer, looked up "Why what's happening?"

"You serious?" Cindy said.

"Do I look like I'm joking?"

"It's New Years Eve numb nuts," Nessa reminded him.

"The biggest party night of my year gorgeous. The night I might finally get whisked away in the arms of my knight in shining... leather," Gordon said, visibly weak at the knees at the very thought.

"Oh, tomorrow is it?" Vinnie mumbled, feigning forgetfulness. "Think I might stay in and watch it on the tele. All that partying, drinking and debauchery just ain't my scene anymore I'm afraid."

The unconvincing excuse earned him a chorus of disbelieving stares. "What?" Vinnie said, irritated.

Nessa finished her drink and stood; she was in no mood to play Vinnie's silly games. "Time we were goin' Vinnie."

Vinnie scrambled to his feet and helped her on with her coat.

"See you tomorrow Ness?" Cindy said.

"Is the pope a Catholic? You'll certainly see me anyway, but I can't speak for Mr pipe and slippers here."

"Isn't he Jewish," Gordon enquired.

"Who, Vinnie?" Cindy said.

"Noo... The pope?"

Nessa, giggling to herself at Gordon's remark, made for the exit closely followed by Vinnie. "See you tomorrow GG."

"Not if I see you first."

———— ⟲⟳ ————

THE 'OLD VIC' CRACKLED with the excitement of another New Year's Eve. Fairy lights, perpetually on the fritz, cast a garish glow over the packed pub. Vinnie, ever the competitor, was locked in a silent battle of darts with his best mate Jack, the tips of their tongues peeking out in concentration. Across the room, Nessa nursed a Jack Daniels, her gaze flicking between Gordon, dressed in a questionable sequined waistcoat, preened for the night's prospects and Cindy, who was deep in conversation (and a touch too close) with a tall stranger who had a questionable comb-over. Even the ever-stoic Landlord seemed caught up in the festive spirit, his gruff demeanour softened by a hint of a smile as he expertly pulled pints and dispensed weary wisdom to a group of boisterous regulars.

"One hundred and eighty," Vinnie bellowed, ripping the darts out of the board with a flourish.

"Forty-five," Jack shot back.

Vinnie squinted at the board, counting under his breath. "Right you are," he grumbled, "one hundred and forty-five, then."

Jack raised an eyebrow. "Pretty sure that's just forty-five, mate. You haven't hit treble twenty all night. Thought of trying dominoes?"

"Dominoes? That's for the bingo hall brigade. Darts is where it's at. Just need a bit more practice and a killer nickname, obviously."

"How about, *Vinnie 'couldn't hit a barn door with a banjo' Vincenzo*," Jack said.

"I like it. Lull 'em into a false sense of security, very clever."

Jack shook his head and laughed. "Sure, Vin. Whatever helps you sleep at night. I'm off for a smoke, need a break from your brilliance." He strolled off into the beer garden, leaving Vinnie alone with his delusions of grandeur.

Vinnie scanned the bar for a challenger. "Anyone fancy a good thrashing?" he shouted at anyone who cared to listen. "Come on guys, I'll give you a ten start."

Silence met him except for the murmur of conversation and clinking glasses. Vinnie sighed. "Ok I get it, can't stand the humiliation, eh? Your loss guys, you could have told your kids about the day you played darts with the legendary Vincent Vincenzo."

Nessa, keen to prevent Vinnie suffering any further humiliation, yelled at him from across the room. "Vinnie, no one's interested. Now shut up and get me a drink."

Vinnie, with a muttered curse under his breath, shuffled towards the bar, head hung low like a defeated puppy.

Pete had just finished serving Cindy and was about to turn his attention to Vinnie when the pub door swung open, momentarily silencing the usual chatter. In sauntered Eddie, his weary grin a stark contrast to his windblown hair. He tossed a lazy wave and a tired smile Pete's way.

"Well slap my arse and call me Brenda, if it isn't Eddie Finch," Pete said with delight, "where the hell have you been? I'm on the verge of bankruptcy here, takings are down by nearly half you old dog."

"Aye up Landlord, sorry to cause you such financial hardship, just needed some time to, you know, find myself," Eddie said without feeling the need to expand.

"And did you?" Pete asked.

"Did I what?"

"Did you find yerself?"

"Eddie shook his head, a defeated sigh escaping him. "Nah, lost as ever, mate. The whole world's a cesspit. But hey, at least there's familiar misery here, so for now, looks like I'm back."

"So, what can I get you Eddie, the usual?" Pete said.

"Yeah, pint of your best and a whiskey chaser please Landlord."

Pete poured Eddie's drinks and slid them across the bar. He was half tempted to let him have them on the house as a welcome back, but it was a fleeting thought before sense prevailed. "Five eighty-five please Eddie."

Eddie looked at his whiskey and looked up at Pete. "What's this?" he said.

"Whiskey chaser. What's it look like?

"You mean it's a sample of a whisky chaser. Give me the bottle Landlord, it's New Years Eve in case you hadn't noticed."

"Now there's the Eddie I love and need," Pete said as he handed over a bottle of *Jameson's*. "Twenty-nine pounds sixty and I've done you a favour at that price."

"Cheer's Landlord, stick it on my tab," Eddie said as he grabbed his drinks and started to walk away.

"That'll be the same tab you've never had then Eddie," Pete reminded him.

"Come on Landlord, give a guy a break," Eddie pleaded.

"You know the rules Eddie, no one's exempt."

Eddie put down his drinks, the festive cheer momentarily forgotten. He shuffled through his pockets, a frantic symphony of rustling paper and jingling coins. A crumpled ten-pound note peeked out from behind a forgotten receipt, but it wouldn't be enough. Disappointment gnawed at him as he recognized a movie ticket stub and a half-eaten packet of mints – remnants of a day that had promised more than just an empty wallet. He dug deeper, fingers brushing past a hole in his lining, hope withering with each empty compartment. With a sigh, he scraped together a handful of loose change, the coins a motley crew representing every British denomination ever minted. He tossed them on the bar with the tenner, his voice barely a whisper, "Will that cover it?" It wasn't a question; it was a plea.

The clinking of coins grew silent as Pete finished counting. He studied the meagre pile for a beat too long, then sighed. "Eleven pound twenty short I'm afraid Eddie."

Vinnie, still waiting to be served, felt he owed Eddie and leant in. "What's he owe Landlord?"

"Eleven twenty Vin," Pete said.

Vinnie slapped fifteen pounds on the bar. "Keep the change, you tight fisted sod," he said as he picked up Eddies drinks and with Eddie trailing behind, navigated the throng towards a cosy corner Cindy, ever the strategist, had secured earlier.

"Thanks son, I owe you one."

"No prob old man... Enjoy. Hey, did you hear about Psycho?"

"No," Eddie said, "what's he done now? Don't tell me he's knocked up Janice, we don't need anything from that gene pool infesting the earth."

"Chopped her up," said Cindy.

"Sorry?"

"He only went and chopped the poor cow up into bite sized pieces and hid her in the wall cavity," Vinnie said.

"Fucking hell, where is he now?"

"Broadmoor, but I'll let Cindy fill you in on the details, if I don't go get Nessa a drink, I'll be kippin' in the gutter with you tonight. Good to have you back Eddie."

"Good to be back. I'll catch you later son," Eddie said as Vinnie battled his way back to the bar.

Cindy sidled up to Eddie and planted a kiss on his cheek.

"For fuck's sake, how much is that gonna cost me?" Eddie said, chuckling.

"That one's on the house you cantankerous old sod," Cindy said holding out her empty glass and eyeing up Eddie's bottle of whiskey, "fancy sharing?"

"Sure," Eddie said topping up Cindy's glass, "half of it belongs to Vinnie anyway, I don't think he'll mind."

Cindy raised her glass, "Cheers!"

"Cheers, here's to the future and let's hope it's a damn sight better than the past," Eddie said. "So, want to fill me in on Psycho?"

"D'you mind if I don't, well not tonight anyway. Rather hear about your latest voyage of discovery."

"Nowt to tell really," Eddie said. "You'd have thought after all these years I'd have learnt wouldn't you."

"Learnt what?"

"Learnt that the grass ain't always greener, in fact more often than not it's just parched earth."

"When you live the lives we lead Eddie, you gotta keep believing there's something better, otherwise what's the point of living at all."

"I guess," Eddie said, resigned, "but in the end it just wears you down. Maybe if I'd found a good woman things would have been different."

"I know that feeling... I don't mean if I found a good woman, I meant..."

Eddie smiled. "I know what you meant."

"You believe in fate Eddie?"

"In the absence of a God, it's as good as anything, why?"

"Maybe we're just fated to be alone," Cindy said.

"Maybe you're right, or maybe it's this damn pub. They should rename it *Pete the Landlord's Lonely Hearts Club*," Eddie said laughing.

"Well, this lonely heart needs a pee, a ponder and maybe a bit of business with those two sad looking geezers at the bar. Chat later Eddie and save me some of that whiskey."

Midnight approached, Pete unplugged the jukebox and switched on the TV before ringing the ship's bell. "OK folks settle down, countdown's about to start."

The room hushed and then collectively started counting down until the chimes of Big Ben started ringing in their ears. Auld Lang Syne roared through the 'Old Vic', a chorus of voices raised in a collective farewell to the year. Vinnie, eyeing Eddie tucked away in the corner lost in thought, strode over and slapped his shoulder. "Come on, you miserable old sod, join in." But Eddie remained silent, a vacant look in his eyes. The ruddy glow that usually painted his cheeks had drained away, replaced by an unsettling pallor. Vinnie grabbed both Eddie's shoulders and shook him gently. "Eddie pal, wake up, you're missing all the fun." As Vinnie's grip slackened, Eddie slowly slumped in his seat, his head lolling to the side. Panic set in as the realisation hit. Eddie wasn't asleep, he wasn't lost in thought. Eddie was gone.

The celebratory anthem faltered as Vinnie's shout, a desperate mix of shock and grief, pierced through the air. Pete froze mid-pour, his face creasing in concern. Cindy spun around on her barstool, the unfinished story she'd been regaling to a couple of hopefuls dying on her lips. Her smile curdled into a horrified gasp.

The melody of Auld Lang Syne dissolved into a stunned silence. Gone were the drunken shouts and the clatter of glasses. The festive cheer that had permeated the pub moments ago had been extinguished, replaced by a cold dread that seeped into the bones of every punter present. The new year dawned, not with promise, but with a shroud of death.

The silence stretched, punctuated only by Vinnie's sobs. But then, Nessa, sprang into action. Shoving past the stunned crowd, she reached Eddie's side and slid him off his chair onto the floor. "Vinnie, call an ambulance... Now," she barked as she knelt beside the body, her eyes scanning Eddie's face, searching for any flicker of life, any hint he might still be with them. Her hand found his wrist, searching for a pulse. A sigh, heavy with dread, escaped her lips as she began chest compressions, a desperate attempt to bring him back from the brink. 'Staying Alive' rattled around her brain as she recalled her first aid training and without realising, she began to sing it out loud, trying to keep to the rhythm of the song, each word a silent plea, a determined fight against the fading beat of his heart.

———— ⌾ ————

PETE, HIS FACE WEARY with grief, polished a glass with a rag that seemed to move more out of habit than conviction. He cast his eyes over the few remaining stragglers. The clock on the wall mocked them with its relentless ticking. The festive cheer that had earlier filled the room had been extinguished, replaced by a suffocating silence broken only by the occasional clink of a glass being moved or a sniffle. The remnants of the New Year's Eve celebration lay scattered around like faded confetti - paper hats askew, balloons now limp and deflated.

Gordon, his flamboyant outfit at odds with the melancholic atmosphere, sat hunched in a corner asleep. Cindy, her mascara smudged with tears, clutched a crumpled tissue, her red dress a stark contrast to the bleakness. Vinnie was slumped in a chair, cradling a half-empty bottle of whiskey. The sobs that had wracked his body earlier had subsided as his gaze kept darting to the empty chair across the room. Nessa watched as Vinnie wandered over to the spot Eddie had taken his final breath, her back ramrod straight, a shield against the storm of emotions threatening to engulf her. Her eyes, though dry, held a haunted look, reflecting the image of her frantic CPR attempts on the cold floor a few hours ago.

Cindy took Nessa's hand. "Did tonight really happen?"

"Afraid so D."

"This ain't a dream?"

"Well, if it is, we're all sharing it."

"Fuck."

"Do you think he knew?" Nessa said.

"Knew what?"

"Knew that he was going to die. You know, like when elephants know and they go away to do it, except Eddie came home to do it."

"I've no idea Ness. What I do know, is that if he'd had the choice, this is exactly where he'd have chosen."

"Did he have any family D?"

"None that I know of. He was a bit of charmer in his youth though, I wouldn't be surprised if there were more than a couple of little Eddie's running around the planet somewhere," Cindy said with a half-smile.

Nessa let go of Cindy's hand and approached Vinnie, wrapping her arms around his waist, and nestling her chin on his shoulder. "You OK hun?" she said.

Vinnie paused. "Yeah, I guess... Did tonight really happen?

"We've just been there and done that. Concluded it was no dream I'm afraid."

"Fuck..." Vinnie said.

"Done that too."

If there was anyone who could lighten a sombre mood, usually unintentionally, it was Gordon. He woke with a sudden start, his voice panicked. "No... No. Get it away from me, it's enormous..."

"Everything OK GG?" Cindy said.

"What?"

"I said, 'is everything OK.'"

"Erm... Yeah, fine thanks."

"Dreaming, were we?" Nessa said.

"I'm... I'm not sure, maybe."

"Big boy, was he?" Vinnie teased, pleased of the distraction.

But before Gordon could even form a reply, a green tinge crept across his face. He lurched to his feet, a hand flying to his mouth. "Think I'm gonna be sick," he mumbled, already halfway to the toilet.

Cindy had seen enough. "OK folks, time for me to make a move, got an early start."

"Early start?" Nessa said.

"Yep, nine o'clock on the dot."

"What you doing at nine o'clock in the morning on New Years Day?" Vinnie said.

"It's not *what* I'm doing, it's *who* I'm doing."

"Do tell," Nessa said.

"Every New Year's Day, same story. Been the same for nine years now. Couple of fancy suits, claiming they need to stretch their legs after a night of the wife's cooking. We meet up, they blow off some steam, and I walk away with a fistful of cash for a couple of hours' work. Not bad, eh?"

"Fair do's," Vinnie said, "but it's four o'clock now, hardly worth going to bed."

"It's always worth goin' to bed sweetie, how d'you think I stay looking so young and beautiful?"

Gordon stumbled back into the bar, still looking disorientated and confused. His eyes darted around, unfocused, like he wasn't sure where he was or how he got there. Briefly, his gaze landed on Cindy and Nessa before he mumbled something and started to head back out.

"You sure you're ok Gordon?" Nessa called after him, concern lacing her voice.

He paused, then mumbled, "Yeah, I'm fine, honestly." His voice lacked conviction.

Cindy stood up, grabbing her purse. "Alright folks, I'm gonna hit the hay. Wanna split a cab GG?"

"Do you mind?"

"Of course not, but no funny business in the back seat, unless you pay of course," Cindy said laughing.

"I think you're safe gorgeous."

"OK guys we're outta here. Catch you later."

"See ya D, bye GG," Nessa said.

"Take care guys," Vinnie said as he reached for a glass on an adjacent table, his eyes landing on a murky concoction that defied definition. Nessa caught his movement and shot him a withering look. He sheepishly retracted his hand.

Gordon saluted them clumsily with two fingers, as he snaked his way towards the exit. "Toodle pip lovers, laters Landlord."

"Take care guys," Pete said not looking up from the laborious task of washing the never-ending line of pint glasses stood to attention along the length of the bar.

"Want a hand clearing up Landlord?" Nessa asked.

"Nah, I'm good thanks," Pete said, "gonna leave the rest till later."

Vinnie felt they'd outstayed their welcome. "Want us to leave?"

"You're ok for five, off out for a smoke and some fresh air."

Pete slid out the back door into the cool night air leaving Nessa and Vinnie with the ghosts of the evening.

Nessa broke the silence. "Can't decide if I wanna forget tonight or hold onto it forever."

"Doubt I'll ever forget it," Vinnie muttered, "but then I'm not sure I want to. I've never seen a dead body before... Well not a live one if you know what I mean."

Nessa smiled. "I know what you mean."

"It's no way to end your days though, is it?"

"Who are we to judge," Nessa said, "not how I'd like to go, but each to their own, I guess.

"Good bloke, deep down."

"I never said he wasn't."

"Bloody brilliant bloke actually... and wise as fuck," Vinnie said before letting out a huge sigh. "Oh Ness, what's it all about?"

"It?"

"This," he waved a hand vaguely. "Life... Us... Them... Pot Noodles."

"Please don't get all philosophical on me Vinnie. It's very late and I'm knackered."

"Sorry scrunch buttocks, it's just got me thinking that's all."

"Yeah, well, thinking can get you in trouble," she said, eyeing him with amusement.

"Maybe I like living dangerously... So, what about us?"

"What about us?"

"You think we'll make it?" Vinnie said.

"You want to make it?"

"Do you need to ask?"

Nessa cupped his face, her eyes searching for his. "Who knows what the future holds Vinnie. But I'll tell you this, for some strange, unfathomable reason, I do love you."

"How much?"

"What?"

"How much do you love me?"

"Don't be childish."

"Do you love me more than Jonny Depp?"

Nessa snorted.

"More than your Jimmy Choos?"

"Hmm... maybe"

"Do you love me more than your worryingly large collection of sex toys?"

"Don't be stupid."

"Ok, two out of three ain't bad... Will we grow old together?"

"I'll answer that when we've grown old. Let's take it one day at a time shall we."

"That's good enough for me. I've got a feeling..."

"Sorry, too tired for that Casanova."

"Not that kind of feeling. Why you gotta bring everything back to sex?"

Nessa burst out laughing. "Probably because I had a good teacher."

Pete pushed open the back door and returned to the bar, a tendril of cigarette smoke clinging to his clothes. He gave a curt nod to Nessa and Vinnie, his eyes a touch bloodshot. He cleared his throat. "Alright you two, sorry to be a party pooper, but time to call it a night. Got a long one tomorrow." His voice held a hint of weariness, but mostly a quiet plea to be alone. He longed for a bit of solitude, the familiar clink of ice in a glass and the smooth burn of whiskey to chase away the unsettling events of the evening.

"Say no more Landlord," Vinnie said, "wouldn't want to out stay our welcome." He stood and offered his arm to Nessa. "Your carriage awaits madam,"

"Why thank you kind sir," Nessa said as she slid her arm through his and turned towards Pete. "Thank you for a most eventful and unforgettable evening Landlord."

"Always a pleasure Nessa," Pete said, "we open again at twelve if you feel the need."

Vinnie gave Pete a thumbs up and led Nessa away into the cool night air with the hope of flagging down a cab.

THE 'OLD VIC' STOOD as a silent monument to a bygone era. Light streamed through gaps in the boarded-up windows, casting eerie shadows on the dust-covered floor. Tables and chairs lay broken and strewn around. The place had a desolate beauty, a quiet whisper of the stories it once held. The splintered remnants of a dartboard lay forgotten on the floor. Gone were the worn wooden tables, the chipped glasses, the very essence of a thousand whispered secrets and boisterous laughter. In their place, a chilling silence hummed, punctuated only by the sigh of the wind.

Vinnie, his hair now a distinguished silver, pushed through a creaking door with a groan of protest. Nessa, her face tired with the years but her eyes still sparkling, followed close behind.

"Don't be stupid Vinnie, we'll get into trouble."

"For what?" he gestured at the desolate interior, "trespassing in a building due to be demolished next week?"

"Still bloody illegal. Come on let's get out of here."

"One last adventure Ness, before they turn it into flats for students with names like Chardonnay and Sebastian," Vinnie said before moving towards a corner, his steps surprisingly sprightly for a man pushing sixty. There, amidst the debris, lay a familiar barstool. With surprising ease, he righted it and placed it carefully at one end of the once elegant solid mahogany bar. "What's missing?"

"Eddie Finch," Nessa said, recalling the fateful night.

"Old Eddie... He was one of life's greats you know."

"So, you said. What exactly was he great at?"

"Buggered if I know, he never told me," Vinnie said, laughing.

Together, they walked the length of the bar, ghosts in a graveyard of laughter. Nessa stopped, her eyes lingering on a specific spot. It was here, under the dim pub light, that Vinnie's clumsy charm had first tripped her up.

"So, what's a nice girl like you doing in a dive like this?" Vinnie said.

"Just passing through, though I have to admit, it does look a bit like something out of a Dickens novel."

"You like Dickens then?"

"Yeah, but not on a first date."

They both burst into laughter, the sound echoing hollowly in the empty space. The decades had silvered their hair, but the spark between them remained.

"Thirty-five years," Vinnie breathed, a hint of disbelief in his voice.

"Thirty-five *long* years."

"Don't say it like that," Vinnie nudged her playfully.

"Like what?" Nessa said.

"Like it's a bad thing." He caught her gaze, his own filled with a quiet tenderness. "Who knew, back then..."

She finished his thought. "That we'd make it this far?"

"Honestly? I thought you were too good for me."

"Well, you weren't exactly wrong about that," Nessa said.

"But in the end, you couldn't resist my irresistible charm, native wit and all-round good looks."

"Yeah, something like that, not to mention your donkey schlong... I wonder where they are now?"

"I'm still witty and charming. The old John Thomas might not perform quite as well as he did in his heyday, but he can still put on a show when the need arises."

"I'm not talking about you, you fool. I mean the gang, Cindy, Psycho, GG, and the Landlord."

A shadow of sadness crossed Vinnie's face. "I read Psycho ended it in Broadmoor about ten years ago, as for the rest I haven't got a clue."

"Do you think they found happiness?"

"Well, if we managed to find it, I'm damn sure they did. Who knows, Landlord may have married Cindy, and they adopted GG who opened a gorgeous gay drag club in Las Vegas, and they all lived happily ever after."

A comfortable silence settled between them. Then, Nessa tilted her head, her eyes twinkling. "One last dance?"

"You askin'?"

"I'm askin'?"

"In that case, I'm dancin'."

Vinnie took Nessa's hand, and they moved slowly to a tune only they could hear. The bar, with its ghosts and memories, seemed to come alive one last time. For a moment, the years melted away, and they were young again, two souls finding unbridled joy in each other's company amidst the chaos of life. As they danced, the sun set behind the boarded-up windows. It was a fitting farewell, a final tribute to the place that had witnessed so many stories, so many lives intertwined.

Their steps slowed, and they held each other close, savouring the silence and the shared memories. The 'Old Vic' may have been forgotten by the world, but for Vinnie and Nessa, it would always hold a special place in their hearts. As they left the pub for the last time, they looked back once more, knowing that while the building might crumble, the memories they made would last forever.

The End.

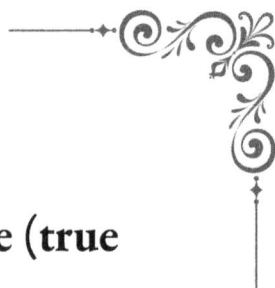

Whispers of Hope (true story)

D espite the boreal blast of a wintry wind piercing through the shattered window of the cramped box room, causing the tattered curtains to dance frenetically, she awoke soaked in sweat. Her shallow breaths materialised as illusory shapes that gracefully snaked towards the ceiling tainted by years of nicotine stains, only to dissipate into nothingness. Dawn's faint glow seeped through the grimy glass, casting sickly yellow tendrils onto the dusty floor. Another day. The mere thought felt like a weight pushing down on her already burdened chest. Each sunrise brought with it the potential for renewed suffering, another chapter in this unending nightmare.

Abandoning the coarse woollen blanket, imbued with the pungent malodour left by countless victims before her, her emaciated and fragile frame trembled uncontrollably. Grotesque visions of her captors laid siege to her mind, leaving her devoid of peaceful slumber. Sleep remained elusive, with minutes stretching into agonising hours, and hours morphing into seemingly endless days, steadily eroding her will to survive with each torturous and tormenting moment.

She rose, her joints protesting at the movement. Each step across the uneven floorboards echoed in the cavernous silence, a stark contrast to the cacophony of screams that haunted her waking hours. She reached the barred window, its iron frame cold against her touch. Outside, the city stretched out, a labyrinth of soot-stained buildings and cobbled streets, devoid of the warmth and vibrancy she once remembered. This wasn't her city anymore. It was a prison, mirroring the one she was trapped within.

As the glacial wind retreated, leaving behind an eerie stillness, the silence enveloped her, rendering her deaf to the world. Caught in a perpetual state of melancholy, her memories of home resembled idyllic illustrations from a storybook, far removed from the harsh reality she had left behind. The laughter of children playing in sun-dappled fields, the scent of freshly baked bread wafting from the kitchen, the warmth of her mother's embrace - these were fragments of a past life, a life irrevocably lost. The purpose of her existence now holds little meaning, save for those who stand to benefit or those in search of fleeting gratification.

Hunger wasn't a guest in her belly; it was a snarling tenant, taking up residence in her gut and demanding rent of every waking moment. The lukewarm gruel left each morning was a cruel joke, a mockery of sustenance rather than a meal. Even water, the most basic necessity, carried an irony she couldn't ignore - its pure essence presented in a cracked earthenware mug, a stark reminder of her fragmented life. In the shard of mirror propped against the damp wall, she saw a stranger. Sunken eyes, once sparkling with curiosity, now mirrored the dull ache in her soul. Hollow cheeks, once flushed with laughter, spoke of stolen youth and stolen hope. The vibrancy of the girl she once was felt as distant as a forgotten dream, leaving behind a pale phantom haunted by the echo of her former self.

The notion of the Lord as her saviour had diminished into a mere hollow sentiment. When she listens to her own prayers, they sound like nonsensical mutterings of a forsaken soul, desperately holding onto the fraying edges of sanity. But even in the abyss of despair, a flicker of defiance remained. Tomorrow might never come, but she wouldn't surrender to the darkness. Not yet. There was a story left to tell, a fight left to fight. Even in the face of overwhelming odds, the ember within her burned, a testament to the enduring human spirit, refusing to be extinguished.

The End.

Milton Keynes UK
Ingram Content Group UK Ltd.
UKHW020014061124
450708UK00001B/145